The
Return
of
Philip
Latinovicz

The Return of Philip Latinovicz

BY MIROSLAV KRLEŽA

TRANSLATED BY
ZORA G. DEPOLO

The Vanguard Press
NEW YORK

Translator's Note

Pronunciation of Croatian Names   Where an English equivalent of the name exists, the names in the text have been given in the English form, as Philip for Filip, Lawrence for Lovro.

Where there is no English equivalent, the Croatian spelling has been given, and the following indications as to pronunciation may be useful:

With few exceptions, the original spelling of Serbo-Croatian proper names has been retained throughout this volume. The following key will help the reader in pronouncing them:

c = ts   as in lots
č and ć = ch   as in change
š = sh   as in marsh
ž = s   as in pleasure
j = y   as in yes
lj = li   as in stallion
dj = j   as in major
i = ee   as in feet
e = e   as in net
u = oo   as in soon
a = a   as in father

The
Return
of
Philip
Latinovicz

It was dawn when Philip arrived at the Kaptol railway station. For the last twenty-three years he had been away from this little backwater, but it was all still familiar to him: the rotting, slimy roofs, the round ball on the Friars' steeple, the gray, windswept two-storied house at the end of the dark avenue, the plaster head of Medusa surmounting the heavy, iron-bound oak door with its cold latch. Twenty-three years had passed since the morning when he had slunk up to that door like the prodigal son; when, a schoolboy in the seventh form, he had stolen a hundred-florin note from his mother and drunk and caroused with streetwalkers and waitresses for three days and nights, and come home to find the door locked and himself shut out in the street. Ever since that time he had been living in the street, and nothing had really changed. He stopped in front of the unfriendly locked door and, just as on that morning, he could feel the cold, iron touch of the heavy, clumsy latch in the hollow of his palm; he knew how heavy the door would feel as he pushed it; how the leaves were quivering in the upper branches of the chestnut trees; he heard the flutter of a swallow as it sprang into flight above his head, and he felt as if in a dream —as on that other morning; he was dirty, tired, in need of sleep, and could feel something crawling inside his collar—a bedbug, most likely. As long as he lived he would never forget that gloomy dawn, that third, last drunken night, and the gray morning.

At the corner where as a boy he had played with his white lamb, there was a building site walled in like a man behind a high wall, and on this high wall there were advertisements for women's corsets and coke stoves; the corsets were slim with tight waists, and a flame flickered under one of the iron stoves.

Yes, there, right under the wall, he had stood that morning unable to go on. He had felt the blood pulsating in his throat, his joints, his fingers, his ribs, his flesh—all of him was a dark bleeding heart—and he had leaned against the wall so as not to fall. He had stood there for a long time under the slim corsets, and his fingers were dirty with dust and plaster because the wall was old, green with mold, and flecked with white patches. A baker's boy had passed by carrying a net full of hot rolls; the rolls had smelled good, and for a long time the boy's shuffling steps could be heard round the corner on the asphalt.

Philip stopped now in front of the old crumbling wall, feeling it with his hand, as if he were touching a dear but forgotten grave. The wind and rain had washed away the corsets; the plaster was flaking off the bricks; and only in one place a tiny blue tongue of the coke flame flickered out from under the painted iron stove. Catching sight of the long-faded advertisement, Philip felt the far-off, dead pictures melting away within him, and he seemed to be all alone, confronting some immeasurably vast space.

Though footsteps could be heard around the corner, there was no one to be seen; nothing but the empty street with the old gray steeple at the end of the avenue of trees, the quiet reflections of the soft morning light on the closed windows and curtains, the flowerpots, the locked doors, the chains, the lions' heads, the stone doorsteps, and the brass nameplates of the tenants, with here and there an old-fashioned bell. A lamp stood in front of the two-storied house. It was the same one that used to shine above the bed where he had gone through the worst crises of his boyhood; night after night he had watched that orange-colored reflection on the ceiling between the dragon's jaw and the wisteria and purple lilacs; the small flame of the streetlamp used to flicker and tremble like a little sick fish inside the glass walls of a dirty bowl.

Everything was gray, and the house looked strangely black, or rather dark brown. The features of Medusa above the entrance door were contorted as if in a death agony; her lips were swollen, the rusty snakes clustered and writhed, and the entrance door was enormous, ironbound, like that of a fortress. The northern side of the two-storied house was windswept, and to Philip it was quite extraordinary to think that once, long ago, his own agonized, unutterably intense childhood had been spent under the roof of this gray-green house with its two stories. They had moved into the house when his mother's career had already entered on its genteel phase: when she kept the tobacconist's shop in Friars' Street and Canon Lawrence used to come openly for a cup of coffee and a game of dominoes.

He knew how everything felt: the latch in his hand, the heavy massive resistance of the door, the long stuffy corridor painted with gray oil paint, the wooden stairs, and the large white-framed window on the landing overlooking the garden. As he stood in front of this locked house no longer his own, Philip wondered what would happen if he went in. He approached the door quietly, pressed the heavy, cold latch; it gave way and the door opened: it was not locked. He softly shut the hall door behind him and slowly, like a thief, noiselessly, on tiptoe, breathless, he crept up to the window on the landing. It was open, and the garden was already full of white morning light. The huge, leafy old walnut tree was alive with the twittering of birds. The old garden was silent, with its four symmetrical white paths, its yellow roses in full bloom, and its glass balls, its dwarfs, and the fountain with little goldfish—all as if untouched and in perfect order, watered, trimmed, as if nothing had happened and as if nothing ever happened in life. Under the ivy-clad wall, beyond the dense evergreens, could be seen the roof of a hen coop. A carpet beater lay in front of the hen coop, the same carpet beater on which Philip had let off fireworks on the eve of Carolina's wedding day. Carolina had lived at the inn with her father, who knew how to skin and stuff birds and give them eyes made of pieces of colored glass. Carolina herself was fat, twelve years older than Philip, and her job was washing bottles at the brewery.

Because of fat Carolina, Philip had gone through the torments of three whole years of pain and frustration. As a precocious, confused, unbalanced child, with deep, dark complexes of moral humiliation within him, full of passionate blood and an obscure feeling of persecution, tormented by sexual longings vaguely connected with various silly, innocent little girls of his own age, Philip had one day felt in his lap the fat, clumsy thighs of the good-natured Carolina.

It had happened down in Carolina's kitchen among the boiling pots and near the red-hot top of the kitchen stove; he had been sitting on a kitchen stool watching Carolina doing the washing, and Carolina, after pouring a pot of boiling water into the wash-tub, had sat down in Philip's lap while she was waiting for the water to cool. Philip had already read Zola's *Nana,* was painting watercolors, had drunk his first glass of beer with disgust and vomited after smoking four cigarettes; and this little boy who played chess and football, who on one hand was still attached to the most childish things and on the other torn by the most desperate viciousness, all of a sudden felt the fat, wet, sweating, burning behind of Carolina in his lap. That accidental, thought-less, harmless gesture of Carolina's remained with him as the most convulsive, passionate emotion of his whole childhood. He remembered how he would gaze at the distant outlines of the Kostanjevec vineyard where Carolina had gone with her vine-grower; how he used to chase dogs, collect shells, and watch capons being castrated, and then spend night after night in delir-ium, dreaming of the irrecoverable transcendent pleasure of the moment when Carolina was in his lap. When he had let off his last fireworks on the carpet beater on the eve of Carolina's wed-ding day, he was on the verge of committing suicide from grief. All that summer he used to dive from the top of the shoulder of the baroque statue of St. Florian into the water under the bridge so that the water above him might be stained with blood. For there was a legend among the boys that once upon a time a miller had jumped from St. Florian's statue and they never got him out, and the water above him had been stained with blood.

Fireworks on the eve of Carolina's wedding day! Blood in the water under the bridge! How much water had already been stained with blood above him, but he was still swimming, he could still move! And that morning when he had come back to this same doorstep like a penitent, like a thief who had stolen a hundred-florin note—and come from wanton and dirty, drunken women—on that morning when his own mother had turned him out into the street in moral indignation, then, too, the muddy and fatally troubled waters above him were stained with blood. How he had shivered at the window that morning, more dead than alive, and how unbearably long the waiting on that spot had been; and the night before when he still had forty crowns and could still have gone far away—that night had been dreadful indeed. And the last night, too—when one florin after another had disappeared and the catastrophe was approaching with mathematical certainty—had been full of ghosts and smelled of death, but now he was facing the most difficult thing of all: to climb another fourteen stairs and ring the bell at the left-hand door on the first floor. In that distant dawn he had stood motionless at the same window for more than an hour, and not even then would he have moved had he not heard the noise of a door being closed somewhere on the ground floor, followed by approaching footsteps. Someone had seemed to be coming up to the first floor. But it was only one of the maids, with a pan of maize-flour in her hand, who was on her way to feed the chickens. So he had found himself in front of his mother's door; a brownish oil-painted door with a brass lock and a glass, brass-framed peephole that looked like a miniature porthole. The little metal circle had been shuttered from behind.

A small metal plate in a wooden frame.

His mother's name and surname. A widow. To him such familiar things, the name and the surname of his own mother.

This was the place in which that woman in mourning had lived, a widow, his own mother, a tobacconist in Friars' Street; and her son, a seventh-form schoolboy, had come home from a brothel; and everything was just beginning.

How had he rung the bell, and when?

For a long time no one had come; all had been silent as the grave.

He had rung the bell once more. The batteries of their electric bell were never well charged, and it always rang feebly. He had been greatly relieved. She must be asleep. She always slept late. And it might be even better to put off this meeting as long as possible.

Then, after long ringing, he had heard the door of the room open and the shuffle of slippers on the wooden floor. It was his mother. The shutter of the brass circle had been lifted and he had felt her cold, pitiless look. He had heard her sharp, cruel voice. She had asked what he wanted. And she had addressed him formally, like a stranger:

"What do you want?"

"It's me, open the door!"

The same sharp, cruel voice had sounded once more behind the locked door, telling him that it did not know him and that he could go back to the place he had come from. That was where he belonged. And again addressing him as a stranger: "That is where you belong."

He had felt as if he were about to faint, but during that whole muffled conversation through the peephole in the middle of the wooden panel, through that mysterious brass-framed circle he had had the feeling here was something insurmountable that could never be crossed. It was a line of demarcation. And when the shutter had dropped and he again had heard the shuffle of her loose slippers on the wooden floor and the door of the room closed inside the flat, it had been clear to Philip that one door was shut on him forever.

So he had turned around, gone down the stairs, and stayed all alone in the street for twenty-three years.

And now he had returned to this remote provincial backwater. It was a spring morning, and he found himself on the first floor of that strange, damp house. It would be embarrassing if anybody noticed a stranger strolling into other people's empty houses in the gray dawn. So, in the same way, on tiptoe, step by step, cautiously, scarcely breathing, just as he had crept in, Philip sneaked back like a thief into the street, where under the thick chestnut branches it was still dark, green, and gloomy.

Birds, water, and meadows, all was buoyant morning—shifting pictures of spring, the flickering of shadows and lights as in a dream—but still Philip could not rid himself of the depression and sorrow that stuck like a lump in his throat. The express had reached the Kaptol station sometime after three, and by now the transparent glitter of a fresh, blue April morning, full of light, was growing brighter above the fields and plowland and around the town. The silky morning wind, the heavy, white, pregnant April clouds, the scents in the fields and the colors in the distance—everything was swelling out in the silent instrumentation of the blue morning's awakening. From the distance, from the open country, across the plowed fields, the bronze morning bells resounded, and above the green copper ball on the Kaptol Friars' Church white clouds were piling up, so that the sparrows on the branches of the poplar trees twittered loudly, heralding an early morning shower.

And there in front of Philip lay Kaptol in its morning calm— Kaptol, the See of Upper Pannonia and Illyria, the famous sixteenth-century bastion against the Turks, situated on the edge of the Sava mud and marshes; the town of Philip's childhood and early youth, from which he had been away for such a long time but where this morning everything seemed so familiar to him and yet so strange, as if he had died sometime long ago and was faintly recognizing the forgotten contours of dead things and events through a veil of incomprehension. Across the promenade, where beds of red and yellow tulips bloomed under the poplar trees, a butcher's van, loaded with raw sides of beef, moved slowly along the line of trees; a bluish calf's hoof was caught between the spokes, so that it seemed as if the wheel would break it. Fascinated by the blue, flayed calf's hoof, Philip began to follow the butcher's van across the bridge and found himself in Friars' Street, next to the gray moss-grown wall surrounding the friary.

At the end of a row of mulberry trees, under the steep roof of a long, low house, next to the first window by the brown fence, there was a tall, green wooden door, shut and locked with a padlock and an iron bar. A tin plate bore the inscription: Licensed Retail Tobacconist.

There, long ago—some thirty years earlier, in fact—had been the tobacconist's shop kept by his mother, Mrs. Regina; and there it was still, as in the days of his childhood, when the water used to drip down the rusty gutter spouts and the cranes could be heard crying in the dark night high in the air above the town. The crumbling brick steps were there still and the wooden doorstep had been gnawed by rats. The iron shutter was broken, just as it had been thirty years ago, and there, behind it, was the damp, moldy, dark room with its rotting floor, where he had so often crouched behind the iron stove in the corner. Philip used to kneel in the gloom, completely alone in the room; from outside only the footsteps of passersby could be heard, from the mulberry tree up to the fence, from the fence up to the wall, along the wall underneath the window and over the open drain, in which greasy green water stagnated, full of bits of straw and poultry feathers. Now he stood on the little wooden bridge looking down into the drain full of straw, garbage, and poultry feathers, and saw a little newspaper boat—that cherished vessel of childhood adventures —caught on a brick, all wet and soaked with water, about to sink. He bent down to lift the little shipwrecked vessel from the stinking pool over which he had spent so much time dreaming about voyages to far-off lands, but as he was in the act of doing so it all seemed more than foolish; so he stood before the window of the tobacconist's shop for a long time, motionless, staring at the spots on the dirty glass.

There, just behind the wall, had stood his mother's polished oval table, and on the table a red velvet-bound photograph album. The red-velvet album, that precious, mysterious book, had brassbound edges and a herald in armor with a bugle on its front cover; from the bugle hung a banner, representing two enormous eagles with outspread wings. The faded velvet album with the gallant bugler was one of those mysterious sacred objects it was forbidden to touch. Such a desecration entailed a punishment that consisted of kneeling for hours behind the stove where it smelled of rats. And there, by the window, on the other side of the bare gray wall, had been a mysteriously beautiful ebony-framed oil painting—the canvas already showing the first spots of decay—of a naked female figure, not more than thirty centimeters wide. The gray-green light fell on the naked body, which had assumed the supernatural color of a transparent apparition and looked like something not made by human hand. His mother, the tobacconist, that most mysterious figure of his childhood—Regina, who was called by everybody simply Regina, though her real name was Casimira, and who, being a Pole, had never learned to speak Croatian properly—jealously kept that mysterious picture of an unknown naked woman in an ebony frame as a relic, and Philip could never discover either whose picture it was or from where his mother had brought it. The picture had puzzled him for years, and it had not been the only secret he had worried over as he sat there by the dirty window, under the torn blind, listening to the wind howling in the attic.

It was by that window that he had fallen seriously ill the night in autumn when the English horses passed in long processions through the town on their way to the Transvaal battlefront—one misty night in October. One could hear the thundering of hoofs across the wooden bridge at the corner of Friars' Street, in a stream of warm reeking horses. They were going to distant, unknown southern seas on their way to the equator, where the strange stars of the southern hemisphere glitter. Black tar-tainted vessels creaking in faraway harbors were waiting for the horses to crowd onto them, that they might transport them somewhere inconceivably far away where boa constrictors creep and poisonous mosquitoes bite. Countless English horses had passed by that night; a host of black, fragile horses' legs thundered by, trembling with excitement, reminding him more of the legs of strange, horseshoed birds than those of hoofed animals. That night his mother had not slept at home. Midnight had long since struck from the Friars' Church tower, but the procession of English horses was endless; they went by interminably, one after another, an endless dark crowd of tails, necks, and hoofs. A mass of dark-maned, neighing flesh that made the windows rattle as in a thunderstorm. Alarmed by the strange thunder, frightened by his loneliness and wakefulness, Philip had crept to the window and lifted the greasy, torn blind just enough to enable him to see the horses' bellies. Peeping from under the blind, he was lost in fascination at this incomprehensible chaos of dark rumps, fetlocks, joints, hoofs, trembling partly with fear and partly with a strange, vague, splendid emotion. And pressing his nose, forehead, and head against the cool glass, Philip had watched the procession of horses on their way to South Africa. It was late in the night, but his mother was not yet back. He fell asleep toward morning when the friars had already rung the bell for early-morning mass, and there was still no trace of his mother. The first thing he saw on awakening was his mother's empty bed.

Regina, the tobacconist, had come home at about eight o'clock, stroked his hair, and told him to put on his velvet suit because they were going to town. She had caressed him and called him Zygmusik. It was a special token of favor and kindness when she put her hand on his hair, particularly if she called him by his real name, and the velvet suit was in itself a symbol of festivity and some unusual event. In the dark blue velvet suit with its lace collar, cuffs, and jabot, it seemed to Philip that he looked grand and distinguished, like a sort of knightly medieval falconer in lace and a velvet cap. Regina, the tobacconist, even though otherwise completely cold in her attitude toward her child, always paid great attention to the decorative side of his appearance. This distinguished her from the circle of the neighbors around the tobacconist's shop, and it stressed a kind of special social defiance, as if to show she was not the same as the other poor tenants of the yard and the houses opposite. The tobacconist's son was always well washed and most distinctively dressed, and it was just this fantastic and doll-like characteristic of his mother's taste that was subsequently the cause of Philip's serious conflicts with his comrades. There were rumors in the town that the father of the tobacconist's son was the bishop, and this rumor had poisoned Philip's childhood bitterly and irremediably.

They made the long journey to town in a cold and unheated railway carriage, and his mother left Philip at a marble table in a café under the glass arch of the shop window. She ordered a cup of chocolate for him and told the waiter to keep an eye on the child and that she would soon be back. In the café Philip was already in a fever: all the straight lines were melting into endless verticals, and the horizontal lines circled around him in perpetual and agitated undulations. His mother did not return until the afternoon. Her eyes were cloudy, tired, swollen with tears, bloodshot. Her eyebrows were ruffled, her face was drawn. Then for the first time Philip noticed that his mother was covered with flour like a clown, and that underneath that white floury mask was another face, sad, gloomy, tormented. He was swinging his legs and eating his third chocolate éclair, when his mother caressed him again and told him quietly, through her tears, that they were going to visit a lady, and that he must be extremely polite there.

"You are my good little Zygmusik, aren't you?"

So he was good and little and Zygmusik, and in addition to all that, hers? Everything was unusual and festive indeed! Then he saw that she had put on her old-fashioned gold jewelry, the earrings with the antique settings she kept in a silk-padded box. Philip could not remember if he had ever seen his mother wearing them before. In her heavy black silk dress with the old-fashioned jewelry, she looked to him very distinguished. Her face was completely bloodless, as white as a corpse's.

It had been a mild October afternoon. As he went with his mother through the park, he had picked three daisies from the lawn and, holding the three tiny, warm, faded flowers in his hand, he followed her into a high, dark, grimy house with glass doors. The glass panes of the hall door were red and green, while the door itself, at which his mother had rung the bell, was varnished, shining, and extremely high. He went in with her, feeling her cotton glove in his hand and a singular warmth penetrating through the material. As he entered and followed her across the dark room and the antechamber, rubbing his feet on the carpets and staring at the various stands and strange objects, he could take in only the fact that there were a great many rooms and that everything was strangely high: the door and the stove, the furniture, the curtains, and the windows. There were thick carpets, the gleam of polished wood and of porcelain in the china cabinet; pictures of hares and deer on silver plates; heavy, fringed woolen tablecloths and armchairs, and he was so excited at the sight of everything that he kept plucking nervously at the three daisies with his sweating fingers.

The woman who received them had a stiff, hairy face and an enormous coal-black coiffure, gold teeth, gold bracelets, and gold lorgnette, and her fingers were covered with rings and jewels. When she touched Philip's chin with her bony hand, he felt the unpleasant and awesomely cold touch of gold. This dark-haired woman gave him a bar of chocolate wrapped in silver paper and sent him to another room, as she had something to talk about with his mother. Meanwhile he could play with Pharaoh next door. Pharaoh was a jay in a yellow brass cage, and when Philip crossed the threshold, Pharaoh greeted him in a hoarse, harsh voice: *"Bonjour, Monsieur!"*

Startled by the bird's voice, breathless and paralyzed with fright, Philip clung to a huge old-fashioned upholstered arm-chair, feeling his fingers slowly breaking through the silver paper in which the chocolate was wrapped, feeling the chocolate itself melting in his hand, not knowing what to do with his little crushed flowers—should he throw them away? He knew his mother was crying in the next room, silently, quite silently, but she was crying; and the jay was scratching about in the cage, turning the swing, cracking nuts, sharpening its beak against the glittering wires. Everything seemed so miserable, suffocating, dark, feverish; everything was sticky, just like the melting choco-late; everything smelled of that disgusting screeching gray bird. *"Bonjour, Monsieur!"*

That night a howling wind brought the first snowfall. Branches cracked in the gale and plaster fell down the chimney —even the rats in the attic were frightened into silence—the foal at the baker's house across the street had broken its leg, and Philip raved all night about the English horses, about the jay that spoke French, about his mother crying. He saw his mother dead, reflected in an extraordinarily bright mirror as if she were sitting in a display window, and on a tablecloth in front of her lay a roll of banknotes, a tiny red-green bundle of banknotes tied up with a purple ribbon. He saw the whole thing clearly before him on a shaggy woolen tablecloth, while the jay shrieked from the next room in French: *"Bonjour, Monsieur!"*

Wind in the chimney, darkness, and his mother weeping in the dark.

He had never before dared to ask that silent woman anything, but that night, when almost in death's grasp, he asked his mother quite naturally why she was crying.

No answer. Hushed sobs.

He rose and went to his mother's bed.

"Mother, what's the matter? Why are you crying?"

As he stood there, barefoot in his long nightshirt, he thought his mother would chase him back to his own bed, but the opposite happened. She took both his hands and began kissing them, and so—he did not know how it had really happened—he found himself in her bed, feeling only how cold his mother's body was, though her tears were as hot as melted wax; so they cried together, while outside the wind howled, blowing chimneys down and sweeping away dead leaves and dead birds. That night he caught pneumonia and lingered between life and death for a whole long winter, damaging his bronchial tubes and left lung for the rest of his life.

And everything had begun by that dirty gray window that distant October night with the English horses.

The drama of a provincial tobacconist! A jay that spoke French! Banknotes on a tablecloth and a repulsive old woman with a black wig! What kind of drama was this? What was the meaning of the mysterious visit to that gloomy old mansion? Where was it all today, and whither had it melted away like mist?

Standing in front of that dirty ground-floor window, so close to the pane that he heard a clock striking somewhere inside, Philip had a feeling that behind the curtain somebody was moving around the room; but when a yellow, sleepy, bearded face appeared from behind the broken shutter, he started in alarm and confusion and walked away with rapid steps down the street to the Friars' Church.

The church was empty. A beggar-woman was sighing loudly in

21

front of the altar of the Holy Virgin, a majestic baroque statue with a crown on her head and a scepter in her hand, wrapped in a reddish brocade cloak with embroidered gold lilies. The vast empty building was damp and cold and smelled of wet ash and rotting rags. Behind the main altar it looked like backstage at a theater: old rags, scraps of cloth, chests, boards, ladders, cobwebs, kerosene lamps, a bottle of turpentine, a pair of pliers. It all looked as if an old performance were still going on although no one knew exactly why. The flags on the altars, the saints' statues, the marble angels, the damp dusk, and the distant twittering of birds around the steeple.

Outside, around the church, were grass-grown graves. On the wide surfaces of the white baroque walls, washed with rain and wind, were swallows' nests and sparrows' droppings; and along by the ruinous ivy-grown red brick wall, the ancient graves of blacksmiths and their wives, respectable tradesmen and venerable abbots and canons of the cathedral of Pannonia, with resounding titles and the medieval blazons of their ecclesiastical dignities.

Under a great slab of granite, in the shadow of the apse, a Count Uexhuell-Cranensteeg was buried; dressed in Louis XV lace, he had ridden here to meet the Turks and died in the Pannonian mud, leaving behind him at Kostanjevec a hundred and twenty empty rooms that have remained intact and empty for two hundred years. There also, beneath a towering cypress, lay the Abbot of the Virgin Mary, his mother Casimira's friend, whom he had suspected for a time of being his father. And over there, somewhere along the main path to the left, all grassed over, with a black oval plate on a massive cross, was the grave of the man he believed to be his legitimate father—Philip, chamberlain and private servant to His Grace the Bishop Silvester, after whom the boy, on his own initiative, changed his name to Philip, although he had been christened after the Polish King Sigismund, and at school they had always called him Sigismund until he entered the grammar school.

Philip's father had died when Philip was only two years old, so that he was not quite certain whether he could really remember the man himself or only his photograph in the velvet-bound album. Philip's father was the Bishop's servant, the chamberlain,

22

allegedly employed by the Bishop of Kaptol on the recommendation of a Hungarian count; but the photograph in the red-velvet album showed him in the count's livery decorated with galloons like a valet-de-chambre, in patent leather shoes and white stockings held under the knee with richly embroidered gold garters. A pale, close-shaven face with deep, passionate wrinkles around his mouth, with healthy teeth; a perfectly impersonal figure, with the cold-blooded, passive look of the born servant; that mysterious father of Philip's hovered over his whole childhood like a shadow at which he shuddered for years. That dead man, whom Philip remembered on his deathbed, lying among pansies and paper lace, began to live in Philip's memory as an increasingly worrying and obscure problem. And here today, after forty years, Philip was still unable to find an answer to the question: whether the decaying livery underneath the oak cross was really his father, or whether it was just a fiction of his mother the tobacconist, who was very much talked about in the town, but who had never given any answer to his questions that would lead to a conclusion unwarranted by the legal documents. And according to those documents, the Hungarian manservant Philip had married the chambermaid Casimira, who had previously served in the cities of Western Europe and spoke several European languages, and there, during his service with the Bishop, a child was born in the tenth month of their legitimate marriage and baptized in the Friars' Church as Sigismund Casimir.

The sun had already broken through the branches of the lime and mulberry trees when Philip walked back down Friars' Street. The tobacconist's shop was open and he found himself in front of the counter; an unpleasant bearded man poured him his *šljivovica,* frowning and squinting suspiciously under his eyelids at the pale stranger who so early in the morning was already snooping around people's windows. Philip drank his *šljivovica* and then had another, lit a cigarette, and sat down on a high empty barrel, steeping himself in the mixture of the old familiar scents.

Those same, unchanged scents of long ago! The entire small ground-floor room—filled with a transparent horizontal cloud of smoke that swayed like a scarf round everything, veiling the cupboard and the wicker stand with its rolls of bread—gave out the acrid and pungently damp smell of the tobacco that had suffused the whole place with its fumes. The scent of cigars, the scent of stale rolls, a sourish smell of brown bread, the mingled smells of *šljivovica* and kerosene lamps and cheap tobacco in pink packages on the bottom shelf. Even the German sausage was still suspended from the same nail on the outer shelf of the glass cupboard with its shoelaces and tallow candles. Looking at those old familiar things, Philip sniffed at his own fingers to see whether he could smell the child's wet sponge and hear the squeak of the slate pencil painfully and clumsily scratching on the damp surface of the slate. There, next to the counter, in front of the glass cupboard near the wicker stand of rolls, a red curtain had stretched from wall to wall, hanging on copper rings from a brass rod and so dividing the room into two parts: the tobacconist's shop itself and the space behind the curtain where Philip had learned to write his first letters, while his enormous childish shadow fell on the curtain and crept along the ceiling like a phantom. At present there was no curtain there, but the old arm-

24

chair, once upholstered in black leather, still remained, leaning with its back against the wall, covered with a tattered, evil-smelling rug, like an old horse. Even thirty years earlier the stuffing had been coming out, a mass of strips, curly feathers, and tufts of dry, bristly, prickly grass; today it was merely the decayed skeleton of an armchair stuffed with old rags and covered with a horsecloth. Even the old, battered, polished table was still there. Philip had played with the drawer of that scratched table for seven whole years. To open the drawer of that worm-eaten table, so secretly alive under its polish (full of invisible movement), was strictly forbidden. But the drawer was attractive and unusually difficult to open, like a secret door, and in the half-light of the dim room glittered a sharp, bare, whetted kitchen knife, so that Philip, gazing at that shining Solingen blade, had the feeling of having crossed the threshold of a dark, cobwebby, medieval armorer's shop. Holding his breath, he would feel his heart beating in his throat in dread lest his mother, in the shop on the other side of the curtain, should hear him. Then in an instant his effort to open the drawer slowly and silently—which very often, with bated breath and fingers excited and trembling, took more than half an hour—would be wasted.

Everything was in its proper place in that damp tomblike room save one thing: the old screen. It had been an old-fashioned English screen in five sections, with a mahogany frame, but the silk had rotted so completely that someone had plastered it over with old steel engravings and lithographs from illustrated papers: English kings with Mary Stuart collars, naked female slaves, falconers, horsemen, counts and countesses, hunters, deer, and generals, Negroes and tropical harbors. The vast surface of a shallow sea rolled onto the beach in green foaming waves, and over there a mast, and on the mast a flag fluttering in the wind; and Philip in a white sun helmet striding boldly alongside the green Congo with a procession of slaves; the jungle exhaling its scents and monkeys screeching in the branches. Outside it was winter. The double telephone wire, stretched across the street from under the old mossy roof on the opposite side of the road, was loaded with heavy wet snow, falling monotonously and unceasingly in leafy flakes. A bird touched the cable with its warm wing, shaking off

25

the wet snow. The falling snow could be seen through the uncurtained upper panel of the glass door; the whole tobacconist's shop seemed to float upward like the gondola of an airship—the tobacconist's shop with its stuffy smells, and cigars, and curtains, and the old armchair, is lifted up and flies, while the screen in front of the divan swells to supernatural dimensions. . . . The guns are thundering before Ladysmith. Fire blazes out of the iron throats and there is a smell of gunpowder; a six-team battery strains every nerve to maneuver a heavy gun into position; the horses' hairy flanks, bloodstained and wounded, their long black lashing tails, their bleeding nostrils, the cracking of whips and the terrified grimaces of horsemen lit up by the glare from the smoky thundering guns. General De Wet, riding a big black stallion, watches the siege of Ladysmith with his entourage, while outside wet snow is falling and somewhere at the end of the street a sledge rattles by. Philip, wrapped in his old woolen shawl with the fringes falling across his knees, like a real traveler, journeys in his chair and watches the count's equerries and falconers, princesses, and kings, contemplates the armor-clad ghosts fading in the evening twilight. From time to time the doorbell rings, a coachman stamps the snow off his boots and buys a roll and drinks his glass of brandy, or somebody drops in to get a packet of Virginia for the doctor; the scent of tobacco and *rakija,* and above the head of the little baroque white-turbanned Negro, a flickering blue bud of flame in case some important gentleman should wish to light his cigar immediately, one of the regular customers of Mrs. Regina, the tobacconist at the corner of Friars' Street.

Those pictures on the gray old-fashioned screen, the only pictures Philip had ever truly experienced in his lifetime. Painting later on himself, writing a great deal about it, he had read as much about the problems of technique as he had written. Nevertheless, even now, he still had an obscure feeling deep down in his unknown self that paintings, if they really were true, living pictures, should speak for themselves at least as loudly as those gray, torn rags had spoken to him in the twilight of that sour-smelling room. In no other picture had anyone ever died so tragically as Przemyslaw, King of Poland, with the lion blazoned on the breast of his cuirass, here, in this tobacconist's shop, in the sooty yellowish light of a kerosene lamp. The lithe tigerish movements, the strange beauty of the bronzed, dark backs of the pearl divers, the lion's bristling mane, the Boer batteries at Ladysmith, the marshals, the horses, the wonderful young women, the whole of that exciting dream had swirled there on the screen like a poisonous green vapor in a magician's retort, and it was with these imaginings, with the ceaseless introspection into and about himself, that Philip's fatal isolation from every kind of reality had begun. It was there long ago, at the very beginning, that he had rejected the direct contact of life; for thirty years he had run after that contact, but he had never caught up.

A carriage stopped in front of the tobacconist's shop. The coachman dropped in to take a small glass of *rakija,* and that hoarse voice, the heavy clump of the driver's boots gave Philip a jolt, so that he started as if someone had awakened him from sleep. Outside shone the bright April morning, dogs were barking and hens across the street could be heard cackling cheerfully and defiantly. He paid for his *šljivovica* and moved toward the promenade under the walls of the old fortress, feeling the warmth of the sun and the scent of the damp smoke in his nostrils.

The café under the poplars on the promenade was already open. There had been a charity performance the night before, and everything smelled of spilt wine and sourish food, while a hunchbacked old woman was raising a cloud of dust and grumbling as she morosely picked up crumpled silver paper, torn streamers, bones, scraps of food, and cigarette ends. Philip ordered a glass of milk. Breaking his third roll with his fingertips and dipping it in his milk, munching without enjoyment the moist, soppy, insipidly sweet mass, completely vague and absentminded, he gazed at the poplars in front of the café windows, at the borders planted with tulips, and at the empty butcher's van, returning bloodstained along by the friars' wall. Contemplating the gray and wrinkled face of the hunchbacked sweeper, her leathery cheeks hard as an elephant's hide, her grotesque movements, her sorrowful aspect, Philip became absorbed in details but unable to give any profound sense to all the details around him.

Nothing but details all around him: the sodden roll, a twittering sparrow, the old hag raising the dust, the early morning—and the weariness in the joints of his fingers, in the top of his head, in his hands, in his thoughts, in everything. Nothing but details and an overwhelming, incomprehensible weariness. Philip had noticed for some time how all objects and impressions fell apart into details under his gaze; only in the most critical days of the war, when everything was breaking up and when nothing was noticeable save a blind piling up of quantities of material—and since man by himself is nothing but an insignificant and petty quantity —only in those gloomiest and loneliest days did it happen that Philip forgot himself in what was going on, losing sight of his own existence. But lately his restlessness had increased and was growing ever more unbearable.

Colors, for instance, the living source of his warmest emotions, were beginning to fade in his eyes. Always before, colors had struck Philip as irresistibly as the torrents of a waterfall, or like the beats of individual musical instruments, but of late the vital force of individual colors was slowly waning and it seemed to him colors could no longer revivify objects or things; as if colors were not veils in which the phenomena of life were wrapped but mere shapes of various form, painted in very pale tints, correctly, like the shapes filled in with watercolors in children's drawing books, without connection, without harmony, without enthusiasm. Empty. Whereas formerly colors had appeared to him as symbols of states and revelations, now his whole experience of color was reduced to a restless and incomprehensible movement of colored surfaces in the streets of gray and sooty cities: the cobalt blue surface of street cars moving horizontally, the khaki-colored cotton patch of the traffic policeman's tunic, the light green shirt of a passerby, and the very pale aquamarine of the Pacific Ocean on a huge map displayed in a bookshop window. Cobalt, khaki, light green, pale aquamarine, as patches, as daubs, as tinted details, and nothing more. Cobalt blue, khaki, light green, against the mud-gray circle of the tire on a car wheel turning very quickly, against the bright *bois de rose* patch of a young girl's dress, or the dark green draperies of a shop window overcrowded with polished furniture; only such relationships of colors in incomprehensible movement, without effect, dead, dull, incredibly empty, without any feeling, without any emotive foundation; worthless, futile.

People pour down the street, faces move in procession; powdered complexions, pale, clownish, with slashes of burning lipstick on their mouths; shortsighted masks of women in mourning, faces of hunchbacks; lower jaws, long waxy fingers with purplish nails, all very ugly. Loathsome faces, inhuman snouts, branded with debauchery and vice, malice and care; sticky, burning faces; carrot heads, Negro jaws, firm sets of teeth, sharp, carnivorous, and everything gray like a photographic negative.

So Philip sat at the window of a dirty city café, watching the movement of the crowds in the street and dreaming of his last coloristic experience in a little southern baroque town a year and a half before, when it was calm golden autumn, and his nerves were not yet as unstrung as now, this spring. It had been a perfectly quiet, soft, oily autumn; the brown tree in the stone courtyard of the monastery—dark brown like worn brocade; the marble knight in armor on the dun bronze slab; the three wax candles in front of the gold-framed picture; the red, sepia-painted, and rain-washed church wrapped in darkness—all in the half-gold heavenly darkness of a dusk full of gleams of a blessed inspiration. A wax candle was burning out on a marble square of the church floor, and the last gutterings of the flame threw broad circles of light and shade into the depths of the church like the flickering of a dying torch; they mingled with the gleam of gold on the pulpit, and the echoes of the friars' sandals on the marble floor of the empty temple in an unusual and intimate sepulchral harmony. It seemed to Philip he had entered a bright green space in a fresh, still-wet oil painting, and in the empty church he was moved by an inner emotion to raise both hands, excited and impressed by the richness of a new world of color that opened before him like some precious metal-framed casket. In that moment of exaltation, standing on the marble church floor with his hands upraised, he looked like a mysterious Delphic statue with two massive vertical legs as if nailed down to the marble church floor, with his hands hovering in the clouds of a fluttering inspiration that seemed very close to him, within his reach, only waiting for him to dip his brushes and start painting.

In the hope of that new picture, of the exultant new departure in the direction of fresh spaces and forms, fresh possibilities of expression, the whole of that autumn passed happily and smoothly as if in a woman's warm hand. The black cowls on factory chimneys, basalt porches with marble piers looking onto the quiet green mirrors of Alpine waters, damp forests with autumnal scents and the misty massifs of mountain glaciers—all this seemed almost within his grasp. The warm vibrations of the last ripe autumn noons above the old roofs of the city, the marble tables in silent mountain inns, the forgotten far-off pains of futile exhaustions, everything looked so shining, so ripe, so finally mastered that Philip felt far closer to the mists, the fish, the hills, and the red apples in the orchards than to anything human either within or around him.

Since then a long time had elapsed, and since then—after those two or three happy autumn days—he had painted nothing at all. For a long time he had experienced nothing worth experiencing; he had dragged himself into cafés, lived among two-legged creatures carrying umbrellas, who, whenever they talked, talked about real things like bread or meat, moving their jaws and their artificial teeth; but it was all futile and offered no reason whatsoever to justify one's existence. So Philip sat now in the café and watched the people passing along the street, musing how strange and enigmatic indeed that movement in the street was. People passed by carrying within them a mixture of boiled fowls' legs, wretched birds' wings, cows' buttocks, horses' haunches, while only the night before those animals had been cheerfully swinging their tails, the hens squawking in hen coops on the eve of their death, and now everything had found its way into human intestines, and all this movement and gluttony could be summed up in one word—life—in western European cities at the end of an old civilization.

Hands. Just what do those thousands of human hands moving about the city streets look like? Human hands that kill, shed the blood of other animals, construct machines, prick with needles; hands hold burning irons, lamps, banners, razors, tools; people carry them in the street as if they did not know what to do with them. They take off their hats, wave their sticks, carry things in their hands—cigarettes, books; one hand holds another hand with the magnetism of physical contact. Human hands are warm; they sweat, grow rough, can be wounded, bathed, painted, make meaningless gestures, follow the movement of human bodies like fleshy ornaments of monotonous size, moving about the streets together with the people, in that long and fruitless human procession that flows and swells between the walls of cities like water. People carry their hands with them, along with their debts, their decaying teeth and their worries, their wives and children, their tired feet, their unhealthy miserable bodies; and they sway their hips and bend their joints; they open their mouths, speak, shout, and here and there a smile appears on human lips. Much of the savage primeval forest still lingers on human cheeks, and unnatural laughter is sometimes heard—laughter that resounds like a

31

silver bell in the darkness—but in the main human faces look tired and expressionless; of wood rather than of flesh. Strange indeed are human cheeks, stiff, hard, as if chiseled; while chains and stuffs and furs all hang on human bodies like superfluous ornaments and mingle with skirts, hair, spectacles, and eyes in a strange unravelable tangle; shortsightedly, wearily, maliciously, and for the most part boringly. All idle and grayish; in fact, just as boring as the sooty pastel gray sky above the roofs and the dirty lead-gray color of the inky reflections on the panes of the closed windows.

Thus Philip in the café contemplated the stream of humanity in the street and thought how he ought to catch that movement on canvas and paint it. The clatter of hoofs on the asphalt, the creaking of heavy axles under the weight of wheels, and the thunder of metal on granite and rails—in some way all this should be caught in its full truth and reality, fixed in a sort of higher realization; but at the same time he felt how impotent he was before all these quantities and how passively he let himself be overwhelmed by them like a crushed and helpless fragment. For how could one paint those floating smells of sawdust, gasoline, oil, dust, smoke, cheap tobacco, glycerine, and tires amid that welter of sounds, and those momentary, almost imperceptible half-silences, when the sound of neither rubber horn nor streetcar bell was to be heard, and when it seemed as if the whole city lay under the soles of a paralytic who dragged his dead shoes along the asphalt, and nothing was to be heard in that moment save the paralytic dragging his tattered shoes along the pavement?

Recently Philip had been troubled by an excessive sensitivity of his auditory nerves; he had long been struggling with the problem of dissociating whole complexes of acoustic impressions from his artistic conceptions. These acoustic impressions obstructed his conceptions to an ever increasing extent, and it seemed to him he would be able to paint again only if he became deaf. When from time to time an idea for a picture came to him, it would as a rule be mixed with some acoustic effect, so that at that moment in his mind the painter's synthesis would disappear; the new sound would arouse within him new associations, and he would waste time in a futile attempt to clarify the image like a bird of prey whose quarry succeeds in hiding itself from sight. Philip would be transported by an unexpected sound, as if by a gust of wind, and would seem to be hovering in space above a futile dark emptiness. To sit motionless for years at café windows, to bite the nail of one's left forefinger, and to break one's head over the fundamental question: Is there any need at all to paint, and if this cannot be questioned, then how to do it?

Crowds pass down city streets, they disappear into the dark, and painting is altogether superfluous for them. Why should all those people need painting? Spurs jangle, and paper flowers are still to be seen in the buttonholes of women's coats, women's breasts stir underneath white linen like waxen globes, voices are low, cheeks pass and speak. Philip had listened to the conversations of passersby for years and had not yet heard a single one talk about painting. Those cannibal-like, coarse, tough faces carry their own misery with them, while painting is no problem to them at all; they have none but their own misery. People move like wax dolls, scratch the napes of their necks, chew tobacco, and leave behind them a cloud of cigar smoke, the reek of their bodies and of misery. Every individual drags around with him the enormous circles of his own existence, his own warm entrails and other persons' warm entrails, from which he has issued like a worm, to crawl and twist, to bite and prick with his poisonous sting, to eat and devour; and others devour him, and have harnessed him, and beat him about the head with a whip. Everything moves in circles of resistance and starvation and horror, and amid all this painting is a largely unknown and superfluous matter.

There is sorrow in every human eye, like an animal peeping out of a cage; human gestures are like those of hyenas, and vulnerable because everything is barred and everything is locked in a cage, and painting is altogether unnecessary in cages. How could one possibly stop those human streams along the streets and begin talking to them about life in terms of painting? The women wear necklaces and snakeskin shoes with colored heels, and their eyes are as clear as spring water. Women dream about furs and silk stockings—not about pictures. People drag themselves along the streets in chains, wheel spokes turn, hoofs clatter, and there is something of the lizard in men's faces, dollish, gray, drunken; everything is weary and drowsy and short of sleep, and in the crowd someone has raised his cane with a silver handle like a drum major's and walks as if marching at the head of a band and as if aware of his destination. How would it be possible to paint such a silly passerby, walking at the head of a mob and wearing a bowler hat? What is particularly important is that he looks like a drum major, and knows where he is going, and where the street goes to, and for him the world is a mechanism that beats as correctly as the watch ticking between nickel plates in his pocket with its hands moving in time, and everything works and moves like a wound-up watch in the pocket of a silly passerby.

Losing himself thus in a series of eccentric and bizarre observations, Philip was fully aware that he was wasting time looking at things in an unpainter-like fashion and that his whole power of observation was slowly disintegrating into trifling analyses of details; but that process of disintegration, those constant digressions, became ever more violent and imperative. There was someone carrying a melon in his hand, someone else smoking a pipe, a woman blinking like an otter—and certainly tonight she would fish in troubled waters—and another man, with deerskin breeches and an accordion, looking as though he had stepped out of a Tyrolese picture. Rodents, termites; pedantic, yellow, clerkish, short-sighted ants with collars of dirty celluloid, destroying one another with poisonous acids in smelly, airless rooms, under whining gas lamps; big bellies full of beer, shining bicycle spokes, and a lady with her hair done like an ancient Egyptian mummy—all the sleepless, ravenous, snarling looks, the hideousness of the body, the misery of the flesh, the futility of vehicles passed before Philip's eyes dully, grayly, incomprehensibly, dimly. Such experiences were growing more and more troublesome and frequent.

Thus would come back to his mind the old, forgotten scent of the dirty wolf's cage in the gray, shabby, stinking menageries he had seen long ago in a provincial suburb in Pannonia. It had been raining. A woman trainer in a braided red hussar's uniform was stroking a long, fat, sleepy snake under a thick, reddish, striped cotton eiderdown; the rain could be heard sliding down the green canvas of the tent, and somewhere a tin gutter spout was gurgling. In the circles of the pictures that represented his life in

34

recent years, amid the smoke of filthy inns and café tables foul with spilt *rakija,* above the bare rows of trees and senseless jangling of distant morning bells, throughout troubled, sleepless nights, the forgotten scent of the wolf in the dirty, dreary, provincial menagerie would come back to Philip like a mournful sound or like a drop of poison, and his condition would become even gloomier and more envenomed. Sickened by that disgusting animal smell that had filled the badly lit enclosure under the wet green canvas together with the suffocating smell of wet sawdust and a smoking acetylene lamp, he would halt, and as if a sharp pain had stabbed the lobes of his brain, he would hold his head in his hands, unable to proceed any farther. From such moods he could escape only through alcohol. To get drunk was to forget.

So he was sitting somewhere on the outskirts of the town and drinking for the second day in succession. It was dusk and half dark in the café, and on a divan by the gas stove a black tomcat was dozing and purring. The inn was under the bridge, and through the window, under the dark stone arch, a poor Jewish funeral procession could be seen passing slowly by in a gentle spring shower; the wooden urn on top of the hearse rocked in a comical way above the black coffin, and the rabbi had a jet-black, curly, Biblical, Assyrian beard. Above the sorrowful procession of long, creased frock coats and umbrellas, the pale blue banner of an advertisement for pasteurized milk waved in a gust of wind; an enormous, unnatural baby with swollen and protuberant watery eyes was painted on the pale blue canvas, and the blue banner spread across the street, the red-brick houses, the gin shops, the windows of old junk shops, the poor Jewish funeral procession, and that forgotten wolf's scent—the smell of half-rotten black meat on a tin plate on the floor of the cage—all these images stood out in Philip's mind in unusually vivid detail but without any internal cohesive power to bind the whole together and give it some sense and unity. At times Philip felt the strength to overcome this disintegration under the influence of alcohol, and the danger of his neurasthenia actually lay in the fact that with the return to soberness things seemed more and more empty and gloomy. Life began to split up in Philip into its component parts; within him the incessant, analytical disintegration of everything

35

grew increasingly active, becoming an end in itself, a process that, for quite some time now, had automatically tended toward disintegration. This mental destruction of everything that came to his hand, or appeared before his eyes, was slowly giving rise to an idea that began to haunt him more and more obstinately from one day to the next: according to his own conception of his subjective life, all meaning, even the slightest, was disappearing. His life had somewhere broken away from its foundations and had begun to turn into a phantom that had no reason whatsoever for existence; and this had been going on for some time, and was growing more and more burdensome and exhausting.

Philip had been living in a four-story house where everything was permeated with the smell of goose fat, gas lamps, and traces of children; where the elevator looked shabby, like a glass hearse at a second-class funeral; a black polished coffin with pillows of dark threadbare plush. To stand by the window and gaze at the murky gloom had been Philip's life for the last two or three years; to watch sick children with their necks bandaged copying designs on the windowpanes all day long. How dark are human dwellings, how evil-smelling are those holes called human dwellings, where children bandaged in flannel rags copy stupid drawings and hold their hands above their heads, unwearied, high up, all the rainy day. Chimneys, roofs, and a thick veil of soot draped over the dark walls like a curtain, every stain of soot leaving a trace like a bedbug's. And the smoke hangs around the roofs, yellow-gray and dirty, like a starving village dog, heavy as a bag of cement, and green as muddy water. The cowls of sooty chimneys in the wind, the fiddlelike screech of the streetcars, the wet, dark gray, slimy streets, the murky light. Philip stood by the window thinking that all those coke stoves and hydrants and gas heaters, so stupidly piled up in one place, had in fact no meaning at all; all those industrial appliances were as dirty as privies and all those piles of excrement, goods, raw materials should be set apart from human lodgings. Water pipes rattle, gas pipes and gas cocks whine, telephones buzz and copper wires on the roofs hum, doors are slammed, musical instruments jangle, dogs bark, and somewhere on the other side of the wall a monotonous drip splashes at regular intervals, like a clock ticking. The dripping of taps, human footsteps resounding in unlit corridors, distant voices heard from somewhere in the depths of the house, the moaning of a recorded Negro sang on a phonograph, and the quivering of Philip's nerves in that acoustic hell buzzing infernally around him—he had ceased to comprehend why all this was happening and why he lacked strength to break away from all that surrounded him, and to do something new with himself and the life about him.

Under his feet the vast grimy city lay wrapped in a pall of soot and smoke in the February half-light, and this was that far-famed Europe, that golden blessed land, with warm blue southern bays where oranges blossom, and terrible sooty northern fortresses where children suffer from tonsilitis and scrofulous girls creep about the streets. How sad Hygeia's plaster images looked in the chemists' dusty showcases. Like the tin of children's toys, so thin and transparent and meaningless are all the barriers of human schemes men erect between themselves and the living truths and reality of life. Just like children's building blocks—religion, silly Christmas customs, idylls forwarding the cult of pure lies, masking commercial ends; buy margarine, chocolate, oranges, vanilla, cloth, rubber goods! People with wallpaper, carpets, parquet, hot-water pipes, glass doors, goldfish, cactuses, and whole showcases of books in their apartments, books no one reads. People have houses piled up to the roofs with China, majolica, aquarelles, damask table cloths, nylon stockings, furs, and jewels. People have their nails polished like ancient Orientals; they take baths in marble bathrooms, drive in heated coaches, drink bitter digestive liqueurs; but in fact they have not the slightest idea of the reality of life or how they should live.

More and more often, and more and more urgently, it had occurred to Philip lately that he might break away from all the soot and smells and go home to Pannonia, where he had not been for so long. To live down there with his mother in the vineyard at Kostanjevec for one autumn, rich, quiet, and with wine in abundance.

The inky dark south wind, the pale moonlight, the mild night with the distant twinkling of lights in the valley. The black branches of the oak trees at the crossroads, the lines of stars quivering behind patches of mist, and here and there in the distant vineyards an isolated shot or two, which echoed and re-echoed across ravines and fields and died away in the cutting near the water mill like a distant peal of thunder. The silence of the fields. Only now and then the whisper of the maize leaves stirring would be heard, as if a woman in a well-starched petticoat had passed along the path and rustled across a hummock. The dirty, muddy Pannonian waters flowed and gurgled under the bridges, and a tin crucifix hung silently under a tiny wooden roof with paper flowers in a box like a glass coffin; a blind man with an accordion had once stood there crying a whole afternoon, but now everything was quiet and there was no one. Pannonia would be sleeping and there would be no soot, no hurry, no nerves. There the nights were still as a pipe that had gone out; no lights, no smoke, no soot. Only the dogs slunk around the fences at night with their tails between their legs and their rumps down, leaning forward on their front legs, ready to jump, with gleaming eyes, friends of fences and hornbeam stakes, in a maze of scents and fresh tracks: there the smell of a peasant's shoe, there a rotten bone, down there a fence, and behind the fence a young duck in a hen coop.

Philip had tossed to and fro for a long time in his gloomy daydream when one night he realized that the time had come to go. Above the sooty cloud in the smoky railway station appeared the illuminated face of the station clock; the black hands against the darkly orange illumined glass face awoke a sense of time in Philip; he felt how time was passing, and how good it would be to start. So he had set out, and now he was sitting in the Kaptol café, and like the smoke of his cigarette, wisps of weary daydreams seemed to float around him—thoughts of the ephemeral quality of human existence in space and time, of the incomprehensible extent of life's reality compared with that flickering phenomenon called the subjective self; and with the trifling, quite insignificant, unreal details outside the subject that constituted the sphere of perception of that subject, which in itself was nothing but a detail in a series of details, and everything only movement and weariness and sadness.

Where is the proof that our "ego" lasts, that "we" are always and uninterruptedly "we"? Where is our measure in actuality? What was there to show that it was the same he who had left this dirty, backward provincial town so many years earlier, when he had sat for the last time in this stuffy café waiting for his train? At that time he had next to him on a chair a newspaper parcel tied with string; a shirt and a toothbrush. The shirt had been torn up long ago, and the toothbrush, too, had worn out long ago, and his body—his constitution in general—had entirely changed, so where or how was it possible for him to prove he had remained the same man who, years before, had started nervously as he had waited for the moment when he would leave everything behind?

A Christian name and surname, the status attached to a certain Christian name and surname, were merely external, most superficial distinctions! Conventional, shallow bourgeois criteria! How could he persuade his "self" with an unquestionably reliable guarantee that he was really the sum of his "self"? By his face? But that face had completely changed! By his gestures? Those gestures today were the gestures of an utterly different man! By his physical continuity? Today there was no longer in him a single atom of his bodily constitution of those many years ago.

On the wall opposite Philip there hung a huge gold-framed café mirror, and to the left and right of the mirror two Empire caryatids on gold consoles bore on their heads two gilt Greek vases with green peacock feathers and palm branches. In the perspective of the mirror's dirty amalgam, in its hazy depths, the whole hall appeared in the distance: the two green parallelograms of the billiard tables, the hunchbacked charwoman sweeping up the perforated lottery tickets, the confetti and streamers; the bareheaded baker's assistant counting out the rolls on an oval marble table for a sleepy waitress to pass around. And here in the foreground, just in front of the gray cloudy glass, was a man gazing into the reflected café; pale, short of sleep, tired, turning gray, with deep black rings around his eyes and a lighted cigarette between his lips; excited, exhausted, quivering, drinking lukewarm milk, and thinking about the identity of his "ego." That man doubted the identity of his "ego." That man suspected the identity of his own existence; he had arrived that morning, not having been in this café for many years.

Strange! Such an unborn "somebody" sits in a mirror, calls himself "himself," carries his utterly vague and cloudy "self" within him for years; he smokes and gets tired of smoking; it makes him feel sick, his heart feels constricted, his head aches, strange greenish circles swim before his eyes, and everything is

40

dim and cloudy, all turning in a circle, and all hypothetical, indefinite, strangely flickering—thus it is to be the thinking subject and to be conscious of the identity of one's own subjective self.

Quite unconsciously taking note of that pale and unknown man smoking probably his fiftieth cigarette since last night, Philip grasped the lighted cigarette stuck to his lip and threw the smelly burning paper into the ashtray, realizing only then how nicotine was trickling down his throat like resin and how his tongue smarted with its revolting, nauseating coating. He took another gulp of milk, losing himself again in a wave of contradictory thoughts that rose in opposition to his hypochondriac restlessness—the resistance of a section of his own personality; he inhaled a gust of wind that, like the fresh breath of a spring morning, streamed through the thick cloud of smoke, spilt wine, and floor polish.

Of course! The identity of the subject could not be established by the face or the grimaces, nor by any external phenomena. His face, his features, the movements of his body were no longer the gestures and movements of his body of those years ago, but the continuity of his "ego" nonetheless persisted somewhere deep down, secretly, obscurely, but genuinely and intensely!

It was the sparrows on the old walnut tree in the courtyard, Carolina's carpet beater, the smell of the stinking tobacconist's shop in Friars' Street, the decayed livery of the chamberlain in the friars' cemetery, the soaked paper boat that had sunk in the drain below the gray ground-floor window from which he had watched the English horses! That unknowable identity was here with him now, under his English cloth suit; under this external form where the watch could be heard ticking in the pocket of his waistcoat; under this flesh, in those restless, trembling fingers (which felt every heartbeat, and in their tips the cold touch of the oval marble table). Under this rich network, under the veil of surface relationships, in the incomprehensible web of his condition, somewhere wrapped away beneath, well concealed, there palpitated and beat that identity of his; and it was no phantom, but flesh, the café, a cup of milk, the reality of the morning and of his return. The material of his suit against his body was warm, and he could feel the milk cold on the enamel of his teeth, and moisture was

41

dripping from the glass down on to his palm, and it was pleasant. The watch ticked in his waistcoat, and the spring of the watch unwound itself in the mechanism, and he absorbed cellulose as he sipped his lukewarm milk, conscious of his soft Parisian shirt. . . .

Much here had changed fundamentally in those past twenty-three years. The last time he had sat in this uncomfortable café, things around him as well as within him were far more wretched than this morning. Then he had finally parted from his mother, then he had been leaving for an unknown destination, hungry, with patched clothes, childishly inexperienced, a man who did not know himself what he wanted—but today he was no longer the same "I"—that was true! From the mirror a different face looked at him; compared with that ragged, consumptive, alcoholic, ingenuously self-confident young adventurer, today this was a gentleman in an English suit; a man turning gray; one who bathed, traveled in sleeping cars, and had left at the railway-station cloakroom his pigskin suitcases with deerskin covers. But between those two faces—the one belonging to a drunken consumptive with one shirt and one toothbrush and the other carrying in his wallet an X-ray photograph of his left lung taken at a very expensive sanatorium in southern Switzerland—a sort of invisible bridge nevertheless existed, in all these sights and objects around him! This gold-framed mirror with the two caryatids and peacock feathers, this muddy Pannonian backwater, this wretched Kaptol street, with tulips and a caged squirrel in the middle of the round flower bed under the lamppost; this café, the mournful friary bell that had tolled in vain over empty attics and chimneys for so many years! This morning he had returned to an old picture he had never mastered, to old worries and cares, the source of the sorrow and depression that beset him, as if he had awakened in his own grave!

In front of the café, below the old ramparts of the imperial and princely fortress, the first chestnuts were already in bloom: the red bricks of the fortress walls, whose redness was striking against the intense green of the turfy glacis, were the only surviving witnesses to the glory of the old fortress, once described in hexameters by poets all over Europe as one of the basic cornerstones of Western culture. The Lord Mayor, who was also Head of the Fire Brigade, had planted flower beds with pansies around the bandstand, and on the house of Boltek, the shoemaker, all one side of the roof bore his surname in huge letters: Humanic. Lawyer Siebenschein's house, with a Nuremberg window at the corner, was still the only two-story house on the promenade side; and a muddy walk led down Friars' Street toward Kravoder, then on to Bikovo, to Biškupec, and then across Lisjak, Jama, and Turčin to Kostanjevec, where he himself was bound, to the village of Kostanjevec, to see his mother, the tobacconist Regina, who owned a one-story house and a vineyard with a vinedresser's hut, and who for years had been inviting him in her monotonous letters. Now at last he had started, and here he was sitting under this dreadful mirror, waiting for the coachman, and everything was so unnecessary and wearisome and pitiful. And the most pitiful of all was the marble woman bent over an urn like a tombstone in the middle of the round flower bed, under the poplars, though it was actually no tombstone, but a statue of Victory laying a palm on the pyramid commemorating "The Great Days of 1914–1918." Someone had chiseled off the first part of the inscription from the concrete pedestal, so that Victory now mourned in her veil, without the pathetic inscription. At the unveiling ceremony Philip had stood in the double row of the guard of honor, stiff with straps and cartridge belts, holding his rifle butt with all five fingers as if they were glued to the wood; and a frock-coated gentleman with an umbrella had said something along the lines of a well-known quotation from a speech made by Maria Theresa at Pressburg, and the drum had sounded muffled as if it were torn.

The contemplation of that bending marble figure—an extremely weak, dilettantish, late secessionist work—evoked in Philip some early complexes. He began to think that the superfluousness of all occasional art, and sculpture in particular, is especially conspicuous on provincial promenades where the pedestals of various discredited monuments stand in honor of that flamboyant time, stripped today of all that once seemed grand about them, so that what remain are only small, unsuccessful statues that look modeled with the sculptor's wet sponge rather than carved by hand;

they were actually common commercial shams, poor stuff. All the eagles and inscriptions, all the eager and obtrusive rattling of bronze monuments as of swords, using statues as an incitement to war, all that was to be viewed in retrospect, from ten to fifteen years' distance; such a small span of years and such a great change in perspective. One had stood there stiff with straps and lead, and today one could hardly remember anything or anybody around that monument! Only the rain falling and the drum sounding as if it were torn. Everything was engulfed in the heavy, thick, gray Pannonian mist.

As is usually the case on such occasions, there was no cab.
One buggy had taken the surveyor on field work, while at the
other cabby's, in a small, bright green hut, next to a lighted stove,
Philip found a toothless old crone munching a roll dipped in
coffee in a red pint pot. She told him that the cabby would be
back sometime in the afternoon, but she could not say when.
There was one other alternative: to wire to Kostanjevec for a
conveyance to fetch him in the morning, and to spend the night
here at the Kaptol hotel. Tired, in need of sleep, upset by the long
two-day journey, shuddering at the very thought of a disgusting
hotel room full of bedbugs, deeply depressed, anxious to leave
this magpie's nest as soon as possible, Philip trudged along the
gray humped side streets off the promenade, looking at the closed
barns, the manure heaps, the haystacks; feeling lost in this noisy
morning idyll and incapable of making any decision at all. From
across the street rang the voice of the anvil; in the blacksmith's
courtyard a fat mare from the Drava valley was being shod, a
well-fed, even overfed animal, and capricious, with blue ribbons
in her mane. The horseshoes clatter, the air smells of coal and
burnt hoofs.
A yellow carriage was drawn up there: it might be a good
opportunity! It was the bishop's coachman, Joe Podravec, who
had driven His Grace's landlady from the bishop's residence to
the fast train for Vienna the night before, and was going back to
Biškupec that morning with a bag of cement. After long negotiations, it turned out that Joe Podravec was prepared to take the
gentleman to Biškupec, and in case the gentleman, say, wanted to
do so, he could even go with Joe as far as Kostanjevec, provided,
say, he was willing to take a short cut across Turčin common, in
which case it was not too far: maybe two hours' drive. And so
they finally reached an agreement, got Milicent shod, drove up to
Löwinger to fetch the bag of cement and a tin tub, picked up

Philip's luggage at the railway station, and so, on top of the bag of cement and the large suitcases, on the high spring seat of Joe Podravec's coach, they finally set off down Friars' Street and then along Illyria and Krajina Streets in the direction of the toll bar near the railway, almost at the other end of the city. The wide road was lined with rows of aged poplars, and the low Biedermeier one-story house by the toll bar had six windows in a row, all carefully closed with heavy iron shutters.

"Them girls!"

Joe Podravec turned in his seat toward the gentleman and winked at him knowingly, waving contemptuously with his pipe in the direction of the closed one-story house with its iron shutters, where "them girls would be sure to be still asleep!"

What a suggestive expression: "them girls!"

But yet! How many profound secrets were buried in the vulgar words of a Pannonian coachman, amassing spittle under his tongue in disgust and moral contempt! The secrets of a distant and sorrowful childhood, when that word "girls" hovered above one's childish cares like a mysterious airship which someone had once seen, though no one had the faintest idea where it might come to earth! There behind the hedge stood a rosebush, where the vet's son Aurel had one afternoon seen one of the "girls" lying naked under a red umbrella. His companions had subsequently searched the whole field as far as the stream, along the hedges and ditches, but no one found any trace of the girl's adventure. They discovered a faded light blue ribbon stuck on a hawthorn and a bronze hairpin, but it was impossible to find out whether those objects really belonged to the adventuress who had been seen sunbathing under the roses. Like dogs with their tails between their legs, schoolboys would slink around the gray, forbidding house, where nobody was ever to be seen, where all was shut and locked, but where nevertheless it was rumored the "girls" drank coffee in the arbor under the walnut tree.

In the sixth form, after a soul-searing year-long struggle, Philip had one day risked the whole of his moral existence and set out at noon for "the girls." It was a July noon. Ducks lay in the puddles in the shade of the mulberry trees; the bindweed with its blue bells clinging to strings along the eaves was drooping in the vertical rays of the sun; blinds were lowered in all the houses. His intention was bold, yet logical. Noon was the most convenient time, as no one would think he was going to "the girls"! The town lay completely deserted, and Philip was as cold as if he had been walking in a dark beer cellar. The vaulted blue sky, the fences, the poppies in flower in the gardens, the poplars, the lime trees in front of the church; a dog ran across the street, and jumped over the fence sluggishly, disappearing amid parsley beds and tomatoes, while Philip moved on, wooden as if under an anesthetic, paralyzed inside, cold, but imbued with a ferocious and awesome strength; he would die on the spot rather than stop! There was no one about; quite alone he walked across the Bishop's Square; yet he had an unpleasant feeling of being exposed, stigmatized, transparent. He felt that everybody knew whither he was bound, and that behind each of the closed shutters someone who knew him was peeping, watching the tobacconist's son, watching him go to a brothel, where after all he belonged, for he was "not born to anything better"! On the pavement in front of the bishop's church a white cat crossed his path, and through the open door of the confectioner's at the corner someone could be heard beating cream in a bowl.

Driven by his restlessness, the fixed idea of his horrible restlessness, like a somnambulist, with waxy hands and cold sweaty joints, Philip had moved in a fever, half blind, trembling, with shaking knees, down Krajina Street, toward the gray, forbidding building next door to the toll bar, with its row of six windows shut with heavy iron shutters, rusted by wind and rain. He had turned into the brick courtyard, where it smelled of pigeons and hens, and everything had an idyllic appearance in the shade of the large walnut tree, and it was all absolutely empty, as if everybody had died. The white glass door to the house, invitingly open, a gold-framed mirror in the hall and red cloth curtains, and on the marble slab in front of the mirror, a porcelain Negress carrying a gold jug on her head and in the jug roses of silk crepe paper. Silence. A rabbit hopped up out of a dark corridor, sniffed Philip's footprints, and vanished in the darkness. The mysterious movements of this dark furry ball made Philip's heart thump in his throat; he thought the creature was a hedgehog, and then even the rabbit disappeared, and everything was silent and death-like once more. Behind a door could be heard a clatter of pots and pans, and a noise as though somebody had slammed the oven door on the kitchen stove. Philip approached the front door and knocked—and already by then he was beginning to think of going back into the road. An old woman with a blue apron and spectacles on her forehead opened the kitchen door, and still stirring some maize-flour in a black iron pot she was holding in her hands, asked him, squinting at him under her eyelids suspiciously and coldly, what he wanted? Who was he looking for?

Then she left the pot on the table, dried her hands, and shuffling down the dark corridor in her felt slippers, passed behind a curtain. The kitchen door remained open; one ring of the kitchen stove was uncovered, and through the grimy circle dark red flames were flickering out, sooty and dark as a funeral pyre. Behind the curtain Philip could hear a door creak, negotiations, talking, stifled laughter, and then, followed by the extraordinarily distrustful eyes of that shortsighted old woman, he boldly advanced, more blindly than consciously, toward the door to which the old woman pointed.

In a damp, musty wave of scent, as if blinded after the glare of the summer sunshine, groping in the dim, insufficient light which came through the open door, Philip could see only basins, backs of chairs with women's clothes over them, geraniums at the window, and postcards on the walls, while from the impenetrable darkness a voice invited him to approach the bed.

There, in a shaft of light from a tiny circle in the shutters, lay a woman with her belly uncovered, enormous and white like dough on a baker's peel. Just that the belly was enormous, swollen, soft, and smelled like yeast under one's fingers; that it had a navel, like a lump of dough on a baker's peel—that was the only picture that survived vividly and ineradicably in his memory.

The "girls"! Where now was that distant time of strange secrets about girls and that white, bulging, doughlike woman's belly with its navel?

Philip rocked on Joe Podravec's spring seat, lost in thought, seeking some concrete way of expressing that motif in terms of painting.

48

Black and white?

Too weak. Too one-sided. In that distant incident the main thing had been the illumination of something that was rotten, raw, bloated, enormous, something mysteriously female, which ought to be treated in the fashion of Toulouse-Lautrec, but again illuminated with the peculiarly unhealthy, unnatural light of rotten flesh. That belly should spread across the whole canvas in a wholly decayed, fluid state, like an overripe Camembert, it should not be the picture of something commonplace, banal, a cross section of a brothel; that belly should be weary; the enormous belly of an old, worn-out woman who had borne many children; a serious, sad, exhausted woman who had ceased to be a Kaptol "girl" and had become a symbol, a formula for the situation in which contemporary woman lives, hidden like a child's sanctuary, but spat upon like a spittoon, something that is looked on with disgust even by a Joe Podravec. Around that bed one should wrap all those invisible veils, those secret burning lusts, the shrinking of innocent fear, and the expectation of something not yet experienced, something transcendental, while in fact there is nothing but a cool twilight in which everything is sour as vinegar! The female belly should be the motif, but a motif completely exposed, dangerous: the motif of woman's nakedness fixed once and for all with shameless sincerity, with the most sensual rapture, with a particular unconcealed stress on the physical. A white naked body, painted morbidly, madly, perversely, like a torso soaked in the light of fear, disquiet, fever, juvenile horror, gloom, stench, the brothel smell of sour feather beds, oil stoves, and dirty cups with crumbs of wet rolls in them, and an irritating green fly buzzing in the dark and beating its wings against the mirror.

Thinking about that distant incident which had happened under the old roof, now concealed by the poplars behind the railway, Philip became aware in himself of spreading concentric circles of associations; the associations grew into a tempest, an infuriating whirl of overstrained imagination which, with its intensity, usually destroyed all his creative ideas in embryo; for in expressing himself on canvas an artist is so limited by the one-sidedness of his medium! It is impossible to paint sounds and scent, and the perfect realism of the picture is unthinkable without sounds and without scents. The fetid sourish atmosphere of the dark room, that brothel-like light and shade, should be filled with the vibrations of a human voice, a hoarse, syphilitic contralto that rolls from the throat like the whistle of a broken reed, a voice as gray as the grayness of the torn sack under the woman's bed. The most important undertone of that fateful incident had been the hoarse female contralto voice; it had filled the picture of that distant July noontide when a young boy had been frightened by the nakedness of a female belly and had run away from the room like a thief, with his heart thumping as if an unknown hairy, greedy beast had stretched out a claw from her bed to seize him.

The woman had told him to come nearer. He did.

To sit down on her bed, and he did.

But as soon as she had taken him by the hand and learned from him that he was Regina's son, she began to talk about the tobacconist as familiarly as if she were a person in no way different from the creatures living in those dark rooms.

"Why? Because she makes love with canons? Or bishops? As if the tobacconist's Canon Lawrence did not visit them too and complain to the girls about that Regina of his who was too expensive for him!"

As Philip listened to that exhausted voice in that sour-smelling twilight, in that leaden-gray cloud of dirty sheets and damp feather beds—the voice that spoke about his mother, while he watched that enormous, bare female belly lying there under his hand, pallid as a brewery mushroom, and smelling of common soap—the sensation of being mysteriously trapped in that loathsome house, as well as burdened with the obscure and mysterious drama within and around the tobacconist's, clung to him like a wet smelly sheet. Aware of an unutterably disgusting stench, he broke away from that pale apparition and rushed out of the room. In his flight he did not forget to fling a silver florin behind him, and he could still hear the clink of the silver coin on some glass.

He had cried the whole afternoon on the embankment under the railway as if someone of his had died.

The monotonous roofs of the Pannonian cottages—thatched like their beehives—the mares and cows in the pastures, the plowfields, the pigs, the slow jogging pace, threw Philip into a deep and vague melancholy, that morose state of mind in which he always approached the most successful realization of his artistic ideas.

Bees were swarming, pigs grunting, cows calving in stables, sick calves slobbering in swaddling bands, the wind was rustling under the fresh, young branches of the elm and oak trees; heavy spring clouds floated over the forests, and Philip was on his way to the vineyard at Kostanjevec after his roving life in the cities of Europe; and he was dreaming of his new composition, a bare female belly darkly illumined by a boy's sad and morbid experience.

The only creative reality is what initially shocks our senses; man really sees only what he notices for the first time. Painting is and should be nothing else but a visionary revelation of the space before us; for, if not that, it has no justification. Otherwise, it is only the sticking together and patching up of familiar and already painted pictures, a mere multiplying of what has already been seen. It is like that boring winter pastime of children sticking transfers onto paper, wetting them with their fingers. Sticking together and rearranging, that is all artistic styles and trends and schools are; but all this had nothing to do with Philip, since he refused to follow any artistic trend, style, or school. And therefore the problem of that naked belly must be freed from his personal, psychological, unnecessary ballast of acoustic or olfactory imagery. That belly should be given a criminal suggestiveness, in terms of Kraft-Ebbing: one should feel how underneath it a child's soul had been violated and murdered!

Pigs were grunting, cows mooing, flies swarming over heaps of warm manure, a multitude of white patches shone out among the

51

wheat and other crops in the fields, reflecting the bright white masses of April cloud; and the coachman, Joe Podravec, was getting bored on his box. His pipe had gone out; the mares were wise and more familiar with the road than he himself, and this odd fellow sitting next to him on the spring seat kept persistently silent, as if he were asleep. But he was not asleep, you could see that. No, he was puzzling his gentlemanly head over something! He had a lot of suitcases: he might be a circus artist or a magician. Or even a Jew, with his merchandise packed in those boxes! Ribbons and combs, or women's silk scarfs!

To break the long silence while they were descending at a slow pace through the Kavadar gorges, Joe Podravec began to talk about himself, about his family and things around him, how things stood with him. How he had been in America twice, but he had no use for America. He had been told by old and experienced seamen, who had pissed often enough in those waters, to look out, for he would spot sea-deer swimming alongside the ship. He had stood on deck for two days and two nights, and wouldn't go to bed; he had waited to glimpse the sea-deer, how they came up out of the water, but not a single sea-deer had he seen. His ship was followed halfway by white birds—"that was true, I saw them with my own eyes"—and then black American birds flew out to meet her—"like black dragons, as you might say"—and by that the seamen aboard ship knew when they were exactly halfway across.

Joe Podravec had been a Uhlan. He had served with the Emperor's Uhlan regiment in Hungary, at Tolna, and he had been captured, too, in Galicia in '15 near Dobra Noč when he still had half a liter of rum left in his flask! He had been at Tehran and Tiflis as well. At Tiflis he had seen only naked Turkish women, while at Tashkent he had sold fish and fought on camels under General Dutov against those red Moscovites. Then he had come back—"God be praised, as you might say"—to Biškupec, twice wounded, twice "mortally ill," but now quite healthy and well, as you might say, nothing wrong with him, and his old wife had a Singer sewing machine, and she could "do all sorts of embroideries on her sewing machine all by herself"!

Listening to the coachman's monotonously empty life story,

Philip felt a distance of unutterable indifference separating him from Joe Podravec. Two hundred million such coachmen, as similar as if carved in wood, lived in the lands from the Pacific to these Pannonian marshes; identical faces, identical hands, identical destinies.

In his thoughts he painted that imaginary belly, combining into a whole with his brushstrokes the bare, soft rolls of flesh around the hips and above the thighs, while this fellow next to him was saying that to make water without getting rid of the wind, "as you might say," was just like going to confession without going to communion afterward!

Joe Podravec had a sewing machine and his wife embroidered linen, while he, Philip, had to deal with things in a symbolic way; playing with colored surfaces like formulas, solving the problems of an abstract, completely imaginary arithmetic. A huge gulf separated him from this Pannonian coachman; truly an incomprehensibly wide gulf! There was a long way between him and the late secessionist movement on the Kaptol promenade. They were two different worlds. And that baroque frontier church, yellow and historical, in the meadow over there, was also a world by itself. It stood there like a sort of a bastion in the mud, and for several centuries now had been speaking to the Pannonians of its fundamental principles and schemes, but without much success; these coachmen's way of thinking had certainly not changed at all for the last two thousand years. The man sitting next to Philip on the box seat was closer to primitive Pannonian man than to Matisse! He was literally a livestock breeder, and how far it was from his calloused palms to Philip's sensitivity of touch for tissue or silk material between his fingers! Two men were seated there on that box seat, one of them an eccentric neurasthenic, a sectarian in painting, a relativist, a fauvist, a colorist; they spoke the same language, and yet actually they were two languages and two continents! Even the marble woman on the promenade, as an outlook on life, was also a separate continent. And all that "Great Time," too, floated in the midst of things like a solitary iceberg, an iceberg that had wrenched away and engulfed an entire world. And that famous Kaptol fortress of Bakacz's, and the Bishop's Palace, and Philip's dead father who had been the Bishop's valet,

53

and his mother, Casimira Valenti, who for some unknown reason had been renamed Regina and who used to be a tobacconist; everything now had its place in space like a series of finished and isolated facts all in disproportion, scattered and incoherent. It was a long way from one phenomenon of this kind to another, and all of them moved along one after the other; unbridgeably, foolishly, fiendishly entangled and sad. The man next to him on the box seat had been a Uhlan and a soldier in the so-called "Great Time." He had kissed naked Turkish women at Tiflis, had fought on camels in Asian deserts; another time he had seen the camp-fires near far-famed Valmy, and had come back twenty thousand kilometers to his Biškupec. This coachman was neither a Catholic, nor a supporter of the Emperor, nor a Russian prisoner of war! He was neither a patriot, nor a citizen; he believed neither in God nor in the Church; he had forgotten his Croatian, and failed to learn Russian; he recognized no sanctity in the Roman sense of the word, either religious or legal, he was overburdened with deadly sins of many kinds; he had certainly killed, perjured, committed adultery. There was just one thing in the world which he feared like the devil himself—a moneylender's bill. But nevertheless, like poisoned rats, even in his own house there were two bills gnawing away! He was called Podravec, had four mares and an Oldenburg stallion, his wife made him boiled cheese puddings, and, "as you might say," sewed and stitched on her Singer sewing machine, and so he sat on the box seat, smoked his pipe, spat, and waited for sea-deer to appear. Two hundred million such coachmen from the Don to the Blatna and from the Volga to the Liao-Yang, rock on their coaches and wait for sea-deer; and everything is in movement, everything is harnessed, everything devours hay and excretes dung, and in books all this is called National Economy.

These two hundred million coachmen are really supporters of the surrealist movement in its most decadent sense. They live in a world that is still primitive, without intelligence, without light, and they themselves are still primitive, dark, primeval. Without duration in time, without any inner driving motive, truly purposeless! The mere existence of matter. Existence amidst objects and events. They are told that they were made in the image of

God, and such practical beings are almost confused at the story of their supernatural origin. In their existence as coachmen, stock merchants, farmers, they are confused and stick close to concrete facts, but even this only partially, and to a certain extent. On the one hand mere dirt, inseparable from the muddy Pannonian marshes where they have stagnated for several thousands of years, these Joe Podravecs speak about their Oldenburg stallions with as much feeling as about a demigod. They regard the Oldenburg stallion's genitals as do Indians, or men in the Congo or the tropics: quite simply and altogether naturally. As naturally as European middle-class girls smell flowers; itself a shameless act, according to Roman morality. Blooming roses in a vase on a young girl's table; a symbol of the eternal sexuality. The way Joe Podravec talked about sex showed a Biblical, uncorrupted naturalness; and in his eyes the stallion's sperm was a valuable fluid, which he collected with his fingers, saving every drop of it and selling it at the highest market price, as his wife sold cream.

What unnatural distances separated this coachman's uncorrupted naturalness and Philip, who as a seventeen-year-old boy had already begun to look at women in the manner of Toulouse-Lautrec (although he had never heard of Toulouse-Lautrec)! What a separation and what a distance, what a development! How had such an individual cell as he been torn away, when was it ripped from its surroundings, its place, its foundations? What was this flying off at a tangent and where did it lead? Did it mean separation, disintegration, or the asylum? A psychosis in the dangerous sense of the word? Everything had in reality lost its original meaning! Eskimos or Negroes, when they eat still warm and bleeding rhinoceros or seal meat, bite into it in a natural way like healthy animals. Negro teeth chew such raw meat quite naturally; the Negroes' munching of raw hippopotamus fat is natural, and their polygamy is also a natural thing, while town people eat like sick cats: they have decayed teeth, they die of cancer, even though they have written thick books about their intestines. All that is urban is sick and scabby. Even these two hundred million coachmen were already gnawed at by the town atmosphere! The town stood for an inevitable, unhealthy deviation from the natural, and from the essential natural foundation of straightforward life! And where in fact is the foundation of life itself, and is there anything that can really be straightforward?

Amid those weary, drowsy images that buzzed around Philip's head like venomous mosquitoes, he was seized with horror at an idea that had been presenting itself to him incessantly during the last two years, now clearly and then more vaguely—his idea of the infernalization of reality.

This idea, doubtless a diabolical and unhealthy conception, was that in life phenomena have in fact no internal logical or rational connection. That life's manifestations unfold and develop one beside another, simultaneously, with the sort of infernal simultaneity of the visions of Hieronymus Bosch or Bruegel; one within another, one beside another, one above another, in utter confusion, in delirium, in ceaseless unrest, which have been from the very beginning. The tall, grimy steeples with dragons' heads, whitened waterspouts, and marble behinds; the fat Carolina; the English horses; *bonjour, Monsieur,* the voice of a caged jay;—and everything melting like the chocolate wrapped in silver paper, everything dragging along like Joe Podravec's coach, everything foolish and swamplike as Pannonia itself! Nude bellies, hidden dramas, sickly childhoods, which drag on a whole lifetime and last forty years—everything lumps together like cloudy steam in numberless variations, and then everything disperses one day like mist, and evaporates like the smell of a privy, all an incomprehensibly immense overflow of something that spreads out in space and is entangled in itself like a satiated boa constrictor; it swallows itself and vomits and turns into stinking pitch. Movement in all directions, a confused circulation of particles without foundation and without any inner meaning; our humanity walks and buries itself, and is reborn and springs up, like water, like mud, like food. It kills itself, devours itself, digests itself, secretes itself, swallows itself; it moves and travels, along the intestines along roads, along ravines, in waters! At one place it begins to fade, and at another it flourishes like weeds on a dunghill; and all this, however hellish in its essentiality, is fleshy and strong and ineradicable within us. There is no one-way direction or development, since everything is entangled, junglelike, marshy, Pannonian, hopeless and dark. On the one hand Philip's paintings, his books, studies, essays about painting, about problems of color, about the creative influence of light; and on the other, beehives and thatched cottages and sleeping cars on fast trains. On the one hand his morbid concepts of the nature of woman; and on the other, at his side, his coachman waiting for sea-deer. Fat red-faced church dignitaries, in the role of asthmatic lovers in violet silk, who have illegitimate children by their servants, by tobacconists; petty things in life with devastating effects. All like anthills turned upside down, rotten roofs, decaying graves. Thus Philip jogged drowsily along, his thoughts bubbling like carbonic acid in a glass of soda water; a process which is rather noisy and produces a lot of foam, but which is refreshing for the nerves; to think in pictures and intoxicate oneself with the endless variety of the changing images.

They passed the morning clamor of Kravoder: the raw acrid smell of ammonia from liquid manure and stables, the lowing of cows and the clatter of oxen's hoofs on the wet road, the quacking of geese in courtyards, the creaking of the inn door leading to the bar, out of which emerged a podgy fat-necked pumpkin-shaped head with a pipe and a fur cap, to see who was driving through Kravoder. For those swinish, red-rimmed eyes, it was most certainly an unusual event; a stranger with suitcases in a carriage.

Either an agent or the new district assessor at Jalžabet? Or maybe even a spy? There are all sorts in the world nowadays!

Red peppers from last year's crop were still hanging at the windows, cheese was drying in nets hung on stakes, cocks were crowing, and hens scurried panic-stricken across the road, right in front of the wheels and between the hoofs; it was a damp, dewy morning, and the warm April sun was breaking through the early clouds with ever increasing intensity. A black foal, with a thick, wavy, streaming mane and a beautiful rounded neck, neighed cheerfully, running alongside Joe's mare, but as they approached a patch of turf he broke away from the carriage and tore down at a flat-out incensed gallop toward the spring at which the stable-boys watered the horses. The water in the troughs shimmered; one could hear the bumping of the small wooden buckets, the chatter of human voices, the flurry and gallop of the black foal in a cloud of dust, all this was gay and full of movement, cheerful, lively.

At the end of the village they met two nuns.

"Ugh, devil take 'em!" said Joe Podravec touching the button of his waistcoat. "We could have done without them!"

Each of the sisters was carrying a basket of eggs and, meeting a gentleman driving in a carriage, they both greeted him piously, and with excessive humility, since he might possibly be an unknown representative of the authorities, and to the authorities it was a good thing to bow of one's own accord. For two thousand years now the church has carried baskets full of eggs, and during that time many authorities have changed both in towns and in provincial carriages. Such a policy of trifling courtesies could never do any harm.

The two somber women in their Toledo costume, with a gleam of sun on their starched headdresses, quickened anew in Philip's mind images of the parallelism of events; those two nuns, with their skirts and rosaries and bizarre white headdresses, like two strange, supernatural parrots, appeared there in front of him like two dark symbols of Kravoder mud. So the centuries can persist parallel with each other for ages, like two alien races in a cage; monkeys and parrots! Those somber women creep about the muddy hovels, steal baskets of eggs from cattle breeders and coachmen, haul them along remote country roads to their anthills. Five thousand years muddy old Pannonia has lain there, with pigs grunting, horses neighing, and those sinister-looking parrots stealing eggs from the Pannonians like weasels, every one with her knight and saint in armor as her patron and celestial lover! Two worlds, next to each other at an unbridgable distance. There was he, a godless, westernized, restless bird of passage, nervy and decadent, driving through Kravoder in Joe Podravec's carriage on a spring morning, with everything stirring, blooming, budding, everything moving like the wheel creaking under him and making a new rut in the road, rolling over so many tracks and footmarks on that road, down which numberless hordes had already disappeared into the mists. Yet all this was really a meaningless chaos!

Like the swish of a bare, shining ax, like the whirr of a steam-saw in the shining metallic revolutions of its keen circular blade, the higher overtones of our time cut like a razor through things and ideas, and vibrate with the clear note of a high-pitched exclamation, like the "a" of a tuning-fork; so, impertinently, triumphantly, there sounded high above Philip's head the zoom of an airplane, echoing like the note of a celestial trumpet. Two worlds in three days: London-Bagdad-Bombay, and the inn at Kravoder with the nuns and their baskets of eggs! The Pannonian mire and civilization!

Above the pig breeders' hovels and mulberry trees, the silvery aluminum guitar with taut canvas wings, a soaring musical instrument, sailed above Joe Podravec's carriage with its sacks and Philip's suitcases. Above all that is static, fixed and immovable, great azure circles of light, and clear sky. Above the roofs and branches and lightning conductors and steeples and peasant carts, which crawl like snails along the muddy roads and creak antediluvially, and get stuck in the mud—a wonderful shimmering flash of lightning. And watching this glittering metallic streak that moved above the earth like a line of silvery chalk across the heavenly dome, Philip felt like taking out his handkerchief to wave to the aircraft in greeting. To signal his presence, like a shipwrecked man catching sight of a white, sunlit ship which, with mathematical precision, sails toward a shining harbor across the whole gloomy morass of present-day reality.

Two months had elapsed since Philip's return to the vineyard at Kostanjevec, and already in the valley the lime trees and acacias were in bloom. Life decays among those muddy ravines around Kostanjevec; it spreads out like a marsh and stagnates like muddy water, in which submerged objects decompose.

At Blato, Mica Trebarčeva had cut her belly with a rusty sickle, and then got blood poisoning and died in agony, and it was thought in Blato that old Mikleuška was to blame for her innocent death. One night Mike, the natural, on his way back from the woods with the pigs, had seen Old Nick jump over the fence at old Mikleuška's and trot away down the road. The swineherd Mike did not know whether it had been ironshod or not, but that the old woman had boiled a hellish brew that night was more than certain; a bright green cloud of smoke had been seen pouring out of her chimney the whole night. And that very same night Mica Trebarčeva had closed her eyes for the last time. The child had also died a day later, God be praised. But it was quite obvious: old Mikleuška had put a spell on Mica because she had refused to marry Mikleuška's one-eyed Francis. Then somebody had set fire to Mikleuška's barn and the barn had burned up, and after that her neighbor Boltek's cow died. It was obvious; a spell. The vet had examined Boltek's cow and said anthrax. So it was impossible to take it to court, but how could the vet know that Boltek's grandmother had dropped molten lead into water, and clearly seen Mikleuška's face in the basin? The matter ought to be cleared up to find out who was right.

At Jama three wolves had attacked Lojze Ribar's cow and devoured it one Sunday, on the holy day itself, at noon. They had come across the common, and that had not happened for a long time. The last time wolves had been seen in plain daylight at Jama was in the sixties, when Archduke Franz had marched against the

Prussians. That must mean something. Rumor spread around the villages, stealing along fences at dusk, leaping across muddy roads, whispering under eaves when it rained, and grew into a prophecy of lean and scanty years ahead. Like the four horsemen of the Apocalypse emerging from the dark clouds would come the lean years: on cadaverous black horses with whetted scythes and funeral torches, with thunder, earthquake, and pestilence; that is how hungry years come. And quite probably a new war was brewing and many other horrors. At Krivi Put the priest's dapple-gray foal broke its leg and had to be shot, and at Turčinovo and Hasan people said they had seen that same dapple-gray foal galloping through the village. Then they saw him on the common at St. John's, alive and healthy. At Kolac a mad dog, or a wolf maybe—"the mischief take him!"—had bitten nearly all the children in the schoolyard and then disappeared without trace. The dead sexton George had been seen several times; he was seen the other night on the watch near the small church at Batina. It was a moonlit night and the door of the vault could be clearly heard creaking in the wind. It might be a good thing to sprinkle the grave with holy water. Graves were opening, people were getting alarmed, rumors were spreading; the other morning Jura Perekov had come back from Russia, and everyone had thought him dead for the last ten years, and so he was regarded by all as a Lazarus; at the women's spinning bees, they were saying he had risen from the dead. People were afraid of him. So, to prove that he was not dead he came one night to the inn at Siebenschein's and hit Steve Brezovečki on the head with a bottle. And lame Matthew of Blato met a black coach one night near the bridge at Bistrica. It was all shining, and it had four lights, two front and two rear. But there was no coachman; only at the back, seated on a golden spring seat, was a general with gold braid and red trousers, wearing a shako. And who was it? Rudolf!

Crown Prince Rudolf in person!

Lame Matthew was so frightened at the thundering of the coach as it flew across the bridge like an arrow, that he could not clearly remember whether it was a four-horse carriage or not, but he thought the leading horse on the left was without a head.

"Yes, Crown Prince Rudolf himself, although he was dead,

traveled at will between Blato and Krivi Put, on his way to Toplice, to the Bishop's Palace, most likely. Judging by all the signs, as you might say, evil times are on their way."

The wheat this summer did not look good at all, and the oats too were all covered with rust because of the mist. There were outbreaks of chicken pox, smallpox, and dysentery, and omens of death, and Kaptol Woods caught fire and burned for three days and three nights. Many trees had burned down there, but if somebody cut himself a whip handle, the Kaptol keepers would shoot him on the spot like a dog. And now everything had burned down; at least it had been a treat for the children.

A pale man had passed through Kostanjevec last night. The dogs had picked up a scent of sulphur after him. Such unknown pale passersby were dangerous at nightfall. They were either thieves, or magicians, or necromancers. There were werewolves, too; they walked like humans, only their feet inside their shoes, so they say, without offense, were webbed. They sprinkled holy water on the grave of Šimun Vugorek and drove three hawthorn stakes into his head, but even so he rolled potatoes about the attic of his widow's house the whole night long. A man from Slovenia was found hanging in the forest of Kostanjevec, but his wallet was there all right, with three hundred crowns in it. What about it? A hue and cry, search warrants for fugitive criminals; somebody was always being hunted. Thieves swarm the whole world over, like maggots in flyblown meat; there is suspicion and mistrust on all sides, and a good thing too, for man is a thief from the day he is born.

To live for a while amid mares and cats, amid village rumors, to feel a rough calf's tongue on his palm, to watch plants growing, from day to day ever increasingly green and lush, with mathematical precision adjusting themselves to the maximum amount of light and sunshine —those were soothing things for Philip's neurasthenia. Having lived for whole years on substitutes for fresh peas, fruit, water, meat; having realized for years how far away were genuine peas and fresh meat; feeling himself cut off from contact with life by the cold tin container of his canned food (and feeling that he himself was inside an uncomfortable tin deprived of both chlorophyll and oxygen), it was quite natural for him to develop a need for the genuine, the straightforward. How good it must be to pick real green peas in a garden, to burst the silky, sweet-smelling pods, to split the milky peas with one's fingernails, to eat cherries fresh from the branch, or eggs which still smelled of the hen and not of sulphur, and finally to sleep as long as one wanted and hear the cock crowing on the roof of the hen coop, instead of the worn-out voice of a vulcanite disc whining somewhere on the other side of the grimy wall.

Everything around Philip was so natural, so real and alive, that it captivated him with its sheer genuineness: he revived in the blue open spaces, full of genuine light and unadulterated scents. A heron's flight, a stork clapping its beak on a neighboring chimney, the people who appeared before him, gray as if risen from the mud, all this unfolded itself like a strange, fantastic play before his eyes. People came along, smelling of dung, of silt, of mud, full of straw and hay, grass and thorns, with no idea of what was going on inside their bodies and souls; everything for them being fleshy and palpable, soft and hard. Set in their habits, huge men, with their horses and carts, and their wine, which seemed to flow from bottomless and inexhaustible barrels; semidrunken

64

shapes in the eternal twilight between drunkenness and fear, at an unbridgable distance from everything urban—and yet stupidly affected by the latest improvements and inventions of the towns—everything seemed to Philip like the commotion in a trampled anthill.

There had stood an anthill with its gray, invisible forces and movements, with its superior order and incomprehensible instincts, but an enormous hoof had trampled on that organism, and now everything was in a state of fear and chaotic disorder. What could be done with that scattered village anthill and how could one approach it? In what way? From which side?

Musing upon the reason things were as they were in the country, Philip Latinovicz, quite naturally, lost himself in everyday utilitarianism; thought of the use of artificial fertilizers, gypsum, or Chilean saltpeter; of plowing with tractors, of merging and uniting the scattered, small plots of land into vast, rational Canadian areas, of raising that twelfth-century way of life to a level twelve hundred years higher! Of lighting everywhere with electricity! Loans? Banks? Cooperatives?

He had seen how some clever individuals had striven and had exhausted themselves in a futile struggle with such cooperatives, in damp gray rooms, usually bare save for a bag of gypsum and a weighing machine with two yellow brass scales on which cooperative vitriol or salt was weighed out. Account books with thick seals were accessible to every member of the committee, so that for whole Sunday afternoons they did nothing else but fuss and quibble over two or three dinars, wondering whether the cashier had taken them. Committees, the combatting of illiteracy?

For the last two million years now we have been walking on our hind legs, but we are all in the main still quadrupeds. And what is the good of knowing how to read and write, when we have certainly been writing for thousands of years, yet only every hundred years is one man born who really knows how to write, and even he is not known or read by anyone?

Should he organize a firemen's meeting? When the people of Kostanjevec got ready for a firemen's meeting, Hrustek, the mayor, who was also a shoemaker and a winegrower, had a gold helmet with a red horsetail. Or should he help the people of Kostanjevec in a more personal way, with his colored canvases, painted in accordance with the program of the most up-to-date Fauvism? All, even the faintest thoughts about painting, seemed foolish to him in these circumstances.

A host of painters live in cities and spread their canvases among the town crowds, like spiders their webs; they chase after dollars in the melee of money and goods. Here at Kostanjevec there would be more sense in selling horse blankets, pots, gas lamps (and even they were not sold in large numbers nowadays), but to paint here was senseless. For whom? Why? Fauvism was pure nonsense here.

The painter's vision had not come to him now for quite a long time. The idea for the composition with the naked woman's belly, when he had driven by the brothel windows at Kaptol, had been his last artistic emotion since his return. Images had ceased to form; all his ideas where rationally formulated; an exceptionally green leaf stirred somewhere, or light flooded a dirty bluish wall, transparent, as in a tapestry, and he would study the relationships of the different planes calmly, geometrically, without any emotion whatsoever. The papers came, but he never read them. Nothing seemed to him more superfluous than the town papers: fashions, hats, football, performances, exhibitions? All that noise and self-importance that makes a town a town; what a lack of proportion! Everything that happens in towns today, the stupid accumulation of goods, the crowds around them; the foolish, noisy self-importance of those temporary owners of machines, soaps, lamps; the shouting, the blood, the quarrels about machines—how could all this be called life in any sense worthy of man? Lust on the lips of weary old women, grimy branches against glowing sky signs, dirty newsprint, his own long weariness with the whole bazaar. Like sparrows hopping amid garbage and horse dirt, the women of the cities rummage among the garbage of the present day, infected veins, saxophones, alcohol, and everything grimy and empty.

But here eternal, blue, clear, calm weather prevails. The breeze stirs a single leaf on a pear tree, and then a long, endless silence follows. On the blue-and-white-striped tablecloth, the old Biedermeier cups look intensely red, madder-colored. And the sun is reflected on the samovar like the sound of the first violin—just a shade too sweet; a bee is buzzing above a plate of cherries; a pure impressionist still life. The bitter taste of tea on the lips is pleasant when it mingles with the first acrid inhalations of smoke; it is pleasant to lie on a deck chair, relaxed, bathed, wearing a raw-silk dressing gown, in the soft current of the morning breeze; the green grass, the dandelion clock in the breeze, the moss-grown roof, the creeper, the vines, the roses—everything is as pleasantly cool as a frosted glass. Everything is full of pollen and the moist smell of earth, good, silent, calm, monotonously blue.

It had turned out that his mother had two houses at Kostanjevec: a one-story house in secessionist style down in the square in front of the town hall, with a drugstore on the ground floor, and on the first floor a surveyor; and a house in the vineyard where she lived alone, on a hill above Kostanjevec, not more than seven minutes' walk away from the parish church by a pleasant winding path between hedges.

This old wooden parsonage of blackened oak, mossy, with an old-fashioned, steep sooty roof, had remained empty after the death of Letovanečki, the Križevac notary public and plum-grower, and his mother had bought it very cheaply, for she was lucky in money matters. They arranged two rooms for Philip in the attic or, as his mother preferred to say, on the first floor. Under the blackened, century-old rafters, where generations of the Letovanečki family had lit candles at one another's deathbeds, in that pleasant little space with four small windows, with a view out over the vineyard to the distant blue hills in the south, Philip felt calm and well. Under the windows was a lime tree in blossom and full of twittering swallows. In the room where he slept was their old red plush-upholstered set of chairs, with the oval table and the old, velvet-covered album with brassbound edges. In that brassbound book, locked with an old-fashioned spring catch, there were many long, fair, handsome faces of strangers, all Polish, on his mother's Valenti side. He remembered very vividly one gentleman in that album with a top hat and an ebony stick whose right hand was touching a cushioned velvet armchair with heavy drapings. In addition there was on the wall an oil painting of the 1840's unknown to Philip: a young woman in white holding in her hand the light blue ribbon of her straw hat. In the room in which his mother had told him he could work, was a blue suite of drawing-room furniture inlaid with mother-of-pearl; it had been left by old Letovanečki and purchased together with the house. But the main decoration of the room was a picture in a heavy gold frame of the Council of 1848 with Governor Jelačić as the central figure. It was a clumsy painting and out of place, and it worried Philip intensely from the first moment, but he had not the courage to ask his mother to remove it; the wish seemed to him too selfish, and he had tried from the first to avoid all unnecessary discussion. Otherwise, everything looked quaint, but not unpleasant; a china closet with gold-rimmed porcelain cups of a light sky-blue shade made agreeable patches of color in the place. It was pleasant to rest one's half-closed eyes on the faded pastel shades when one was still half asleep, listening to the bees buzzing outside, and the wind playing with the curtain on the rod. It was morning, but one did not know what time it was. A fly circled the room and disappeared at a tangent through the open window, and somewhere a hen clucked softly. Everything had a lapidary quality, everything stood on some base, everything had foundations, roots, three dimensions. Living like this, a man might himself acquire three dimensions: go back to Euclid, develop backward to the stage of a real contact with matter, and be himself changed back into something material.

The other night Philip had dreamed about a pale, strange, unknown woman, with whom he walked along a steep street, which might have been somewhere in the south. And again everything was gray, sticky, vague, barely illuminated with blood-red lamps that gave a smoky dark orange light, as if the bulbs were giving out. And there were many black pillars there, all freshly painted and smelling of tar. The passersby, shouting and sweating, trudged up the steep southern street pushing a bulky iron-covered machine, like a sort of tank, immobile and heavy as a mammoth. Heavy, swollen human hands clutched the spokes of the iron-bound wheels, some half-naked stevedores pulled the spiked, iron, wheeled plates apart, and it all looked like a dismantled ship's boiler, from which flickering flames licked and burned the men's flesh, hair, and faces; the flesh hissed in the fire and everybody began to shout and take his hands off it and the iron monster of a boiler rolled down the slope. Philip had the feeling that it would go plowing across the town along the rows of houses, smashing all the things under it like toys. With elemental force the grimy boiler rolled down the slope, and just at that moment of horrified uproar, Philip felt the unknown woman quite close to him, felt that he had only to stretch out his hand to pluck her as one picks an orange from a branch. As soon as the monster had rolled away, his own screams startled him from the warm entanglement of sleep, and feeling a sharp pain, he was immediately wide awake. Ruddy rays of light were penetrating through the square panes into the darkness of the room; flames were reflected on Governor Jelačić's face in the picture of the 1848 Council, and one could see the Governor standing talking to the Croatian nobles and dignitaries, lit up by the glare.

"Fire, fire!" shouted voices in the dark.

"Fire!" The old forgotten cry awakened in Philip a vivid feeling of his Pannonian background. He himself did not know why, but at that moment he felt most intensely a kind of basic connection with that region; he felt at home.

And as if all this were quite normal, carried away by the enthusiasm stemming from his adherence and loyalty to Kostanjevec, he hastily put on his clothes and dashed out into the night. A fire had broken out at Hitrec, the head roadman's, immediately below the vineyard, near the road. The barn, the stable, the enormous haystacks and the house, all were in flames. They had rescued all the livestock except the Siementhal bull which was still in its stall. Hitrec was yelling desperately for his bull. The bull was not insured, they must get him out, it was all the wealth he had in the world.

By that time the rafters of the stable were red-hot, and it was only a question of minutes before everything would collapse in a blazing mass; pitchforks, and rafters, and the whole wooden structure would burst into flames like straw. For Philip, it was a challenge: to face that blazing inferno of beams and planks and feel his own strength growing to a decision; to rush into the blaze in front of the whole terrified population of Kostanjevec and rescue Hitrec's uninsured bull.

69

Afterward Philip analyzed the event in the minutest detail: the strangely intimate mysterious effect, as of an ancient calendar, of that old-fashioned, forgotten cry of "fire," and his queer, exciting, interrupted dream about the grimy boiler that had rolled down the slope like an avalanche—which had, in fact, been nothing but a subconscious feeling of anxiety, caused by the shouting and the alarm of fire—his subjective search for an obscure yet positive foundation in his own anxiety complexes, could all be regarded as contributing to his mad act. But what had so compulsively urged him into that inferno to fetch Hitrec's bull, he just could not understand. He had pulled a blanket over his head and dashed into the burning stable. In that glare, in that volcanic, blazing forest, under a stream of fireworks, it had dawned on him that the bull might even tear him to pieces, and what would happen then to his two Modigliani portraits? He did not think about his own paintings, but about his two Modiglianis and what would happen to them if he were torn to pieces by Hitrec's bull which was not insured. But the bull instinctively felt the panic of the moment and followed Philip as calmly as a child. From Turčinovo to Kolac and Batina, from Mračni up to Krivi Put and Jama, Philip's fame grew like a mushroom overnight. And everywhere he was known as the gentleman who had rescued Hitrec's bull.

Philip's own mother became a new and unpleasant source of his anxieties. It is not true that the life of old people is an idyll pursued amid the glitter of old polished furniture, a turning over of old recollections and sweet-sad tales at dusk by the soft light of a milkily glowing lamp. This old woman, who was over sixty, was unusually particular about her appearance, constantly gazing at herself in her mirror and talking about her good looks, like a capricious old maid. Her body was already soft as a sponge, but in her veins an incredibly thirsty blood still flowed. She complained of shooting pains in her joints and wrapped herself in flannel at night, but in the daytime went about in a suit of raw silk or in a white dress with an orange parasol. From those aching joints of hers, from that tired body, there welled a profound vitality, an enthusiasm for life's experiences, a talent for life. She rejoiced in small things —all qualities that were absolutely alien and strange to Philip's nature.

It was a real pleasure for her to buy all sorts of things, even the most trifling; candles, raisins, soap, chocolate. Parcels had become the joy of her life, and no matter how foolish it was, her purchases were delivered to her from the shop in the municipal square in specially wrapped packages. She enjoyed wagonette excursions and the arrangement of picnics; together with the Honorable Silvius Liepach of Kostanjevec and his sister Eleanor, widow of Rekettye de Retyezát, and the wife of the Governor's counselor, she arranged picnics the whole summer, each one more foolish than the other. Birthday parties, name-day parties, holidays, and various church saints' days were all items of which she took conscientious note, and from the feast of St. Rock of Kostanjevec to that of the Madonna of Turčin, she knew the day of every saint, male or female. In those years during which Philip had not lived with this woman for more than five or six days at a time, she had completely changed. In his early childhood, Philip remembered she had been a silent, morose, unsociable, gloomy, reserved person who was eaten up by something within her, who carried within her a secret ailment, but was too proud to admit anything about it to anyone. Pale, dressed in mourning, with a calm, waxlike expression, carrying a prayer book in her hand, she used to get up to go to early morning mass both in winter and in summer, with the same persistency. She knelt in church, stiff and cold, and knew how to torment Philip to the point of insanity with her kneeling. He got weary—he could feel his knees growing stiff with kneeling. How cold the stone floor of the church was, how hungry he was getting—while that woman knelt speechless and motionless, gazing in front of her without even moving her lips. And in the shop, where at one time she sold cheese, salami, and sardines to gentlemen of the county court and the country committee, she never once gave Philip a mouthful, nor did she take anything herself. Now, in the house at Kostanjevec, the beating of cream in a bowl could be heard all day long, all the quilts were filled with goose feathers, everything was soft, cushioned, and smelt of vanilla and spices, and great attention was paid to the quality of the food; she bothered Philip from morning to night about what they should have, whether he wanted sturgeon mayonnaise or grilled Emmenthaler cheese.

From the very first day Regina began to get on his nerves, with her incomprehensible love of strong scent, eau de cologne, face creams, perfume. All those flasks of eau de cologne and salts on the polished surface of dressing tables and nightstands, those vital accessories for aged people—cosmetics, wigs, cushions, pads, toupees, hairpins, creams, oils, hair- and eyebrow-dyes—all this began to irritate him intensely. The old lady used to take two baths a day, and the fat Carolina, who had entered her service as a widow, massaged her for a whole hour after the morning bath. And those bed warmers, prayer desks, rosaries, holy images, consecrated water, mixed up with fashion journals and foolish multicolored rags and patterns, and the silliest thing of all in the whole maddening house—her French bed-warmer, which kept the bed at a steady temperature of 14° Reaumur—all this from the first seemed very strange and problematic to Philip. Life under that roof was more like the life of wax dolls than a human existence. Considering his mother's way of life—abnormal in every sense of the word, it became clear to him that her self-tortures in the faraway hell of the tobacconist's shop had represented a diabolical distortion into suffering, which was today translated into some sort of imaginary "pleasure."

On the very first day of Philip's return—immediately, the same evening—she related to him at table the whole of her romance with His Excellency Dr. Liepach of Kostanjevec; she who had never in her life spoken a single word to him about herself or his father, talked to him about His Excellency Dr. Liepach of Kostanjevec, former District High Commissioner and tenant-in-chief on the estate of Count Uexhuell-Cranensteeg, speaking with such vehemence, for two whole hours, that white saliva bubbles began to foam at the corners of her lips. She talked about the dilation of his heart, and how the physicians in Vienna believed that he would not survive Christmas, and how much calcium and sugar sediment he had in his veins, and how their connection had already lasted three years, and that now it was he who insisted that they should get married before the Feast of the Virgin! But she was unwilling to proceed with such haste. First of all the condition of his health was questionable in every respect, and then he had his sister Eleanor too; she knew that lady very well, and "had heard somebody say" that they were hoping Regina would leave her two-story house to Eleanor's daughter—which, of course, she would not dream of doing. Then Philip learnt that apart from the two-story house in the town in Jesuit Street, his mother also had a ground-floor house with a garden in the suburbs of Kaptol, near the railway line, and its price had gone up because an oil company wanted to buy it to build a station of its own on the railway.

And then the fuss about her portrait began.

His Excellency Dr. Liepach had read a book of Philip's about painting—and had brought it to her, but she had never had time to read more than the first three pages. She had, however, told everybody that as soon as her son returned from abroad, he was going to paint her portrait. It was natural for a son to paint a portrait of his own mother "if not from artistic motives, then at least for family reasons—to have something to remember her

73

by," and he could not refuse to do that for her. So at last he stretched his canvas and opened his paint box, and the torture began.

To paint that parrot with her toupees and mandarin wig, with her thick artificial plaits, her glittering silver hairpins, that greedy, sensual face with its protruding upper jaw, that lustful mask that was his mother's, though even now he did not know who his father was—to paint that, he would have to paint a parvenu brothel madam sitting in front of him with her legs apart, her fingers covered with rings, with a gold lorgnette and gold teeth, with all her hairpins and face creams and warmers. It would have been a psychoanalytic caricature on canvas, and not a portrait to the taste of the eighty-year-old District High Commissioner, His Excellency Dr. Liepach of Kostanjevec. Moreover, in what setting should he paint her?

In natural surroundings?

In pure white silk with her orange parasol, in a Panama hat and a green ribbon in the shade of an apple tree in the garden? At teatime, against a blue and white tablecloth in the shadow of a samovar? In her unfortunate Louis XV drawing room, that impossible interior, which looked like the display window of a provincial furniture store?

That was how his planning of a picture usually began: the detailed consideration of the subject itself, the helpless, decadent, artist's fear before coming to grips with his subject. He had an intensely personal conception of her, though it was anything but conventional. As he could not make a caricature of her, he thought the color of her flesh—the contrast between her dyed black hair and her complexion—would look best in white; he would have liked best to paint a portrait of her sitting in front of her dressing-table in an old-fashioned white dressing gown, but she of course refused to hear of such a thing. She insisted upon a portrait in black silk.

He had once seen this woman in black silk, long ago, many years earlier; it had been an unusually impressive experience in that strange gilt café when he had waited a whole day for her. Then for the first time he had seen her tired and old, and today, so many years later, he himself was far more tired and old than

74

she was. And no matter how contrary this was to reality, his early impression that her face was like a clown's, white, as if covered with flour, began to come out under his brush as he progressed further with the picture. Her feline grimaces, her affectations, her false amiability, her artificial laughter, her hypocrisy and feigned Catholic nunlike modesty, all constituted the spiritual layers that he had to penetrate in removing the mask, like a death mask, of this woman who sat in black silk before him.

With the first strokes of his brush the pale mask appeared as the foundation of a sallow clownlike face in black silk, with an old brooch. The wrinkles around her lips, her extremely sensual lively eyes, large, sunken, burning; and beneath those dark eyes tired rings, like the shadows of vice. And behind all this a tired face, unnatural, false, really a monkey's face; an unusual, wrinkled, nervous physiognomy. The first two days—while the face was still only roughed in, the fluidity of the first strokes, under a mass of undifferentiated colors, while the features could only be guessed at, and everything was still a conventional distance from reality—the old lady was satisfied, and expressed her approval in phrases that bordered on rapture. But later on, when the brush in the son's hand began to penetrate more and more sharply under the mask, when the fine hairs of the brush began to remove the epidermis like a razor, when the rouge began to melt under the artist's piercing glance, the mother, confronted with that shape in black silk which was beginning to appear on the canvas under the artist's hand, grew more and more perturbed. The more the turpentine-soaked brush took away from that face all that was adventitious, artificial, cheap, affected; that thick layer of make-up covering the secrets under the skin; the more the hidden face was revealed as with the cuts of an anatomist's knife, the more her peevishness increased. She grew irritable; she began to be tormented by afternoon migraines; she missed sittings on various pretexts, and finally one morning before work, when Philip, smoking his first cigarette of the day and completely absorbed in the canvas that had already begun to attract him, had forgotten that his mother was waiting for him, she started to tell him something, but could not go on after the first few words. She burst into tears, convulsively and unaffectedly.

75

Philip wanted to explain things to her. He said something about the subjective creative factor, feeling how false his phrases sounded, but she could not suppress her tears, and her voice was broken and hurt.

That a son could look upon his own mother in such a way as he, her only son, had looked on her, was a sad thing indeed!

So he put his brushes back into the paint box, carried the unfinished painting to his room and turned it to the wall behind the wardrobe, and there it remained.

The circle around His Excellency Ex-Commissioner Silvius Liepach, gentleman, of Kostanjevec, grew increasingly irritating. They used to come over to the house at Kostanjevec as if it were their own property, and behaved in it as if in their own house: the old District Commissioner and his sister Eleanor, wife of the Governor's Counselor; her daughter Medika; and their nephew Dr. Tassillo von Pacak-Kristofi, nephew also of the Bishop of Kaptol, Silvester Kristofi, in whose service Philip's father had been a servant. Philip watched these people chewing with their porcelain teeth, talking about the latest homeopathic methods of treatment, about veronal, about music, about spiritualism, about anthroposophy, and at times it seemed to him as if he were dreaming. Among fifty thousand houses he had had to come to such a decadent one, and that decadent household was in fact his so-called "parental home."

Her Excellency, the wife of the Governor's Counselor, Mrs. Rekettye, was a conservative lady in the style of the nineties; her world remained one of old-fashioned corsets with whalebones and of vaseline as a means of enhancing her natural charms. Thin-faced, with a Spanish lower jaw, disproportionately tall, in old-fashioned white stockings, Her Excellency went about like a dilapidated ghost from a highly picturesque world; a world of beauty that was eternal, of a god who was incomprehensible, and of King Leopold of Bavaria, who galloped like a fury through forests at night accompanied by torchbearers. She moved about in society and spoke about Casals, insomnia, and bizarre spiritualist séances, and was actually dying of the fixed idea that she suffered from cancer. Her husband, the Governor's Counselor, von Rekettye, had died of cancer three years earlier; the whole of his last five years she had done nothing else but watch the cancer slowly devouring his body, imagining to herself how all that mass of teeth, intestinal wind, and heart beats was really nothing but a disgusting and incomprehensible sarcoma gnawing and devouring its own self, as it was in the beginning, is now, and ever shall be, world without end. Bald from her last year's attack of erysipelas, Her Ladyship the wife of the Governor's Counselor wore a thick jet-black wig, and a black velvet ribbon round her neck. Bony and unusually tall, she moved about the rooms like a scarecrow. Like an old raven, she chewed her pills and talked continually about how she was dying of cancer.

She knew for certain that every moment of her life was numbered, for she could tell from the bluishness of her nails that her cancer was growing steadily. Everybody was paid to deceive her and all lied to her face, both physicians and servants! After all, cats were the nicest creatures in the world. She was dying, but nobody wanted to tell her the truth. Everybody was acting a part before her, but she saw through it all.

His Excellency the District Commissioner, Dr. Liepach of Kostanjevec, had spent his happiest moments in the glamor of the Austrian Empire and so he spent the rest of his days dreaming about that far-off "unforgettable era which would in all probability never return."

All that delightful gaiety had been engulfed by this unpleasant, loathsome, democratic-materialistic age; nobody's position had improved at all, and the sublime culture of the days of Franz Joseph today lay in ruins, like some ancient temple in a painting by Böcklin.

Contemplating the hateful events about him somewhat elegiacally, His Excellency would weep silently over the ruins represented by his souvenirs, the most magnificent of which was the gilt-edged invitation to a most illustrious court banquet, on the occasion of the distinguished visit of His Majesty the King and Emperor to our capital, the metropolis of the Kingdom, in 1895, in the month of October. A clipping from *The Popular Gazette* for October 14, in which the names of the dignitaries who attended this most illustrious banquet were printed, and where amid the names of counts, princes, dignitaries, and bishops, that of His Excellency the District High Commissioner, Silvius Liepach of Kostanjevec, was included as one of the distinguished guests—

78

this faded newspaper clipping, together with other similar treasures, he kept as a valuable relic, in a padded box covered in purple velvet. The picture of that most illustrious banquet in the great hall of the Governor's Palace remained etched unforgettably on Silvius Liepach's memory, and his memory bore the seal of that spectacular event, like the wax of the Royal Seal with the three initials of His Most August Majesty the Emperor's name.

Next to His Majesty, on the left, was seated His Most Serene Highness, the Archduke Leopold Salvator, wearing the uniform of a colonel of the artillery with the insignia of the Golden Fleece; then the Lord High Chamberlain von Szabadhegy, Captain of Cavalry; then His Excellency the Hungarian Prime Minister, Baron Banffy; and then Count Pejacsevich, Privy Councilor and Supreme Master of Court Ceremonies; on the right, His Eminence the Governor, Count Khuen-Héderváry; then Legal Privy Councilor and Master of the Ordonance, Baron Fejérvári. And in the illustrious suite composed of counts, governors, ministers, chamberlains, legal privy councilors, and Knights of the Golden Fleece, in that distinguished circle of bishops, chairmen of the High Court of Justice, aides-de-camp, Supreme Masters of Ceremonies, and Court representatives, in that brilliant bevy of members of the noble House of Peers and other, lower, legislative bodies, there at that honorable table, covered with glittering gold dishes and crystal glasses, was seated the High District Commissioner, Silvius Liepach of Kostanjevec, forty-seventh in order, between von Ludwig, President of the Royal Hungarian Railway Administration, and Major General Count Wurmbrandt, representative of the loyal and faithful Regional Administration of Koran and Glina, and opposite the worthy Master of the Royal Kitchen, Count Wolkenstein.

Between two royal hunting parties who had shot a hundred and sixty-two pheasants, seventy-three hares, three wild bears, and one roe at Konopište, the Emperor had left for St. Marcus' Square to return by express train to Ischl, where he killed forty-three stags and seventeen does; but in the meantime, like a demigod and a supernatural being, he had extended his Imperial hand in the flesh to that most illustrious gentleman, Silvius Liepach of Kostanjevec, and thus touching that blue-blooded mortal with his right hand, consecrated and anointed at Jerusalem, he had sanctified and consecrated him for a whole human lifetime.

Silvius Liepach, gentleman, of Kostanjevec, sat in front of his velvet box turning over his dear and precious relics. The number of *The Popular Gazette* containing the news of his promotion to a higher grade as Secretary to the District Commissioner: "The Civil Governor of Croatia, Slavonia, and Dalmatia, has approved the appointment of Dr. Silvius Liepach of Kostanjevec as Secretary to the District Commissioner."

That was a fragment from a dead, faraway time, when the young Secretary to the District Commissioner, Silvius Liepach, stood on the threshold of life, through which he had passed as through a series of brightly lit rooms, and now he turned the pages of letters and faded newspaper clippings, and everything was behind him like the dusk behind a horseman. On that day, July 12, 1880, *The Popular Gazette* reported among the local news the death of a newborn unbaptized female infant whose surname was Cerić, who had been born to a servant-woman in Mesnička Street. As the child, according to the findings of the town physician, might have been strangled, the servant Mary had been taken into custody pending trial; and that was the only sensation reported from the capital of the kingdom. . . . The Count Uexhuell-Gyllenband-Cranensteeg, General of the Cavalry, had arrived in the town and stayed at the Empire Hotel, and amid excise duties, taxes, and rents, the Secretary to the District Commissioner prepared himself for his brilliant career. And when he had been nominated High District Commissioner, *The Popular Gazette* had carried a whole article under the headline: "The Career of the Hon. Dr. Silvius Liepach of Kostanjevec."

The recently appointed High District Commissioner for Koran and Glina, the Hon. Dr. Silvius Liepach, was born on August 3, 1856, at Zagreb, son of the Hon. Silvius Liepach, landowner. Having graduated from the Law Faculty at Vienna where he took a doctor's degree, and having completed his one-year voluntary army service with the Royal and Imperial Fifth Cavalry Regiment of Uhlans at Virovitica, the youthful doctor in 1879 became probationer secretary to the existing subdistrict of Zagreb for political service. The same year he was appointed Assistant District Secretary, and within a year District Assessor, to be nominated a year later as District Secretary in a higher grade, assigned to the Royal Croatian, Slavonian, and Dalmatian National Government. From that time he served with the Royal Croatian National Government, under which he was appointed First Secretary, grade one, and in 1889, Chief Secretary to the National Government. In that capacity he served until the decease of his late father of blessed memory, landowner of Kostanjevec, when for family reasons he felt it necessary to resign from the civil service and to devote himself to the management of his estate, which represented an imposing and substantial property. In a royal edict of October of the same year, the resignation handed in by Silvius Liepach was accepted. When, however, on the death of the Honorable Mr. Lentulaj, abbot and member for the district of Lonjskopolje, the position of member of the Assembly fell vacant, Dr. Liepach accepted the offered candidacy, and in the elections of December 2, 1894, was unanimously elected member of the State Assembly of the Kingdom of Croatia, Slavonia, and Dalmatia. As a member elected by popular acclaim (he had been elected unanimously by seventeen electors), he of course joined the National Party, in which he began to play one of the most prominent roles, particularly distinguishing himself in the Budget Debate of the same year. Enjoying from the days of his service with the Administration the deserved reputation of an excellent, efficient, and, above all, conscientious administrator, he has now been appointed District High Commissioner for Koran and Glina, as a personage regarded as especially reliable by His Excellency the Governor, who by this selection has shown once again his extreme aptitude in the choice of his chief colleagues. The Honorable Dr. Liepach of Kostanjevec is now at the height of his powers, enjoys good health and, by his tactfulness, his extraordinarily diligent and faithful service, will do credit in his new post to the people he serves and the country which has honored him with such confidence.

"Particularly distinguishing himself in the Budget Debate of the same year"—this comment in *The Popular Gazette* was a bare statement of something that had marked a turning point in the career of the District Commissioner, Dr. Liepach. During that same Budget Debate the paper *Pester Lloyd* had carried an article signed "An L. P. Landowner" that is, a Lonjskopolje landowner. It was never stated anywhere, but it was known that this article signed with the initials "L. P." was written by an estate-owner of Kostanjevec, who by this article, in addition to the fine epithet "a capable manager," now acquired the indirect title "of a recognized authority of constitutional matters." In that notorious and, according to an opposition paper, translated article, estate-owner Liepach expounded his "constitutionally scientific" ideas as follows: "Today, as regards politics, we live on mere fictions. We call a certain country Croatia, although in fact it is not Croatia, but has acquired that name only since the end of last century; we call another country Slavonia, although it is likewise not Slavonia, but ever since the establishment of the Kingdom of Hungary has been as much a part of Hungarian territory as Bihar or Szabolcs, a component part of the Kingdom of Hungary. And with these pseudonymous territories we carry on negotiations as one state with another; we accept allegations whose meaninglessness has long been exposed, which are contradictory to documents and laws, and against which our honest convictions, based on the evidence of recognized authorities on constitutional science, revolt."

Having thus "particularly distinguished himself" by this unsigned article in the *Pester Lloyd,* the great landowner of Lonjskopolje and Kostanjevec, Dr. Liepach, was nominated District High Commissioner and the door to the very highest possibilities was open to him. For his failure to become Deputy Governor, his wife Eleanor was to blame; on the occasion of the Imperial Reception Ceremony at the Municipal Ball sponsored by the Croatian Sokol Association, she ostentatiously refused to take leave of Her Excellency the Governor's lady, Margita Khuen Héderváry, because she was offended by the whole arrangement of the ceremony, in which she, the wife of a District High Commissioner and a nobleman, and herself of noble descent, of the family of

82

Somsich de Gáldovo et Turócz, was in her own personal opinion placed seven places too low in the ranking. In the circle of most eminent, illustrious, and highborn ladies who were to represent before His Majesty the elite of our municipal society, Madame Somsich had been placed twenty-fourth in line instead of seventeenth, and when she had approached Her Excellency Countess Khuen to explain to her, as the Governor's wife, this obvious slight misunderstanding, that lady had uttered not a word in response, but ignored her interpellation as if it had not been made at all. Everything was quite clear. The Governor's wife—Countess Khuen Héderváry, whose title Countess Khuen dated from 1361, who was also Countess of Lichtenberg and Baroness of Neu-Lembach as from 1573, Lady of Nuchtar, de Hédervár and Vicze, born Countess Teleky, of a Hungarian noble line recognized by King Sigismund five hundred years earlier—was standing by the balustrade with Baroness Inkey, born Ludmila Theodora Maria Gabriella; Countess Deym, daughter of the Czech Count François de Paul Maria Zaharia Anton Wenzel Deym; and Countess Maria de la Fontaine and D'Harmoncourt-Uverzagt; and with Countess Juliana Drašković-Erdödi, wife of the Lord of Trakošćan and Lady of the Order of the Great Cross and Star, and daughter of the Honorable Commander, *ad honores,* of the Royal Bavarian Order of St. George, Erdödi of Štakorovec, and this uninvited woman approached her—such a puffed-up Slavonian woman—and accosted her in such an impossible manner that the Governor's lady could really do nothing else but reply not a word. First of all, the order of the reception had not been arranged by Her Excellency the Governor's lady, but by the Royal Master of Ceremonies, and then, What did this person want, who was she in fact, and what was the wife of a District High Commissioner anyway? How ridiculous!

So when after the reception the Governor's wife took leave of the ladies who were present, and when she approached "the twenty-fourth" and extended a hand to her, this nameless "twenty-fourth" refused to shake hands with the Countess Margaret; and so a scandal broke out that was far greater than that caused by the burning of the Hungarian colors.

"I was the twenty-seventh, yet you did not consider it enough to be the twenty-fourth," grumbled Silvius Liepach, agitatedly discussing the incident with his wife, and foreseeing quite correctly his own ruin.

His Excellency the Governor, who by the appointment of the Honorable Silvius Liepach as District High Commissioner had "displayed his unusual aptitude for selecting his right-hand men," finished with that right-hand man very quickly after this scene; the District High Commissioner, Silvius Liepach of Kostanjevec, returned to Kostanjevec for the Christmas holidays and never left it again. The sudden death of his wife, Eleanor Somsich, from appendicitis occurred there about Whitsuntide just before the outbreak of the war; there he also outlived his only son Silvius, who fell in the famous cavalry assault near Raw-Ruski in '15, as Lieutenant in the Royal and Imperial 5th Regiment of Uhlans. He also had the experience one October night, in his nightshirt, coatless, in his underpants, of seeing "certain ruffians" set fire to his house at Kostanjevec. Then "certain democrat canvasers" arrived and distributed "among these ruffians" his best four hundred acres of plowfields, so that now he could hardly make ends meet at Kostanjevec—overburdened with debts and uncertain whether he might not simply be turned out of the house one day by Jacob Steiner, and finish his days in a ditch like a vagabond. Philip's mother's assumption that "those people at Kostanjevec reckoned on getting her two-story house" in Jesuit Street was therefore, in all probability, not unfounded.

Silvius Liepach of Kostanjevec could no longer adapt himself to events and things around him; keeping up with life's tempo was gradually becoming too much for him. Dreaming vaguely over his relics and securities, he stared at the pale blue forms of the Austrian life-annuity payments and the deposit receipts of the Austrian Credit Bank as at playing cards for some fantastic, distant games long forgotten; all those once-valuable things were as worthless today as thumbed playing cards, and of what use to him were those securities bearing the signatures of governors, ministers, and dignitaries of an empire that today lie discarded, sprayed with naphthaline like his brown court dress! How much trouble he had taken in the building up of the personnel of the District High Commissioner's Office in the eighties, and where today was all that host of hangers-on, cringers, underlings, climbers, aspirants, candidates, and undergraduates, who used to pass in crowds through his anteroom? What a pall of gloom had descended since those times when the royal monopolies, and roads, and railways, and offices foamed with the Governor's champagne at the appointment of the new contractual civil service apparatus, when truly "disinterested idealists" had tried to raise the standard of living of that unfortunate "peasant stock" of ours.

From cholera and marshes and floods to scientific farming. And the gratitude of those cattle and vermin! They had broken into his house and set fire to the roof. Incomprehensible indeed!

As a young "gentleman" with a Vienna doctor's degree in the eighties, he had been extremely particular about his clothes. His Chesterfield coat with braid-edged lapels was elegantly fitted at the waist with three seams; checked trousers, pointed suede shoes, silk hat, everything first class from the best Vienna tailors, everything discreetly marked this young squire as a man with a good sense for an elegant but not ostentatious style of dress. Even today his old black paletot was still his best garment, while his tailcoats, his Welsh-mohair havelock, his evening dress made in Budapest, all hung neatly in the wardrobes and were aired every other week, although among those clothes there were some he had not touched these forty years.

Paying his daily visit to his friend Mrs. Latinovicz-Valenti, Philip's mother, in his light gray jacket, with cream spats, an ebony stick, white tie, and dazzling collar and cuffs, he looked like a gray doll from a strange old album. Meticulously bathed, completely gray, close shaven, still fairly alert, he did not actually make an unpleasant figure; but Philip could not reconcile himself to Liepach's very existence. In the first place, the old man always addressed Philip's mother by her full title, Madame Latinovicz-Valenti, in the old style, distinctly, slowly, and ceremoniously, as if pronouncing an extremely distinguished and prominent society name, with a particular stress on the Valenti, as the surname of her brother, a Fieldmarshal-Lieutenant in Vienna, whom Liepach had known personally at one time and as a guest in whose house he had felt extremely comfortable. In addition to all this, Philip suspected that the old man had known his mother in the obscure days of the Bishop, and so knew far more about her than he himself, regarding her from an angle altogether unknown to Philip.

The old man had more or less successfully kept his skin smooth by means of creams and pomades, except his hands. His hands looked literally condemned to death. Unusually sensual, greedy, and selfishly restless, the hands of the old bon vivant snatched at things avidly, as if grasping at life itself from the already dark approaches to the grave. How greedily he used to warm his bloodless palms against the warm surface of the porcelain teapot! How revoltingly he would touch Regina's hands even in the presence of strangers! How eagerly he would roll his cigarette and, licking his lips, put it into his ivory cigarette holder! All this had a repulsive and irritating effect on Philip. To him all that went on in that house at Kostanjevec began to seem almost blasphemous, it was like a dance on graves, a Dance of Death, hollow and empty, altogether morbid and unhealthy. With all the talk of two-story houses, dull Viennese jokes, tea and dinner parties, it was a concealed and conventional comedy cracked underneath like an old jar from which a morbid and festering human passion slowly drained away. The old man would drop in toward evening, or even at teatime, and then stay usually until after supper and late into the night. They talked about spirit-rapping, about submission to the Lord's will, about a certain higher resignation in old age, from the point of view of which all human passions and efforts seemed rather ridiculous. They talked about the far-off experiences and delusions of youth; about dogs, cats, and servants; about clothes; about cooking; and about concerts; about the importance of dogs' digestion, about dogs in general and at great length, and of the ingratitude of servants; about ear and throat ailments; about the incredible diseases of the heart; about mallow compresses and diets. All this politely masked and insincere chatter was infinitely monotonous, and when the two of them remained alone in the dusk in Regina's room on her velvet upholstered divan, a long silence would spread its wings over the room. Returning unexpectedly toward evening one day, Philip passed under his mother's back window overlooking the garden, and as the curtain was stirred by the breeze at that moment, he caught sight of his mother sitting on the old man's knees in the twilight. He felt sick and he was ready to pack his things the same evening; nevertheless he stayed. He began to restrain his excessive sensibility; his exaggerated dislike of bodily contact, even of the touch of his own body, had always seemed to him unhealthy. So too he had always to force himself intellectually to touch the body of a woman with whom he wanted intercourse, for he dreaded such open contacts as something particularly shameful.

"Silly! Even the life of old men, like that of other organisms, is nothing else but an expression of the body and the physical. It is a human instinct making for the perpetuation of life. For duration. For the prolongation of duration. To condemn such instincts in old people is illogical if one does not condemn them in the young."

That was logical, but nevertheless, in his inner self, Philip could never reconcile himself to that old man. But the old man, feeling this unpleasant newcomer as his latent adversary, was particularly charming and kind to him. For months he kept inviting him to his home at Kostanjevec to show him his books, his collection of weapons, his family portraits—which should be restored, although he was not competent enough to undertake it—and for two months Philip kept on declining the invitations.

The old man had an allegedly very valuable copy of a Palma Vecchio painting, and as there was a chance of his selling it in the town, he once again asked Philip to come and assess its value for him. For the first time since his return Philip had a violent and very nearly offensive argument with his mother over this picture; then he gave in and the next afternoon set out for the château.

This so-called château of Kostanjevec was a pleasant one-story baroque building, erected in its day on the edge of the forest as a residence for Cranensteeg's steward; while Cranensteeg's own dwelling at Kostanjevec, an enormous edifice with a hundred rooms, stood three kilometers away from Liepach's house, which was built on a hill like a fortress. Isolated, with its own bridge and tower, it commanded an immensely wide horizon. The Liepachs had bought the smaller mansion in a very shabby state in 1875, but after reconstruction and the planting of poplar and birch trees, the one-story house had acquired a quite respectable aspect; with a paved ramp for carriages and a terrace on the first floor, it looked like a summer residence in the middle of its park. Old Liepach, walking in the shrubbery in front of the château, welcomed Philip warmly, intimately, as a good and dear acquaintance, who by this visit had done him not merely a particular honor but an exceptional service. Taking his guest through the ground floor, which was decorated with old chests and brocade curtains and church candlesticks, he showed him onto the terrace. There Dominic served tea with sweet cream, chocolate cream cake, and melon. The old man in his shabby coffee-colored livery, with enormous white gloves splayed out like an old tortoise; that other old man in his light gray jacket, who used the familiar "thou" to Dominic, while Dominic addressed him as Your Excellency; and the tea, and the cream, and the melon, and again the two old men—everything seemed ludicrous to Philip.

The Palma Vecchio was of course hopeless, and the family portraits of no particular value, worthless rubbish from the eighties, painted in an old-fashioned style to make the Liepach family look as ancient as possible. The library was quite impersonal and empty, with three leather-bound volumes of *Ephemerides politico-statisticae Posonienses* as the only rarity today. With a slightly exaggerated gesture, almost solemnly, old Liepach took a pigskin-bound annual volume of the Pressburg Information Bulletin and pathetically opened it at one page, marked by heavy red moiré silk ribbon. If Phillip was interested in a little curiosity, he would take the liberty and have the honor of drawing his attention to something which was of particular importance to the Liepach family, the Declaration of Pressburg, according to which the Liepachs had been raised to the rank of nobility in 1818.

And indeed against the date of December 5, 1818, was the following inscription:

"To Mr. Anthony Liepach, Councilor of the Illustrious Royal Hungarian Financial Division, in recognition of meritorious service to King and country for more than forty years, and to his son

Anthony, military notary, His Serene Majesty has graciously been pleased to grant the rank of noblemen of the Kingdom of Hungary."

On the front page of the Pressburg newspaper, below a gray steel engraving of a symbolic half-naked female figure surrounded by clouds, carrying a book on her winged head, appeared the calligraphic signature of the first Liepach nobleman, written with a quill pen, in clear-cut and scrupulously spaced strokes, *Antonius Liepach, nobilis in Monarcham et Patriam meritissimus.* Above this, in pencil, probably in a woman's hand, now quite faded, was written, *Flossmann: Polka Potpourri. Seitz: The Witch of Boissy.*

"As silly as the Polka Potpourri," Philip thought as he looked at the faded newspaper account of the Liepachs' Patent of Nobility, and he did not know what to say to this old blue-blooded aristocrat whose fate it was to be one of his mother's last cavaliers.

Above the bookcase, under glass in a gilt frame on the wall, like a four-color oleograph, hung a reproduction of Benczur's famous "Hungarian Millennium," representing the estates and nobility of the Kingdom of Hungary, Croatia, Slavonia, and Dalmatia making a presentation to His Majesty the King of Hungary, on the occasion of the thousandth anniversary of the foundation of the Hungarian Kingdom. In a baroque state apartment in the Palace at Buda, among the crowd in ceremonial robes, stood the Knight of the Golden Fleece, Count Khuen Héderváry, the Royal Standard-Bearer, and amid the violet of the prelates' and bishops' cloaks, the cochineal red of the brocade-upholstered walls and the cardinals' gloves, amid the undulating mass of banners, standards, and silk hats, stood out the pale face of the late Empress Elizabeth of blessed memory. She was under a canopy, in mourning, and at her feet, across the floor, the Croatian colors were spread in front of the sovereigns as a gift appropriately betokening the sentiments proper to the occasion of the thousandth anniversary.

"This senile old gentleman has a Benczur in his library, and wants to discuss painting with me," was the only impression of which Philip was dimly aware in a distant part of his mind; he turned the pages of *Ephemerides Posonienses,* and contemplated some tempera paintings on the ceiling, and did not know what to say to the old babbler, who inundated him with phrases and tributes. He had read one of Philip's books; he had heard of his spectacular success in London, and after all it was no trifling matter to be a regular illustrator of a big city paper, and to have made his way quite alone and unaided to such a position as Philip had succeeded in acquiring abroad.

He let the old man torture himself in his embarrassment, and himself stammered something as if talking to a foreigner; then he suddenly got up and took leave of Liepach, and everything looked extremely clumsy and foolish. On his way home he had an unpleasant taste in his mouth as if he had eaten a piece of stale putrid meat.

"Where did they come here from, to Kostanjevec?" mused Philip, thinking about the Liepachs as he descended a gently winding path from the forest toward the vineyard, along the edge of the plain which was already flooded with the evening light of early summer. How did such mental poverty differ from that of Hitrec, the head roadman, for instance? Hitrec also had a gold-framed three-color print entitled "From the Days of My Service" in his attic room. Yes, that Uhlan in a blue Uhlan's uniform riding a white mare, with the photograph of Hitrec's face glued in, was Hitrec, of the 12th Royal and Imperial Tolna Regiment of Uhlans. That head roadman galloping on a white mare, with his cavalry saber drawn, under the Imperial coat of arms and the banners of the Empire and of Hungary, was another stuffed dummy like the Honorable District Commissioner, with Benczur's gold-framed fantasy of the baroque state apartment in the Palace at Buda. All was in complete darkness. And the gloom could be illuminated only by means of the Niagara Falls and phalanxes of new imaginary people, and not by any Liepachs or any noblemen like them with patents of nobility dating back to 1818. These were the intelligentsia who made a note of a Polka Potpourri as a cherished musical memory of an artistic event, and had old Dominic wearing a livery, playing his part as if nothing had happened in the world.

All that evening Philip could still hear old Liepach telling him how in his day aromatic Karbol-Essenz was used as a universal disinfectant, how saccharin had disappeared from the market, how the Hungarian system of district administration was the best administrative system in the world, so that the English had even introduced it in the colonies; the Hungarian system, if you please; and so he was tormented late into the night and could not get to sleep. The first signs of dawn were already beginning to appear above the woods and a quail had begun to call from the wheat when he threw away his last cigarette.

It was a warm summer night with a full moon. Philip sat till midnight at the Crown in the town square, turning over the pages of the *Daily Mail* and some foreign illustrated magazines; then he drained his fifth cognac and soda, paid his bill, and walked out into the green moonlight, into the open. He felt how light he was, how masterfully he strode, and how good it would be to go far away, into the silence. He had a physical need to get away from everything human, and to be alone with quivering branches and silent green distances. Once, long ago, twenty-three years before, on a summer night, he had walked in the same way alone along a wide white road, where the dew glittered on both sides like broken glass. It was a warm summer night, there was a scent of hay in the air, and the boys were waltzing with warm, white girls. The hay smelled pleasant, and everybody was intoxicated with it all: the summer night, and the fiddle, and the semidarkness, and the girls' soft waists; youth, clear as a drop of dew, lonely as a dewdrop in the dew-drenched night and light as the wind in the nocturnal branches. The distances were green, transparent, liquid, and the starry dome so glowing, so phosphorescent, so close, as if within the reach of one's hand. The laughter, the girls' voices, and the dark figures of their chaperones—all this was now behind him; the small town with its balconies and the copper balls on its steeples and the open windows with their fluttering white curtains. In that contact of the flesh, in the ecstasy of warm bodies swaying under the white moonlight, to the murmur of the stream, the rustling of dark branches, and the warm fluttering of wings, he had moved as though lit up by something physical inside him, full of the music, excited by the warm closeness of a childish female body, he himself still a child in childish rapture. That was the night he had taken the fatal step that led to so much suffering, to his foolish romance, running after the little simple-minded provincial girl, because of whom he had squandered his mother's hundred florins and wasted the whole of his youth!

"How strange are the blind motions within us, how human bodies resemble mysterious magnetic poles, and how we all move according to certain obscure and incomprehensible laws that rule our flesh! So something awakens a youth of seventeen, something like fate diverts his steps; a mere kitten, a shallow, narrow-minded, freckled little girl becomes that fate which a man has to drag about with him like a millstone all his life!"

Absorbed in his thoughts, he had left the path, and walking along the bank of a stream, through a moist dark gully, dank with the spray of a waterfall, he found himself in a glade on the edge of an oak wood. There, in the shade of some tall, dark pine trees, stood a shack with a thatched roof, as white as linen on a lawn, flooded with the light of the full moon as if whitewashed.

There he stopped. Everything around him was still and silent. The night was dark, and he felt the pulsing of his heart in his throat after his rapid walk. In the dead, green silence, the ticking of a clock could be heard in the shack, from under the thatched roof, where there was a sourish smell of large maize-flour loaves, sooty jugs, and smoke under the eaves. The quiet, monotonous movement of the wooden mechanism with its clumsy, rusty-iron pine-cone-shaped weights suspended on chains.

Tick-tock, tick-tock.

Silence and the pleasant, wise, decadent passage of time like the gurgling of a water clock. The white lime-washed square of the walls under the thatched roof, the faraway murmur of the stream, and the fluttering of the wings of a bird awakening in the branches, all seemed to Philip to represent some great, momentous emotion. In the distant, green, glittering web of the ripe summer night twinkled the lights of the heavens and Philip breathed calmly and freely, feeling the blood circulating within his body according to its own logic, and his flesh burning and fresh, still quick with life. He felt that he was slowly overcoming his impotent depression and that the strength of his emotions was returning. Today, after a long break, he had again painted a picture. . . .

At noon he had been walking back home after bathing in the

stream when he saw in front of him the broad whitewashed surface of a wall illumined by sunlight; a child was turning towards
the sun and his shadow fell across the wall. The child held both
his hands stretched out and was murmuring something inarticu-
late in his childish voice. It was a dreadful sight, for Philip suddenly realized that the child was deaf and dumb, and its inarticu-
late cries were animal-like, horrible. Holding out both hands
horizontally, the deaf-and-dumb child, more with his throat than
by ear, was imitating the voice of a priest chanting in front of the
altar. His hands were stretched out as if in blessing, and the raised
arms cast shadows on the wall, like strange, unnatural snakes;
their shadows crept along the wall, writhing like independent
creatures in flexible movements, shadowy, enchanted, and the
child howled desperately, from the depths of his throat, as if obsessed, imbecilelike, affected by the sun, and as if in the delirium
of sunstroke;—and all this was a spasm of nervous energy, an
epileptic vision, rather than reality. The animal-like voice of the
deaf-and-dumb child quavered in the blazing sunlight, throbbing
in painful waves, radiating in the glare of the sunlit wall, seem-
ing to fill all space, under the roof, above the steeple, above the
row of trees, and then to hang like smoke failing to rise because
of the sun and the sultriness of the day.

Obsessed by this horrible sight, Philip came home, picked up
his canvas, and painted the child howling in the sun at noontide
in front of a whitewashed wall. The voice of the deaf-mute child
seemed to haunt his canvas like a cracked bell, and the dirty,
paralytic, imbecile body in the sunshine, the convulsive fear of
something dark and deaf and dumb within and around ourselves,
the tremor of the red vocal cords in the throat of the deaf-and-
dumb child, Philip transferred to the canvas with such a direct-
ness of expression that afterward he himself was taken aback by
the demoniacal strength of his own strokes. The mute throat with
its small, red, fleshy tongue, the slobbering movement of those
mute lips and salivary glands, the blind meaningless waving of
the hands in the sun, all in front of a wall white as cheese—it was
a subject for Daumier, but much more difficult than Daumier's.
He had skipped his lunch and gone on painting until teatime, and
now, standing in the moonlight, in the open, under the stars, with

94

the nightbirds, the quivering branches, his flesh crept with excitement; paints still flowed from his tubes; there was still strength in his nerves, and ecstasy in his blood. He was alive and felt how good it was to be alive!

Emotions kept coming back one after another, like birds on their way home from Egypt, flying in noisy flocks. In the green evening twilight, Philip sat in a wicker armchair on the veranda and, watching the swallows circling around the roof in swift, darting curves, meditated on how cruel and bloodthirsty life really was.

Even that idyllic bird which is so dear to men, that bird whose nests, according to popular belief, bring happiness, and about which even primary-school children write enthusiastic poems in their notebooks, that tiny black-winged bird, twittering around our attics and steeples, is in fact no better than a shark. Its twittering, which is so dear and familiar to us, there in the early evening green, is in reality a signal of terror to the world of gnats, for those small creatures are as afraid of the arrowy rush of swallows' wings as we are of a tiger roaring in the jungle. And so some sort of incomprehensible roaring and swimming, soaring, flying, and devouring goes on everywhere. Sharks eat tunny, but the tunny eat smaller fish, and smaller fish eat flies; and swallows eat mosquitoes, and mosquitoes spread infection, and all this is interconnected; things devour one another according to mysterious laws, foolish as Aesop's fables for children. Fungi grow under old oak branches, and people eat them and get poisoned and have convulsions for three days, like the shoemaker's Anna, who was poisoned last Thursday, and they didn't know whether she would live or not. And cows have anthrax, and are affected by hoof-and-mouth disease and liver-fluke; and everything is muddy, everything rots in the marshland, and everything has horns and fur and is hairy and covered with skin; of all this fauna only man is naked as a Greek marble, and has some imaginary and unnatural ideas of the beauty of his own body and of the bodies around him. Around that naked man, nevertheless, there vibrates an invisible aura of something metaphysical within us, and one could look at things from one point of view, causally, like concentric rings of pictures emerging one from another, like ripples on water into which someone has thrown a stone; but they could also be considered from a higher point of view, like the old steeple at Kostanjevec which still sings its old Renaissance song about cardinals and Roman churches. And then there was the Pannonian mud, and above it the air route: London—Bombay. And in all this, among all this, he too existed, an academic painter, Sigismund Latinovicz, who had taken the name of Philip, and signed himself Philippe, and had come here to see his mother, the tobacconist; and there was that simpleton Mike, driving Sultan, Hitrec's bull, which he, Philip, had rescued from the burning stable, and all was rather vague and muddled. If anything at all was clear in this tangle, it was the emotions of the artist. The formal mastery of matter through emotional transference, and nothing more!

Thus Philip sat in the twilight and listened to a stork clapping its beak like a castanet on a neighboring chimney, to the shepherds' voices echoing from the stream where they watered their beasts, to the swallows greedily circling around the chimney like birds of prey, and vividly and rapturously he felt flowing into him those multitudinous expressions of life. Images circled around him like birds, around his funeral mood and inner depression and around the vineyard and the plowfields, and the tracts of woodland fading in their heavy, velvety green, like old-fashioned damask, and disappearing in the vague brown tissue of the distance.

Along the road, on the other side of the hedge and fence, passed some winegrowers carrying sprayers on their backs, and one of them had a pipe that glowed very brightly in the dusk, reddening his cheeks, so that it looked as if he had been flayed. Softly and inaudibly the winegrowers, with their heavy stiff peasant shoes, green with the sulphate as if made of copper, disappeared in the gray light of dusk. The copper-green shoes of these passersby, the quiet passing of their shadows in the gray haze lit by the glow of the pipe, made another picture in Philip's mind; a watercolor, a little too delicate, almost too feminine in its shades, but indescribably fine in color, overflowing indeed with a morbid yet glowing light. And everything around him became fuller and fuller of pictures: three ripe peaches on a green plate bordered with tiny blue flowers, against a tablecloth with red and blue stripes, and lit by the last red glow of evening, a rich range of colors fading into the golden color of the evening. The undulating fields of ripe corn billowing in the wind, in smooth, parallel waves, like ripples on cloth; dark, placid, infinitely serene. Bleeding fish, with unusually red gills, in front of a green wall, on a dish of old grayish zinc covered with a wet gray sheet of dirty newspaper, on which one could still make out the faded print in dirty, illegible, straight black lines. And the leaves, and the branches, and the perspectives of richly draped sunny days, still lifes on washed-out tablecloths, the movements of pale sickly faces, the diffused light and silence of dusk; it was all a ferment of imagery, through which, as through a silvery veil, Philip could feel two blue, troubled woman's eyes. He suspected a woman behind all this feeling of restlessness, he felt with all his senses that such a profusion of emotions within him was aroused by some woman with her sensitive fingers, her fragile waist, and her strange bright gaze.

From the very beginning, from the early days of his youth, a woman had had the power to transport Philip from his gloomiest depression into ecstasy, and from foolish raptures into despair, when he would crawl on the verge of suicide, feeling trampled underfoot and broken like a crushed snail without a shell, slimy, mud-stained, and hurt. Morning mass, communion, and confession in those faraway vanished days at Kaptol, everything was steeped in dreams about women, like a girl's album in the scent of braided locks of hair and pansies. Those distant communions and confessions had been his first blasphemies and lies, because in them he kept silent about his deadliest sin; his excited daydreams about girls, sinful foolish daydreams about bodily contacts and the pleasures which those incomprehensibly mysterious creatures concealed in their laps. And divine service and vespers, with the small servers swinging their silver censers, and carrying gold brocade canopies and banners, everything was even then interwoven with carnal dreams about the great mysteries of the flesh; and those mysteries crept like venomous serpents into his first books, into holy pictures, and into those first intimate conversations in hidden corners, behind walls and barns. The cathedral church and its shadows, the towers of Kaptol, the ringing of bells on holidays, from Lent to Quadragesima—all this in the richly manured plain, cattle-breeding, muddy, crowded with livestock, full of the noise of cattle fairs. And through it all moved small schoolboys with secret clippings from calendars; and mysterious prayer books in which one could find the picture of the devil in a lecherous round with witches, or golden-haired Venus in Faust's retort; or a three-color print of a wonderful nude, stolen from some locked cupboard; a dreaming naked goddess with a swan, her hand curved seductively below her breast.

In the abundance of this barbaric peasant world, among the piles of cabbages, pumpkins, beans, fish, meat, and bacon, the fat piles of bleeding pork, thick rich fish, kale, lamb's meat, lard, butter, eggs, and poultry had lived a small schoolboy who attended a grammar school, one who for whole days hunted and scratched in the sand along the bank of the river, in the hope of finding in the mud and gravel a tiny bronze Roman statue of Aphrodite sleeping with her arm lifted above her unruly hair. A schoolmate of Philip's, while swimming, had found a naked Roman Aphrodite stuck in the sand, and that had been the biggest event in the annals of the Bishop's Grammar School for the last fifty years.

The whole atmosphere around the tobacconist's shop was unhealthy, especially in the physical sense of the word, so that in the nervous child, who already had a tendency to perversity, contact with the great, mysterious question of sex was bound to become acute and strained to the point of quivering sensitivity. The fundamental question, so delicate in itself, and at the same time so comprehensive, which had tormented him for the whole of his life and which he never dared to formulate distinctly, so that even now it still remained unsolved for him was: Who was really his father? An unpleasant wave of tobacco scent from the tobacconist's in Friars' Street had enveloped all those strange and indistinct goings-on between his mother and various people who passed through the shop, things which remained incomprehensible and mysterious to him, for on the divan behind the curtain and the screen, those carnal secrets were shrouded for him from one day to the next in an increasingly mysterious veil. The eyes of the

99

whole city, those agitated petty eyes of an entire small town, were on the dismal gray tobacconist's shop, on his mother, and particularly on Philip, a child of lechery and sin; and this developed in him strange and morbid inclinations toward that very sinful lust that is within us all, so that his open flight to the brothel at the end of Krajina Street was the revolt of a strong character who, in defiance of all, wished to cast mud upon himself before the whole world. Around the cathedral and the cathedral city flitted the shadows of the clergy, friars, and nuns, black apparitions emerging and vanishing from the bishop's courtyard; and his mother, Regina, sat behind the counter of the tobacconist's and dealt in cigarettes and rolls; canons came in and officers, humbler government officials and cabdrivers, and talked to his mother in a way that was unutterably painful to Philip, so that he did not know whether all the rumors about his mother were hellish fabrications or the truth.

And afterward, in the lean and hungry years in the fifth form of the grammar school, at the bishop's orphanage, in a bed full of bugs, with his throat parched and thirsty, he passed whole nights without sleeping, restless, agitated, delirious. The gray-green walls, the wrought-iron bars at the windows, the black lacquered crucifixes with the pink-and-white figure of Christ and whole rows of wooden saints in the corridors—clumsy saints in light blue gowns and red mantles with paper flowers in their hands— and Philip lay wide awake, gazing at the dull monotonous flickering of lamps before the holy images, and dreamed of Rezika. The only bright spot in the whole of that fetid house of torment and bug-ridden beds was Rezika. With her strong legs, bulging as if swollen, bare, red, and fleshy, and the rustle of her petticoats; with her massive arms, red and chapped, and her sleeves rolled up above the elbows, she was the dream of the whole orphanage; and it was even rumored among the boys who left last year that she was not averse to occasional love affairs, so one never knew one's luck. Perhaps it would be worth taking the risk, of stealing through the refectory, and after the refectory descending the dumb-waiter—by this adventurous route one could get to Rezika's room. So Philip had got up and stolen, quietly, barefoot, to the refectory on the ground floor where on a golden pedestal near the entrance door a wooden statue of St. Joseph blessed the inmates of the bishop's orphanage. Cold and empty, the refectory stood deserted and dark with its tables of soft wood, its dirty tablecloths covered with stains of beans and soup, its broken saltcellars and its endless rows of plates laid ready for tomorrow's soup. He upset a stool and it made a loud noise like an overturned praying desk in church, echoing hollowly and long, and then there was silence. From outside, in the distance, could be heard an engine wailing somewhere outside the station—but here rows of long tables covered with white tablecloths stood like coffins—and the dumb-waiter was locked. Light shone through the holes of the wooden shaft; the nuns were already up in the kitchen and busy preparing the children's soup.

It was getting light. How foolish and futile had been those melancholy moods of a child's excited heart locked in that big, gray, evil-smelling, ugly house! There they ate beef cooked to shreds and they had found rats in their boiled vegetables and old stockings too. The large, bare surfaces of the courtyard walls were wet with rain, leaking gutters gurgled all night, mildew stains and mold crept across the vaulted ceilings of the ground-floor classroom, where yellow sooty kerosene lamps smoked, and just as he had then dreamed foolishly of girls' voices, movements, and hair as things far beyond his reach, so he had remained foolish up to the present day. All his physical raptures had remained unrealized and in the main unrealizable. He could dream about women when he was alone in his warm bed, but at every actual bodily contact, Philip had an unpleasant feeling of waking up, as of getting up sleepless and naked, yet drowsy and tired, in a cold, stuffy room, and walking across bare stone while the wind howled in the wires and lightning conductors and around the building behind the walls all night. In the steam of macaroni or bent over a washtub, elusive as a ghost, unattainable yet alive, through the veil of half-sleep, the warm Rezika was still there with him, and then would come the reality: long corridors filled with the smell of soup, a wretched kind of soup with stale, brown bread; miserable mornings, when the fields were mantled with frost, and Philip was compelled to go to early mass in the cold church, where one's breath condensed in thick drops, and the hair in one's nostrils stiffened, and the holy water in the font froze. There they knelt at the cold praying desks, and half asleep after a delirious night, he would copy mathematics exercises with his frozen fingers by the light of the altar candles. The secrets of the flesh, the unhealthy secrets of the flesh in children's sickly bodies . . . wet snow falling outside . . . and he was sure to fail in mathematics.

Old Liepach was giving an afternoon coffee party in honor of his dear friend Countess Orcyval. Among the guests invited were Casimira Latinovicz and her son. Philip, to his mother's great amazement, had accepted the invitation. He knew that an invitation to this very genteel gathering of the élite of Kostanjevec had also been sent to Madam Xenia, the cashier—or as Steiner the innkeeper himself called her, the manager at the Crown. Bobočka Raday, the divorced wife of a Minister called Pavlinić, had taken over the post of cashier at Steiner's a few months earlier. This Madam Xenia, with her graying hair, hoarse contralto voice, and bright, girlish, light aquamarine eyes, was the chief reason Philip had not left Kostanjevec. He had heard so much malicious gossip and scandal about this woman among the people of Kostanjevec— how she had caused the failure of several banks; how she had ruined and incapacitated her husband the Minister; how she alone was to blame for the arrest of her last lover, lawyer Baločanski, whose wife had then committed suicide by jumping from a second-floor window—that this mysterious lady cashier who always dressed in black began to interest him. After he had made her acquaintance, it was a pleasure for him to go to the Crown and chat with her about the most ordinary daily happenings and even to breathe the air in her vicinity. Her gentle aquamarine gaze brought him a certain special peace, so that to sit at the Crown, at the table next to the cash desk, with his copy of the *Daily Mail* and a cigarette, became a daily necessity. To the party arranged by Liepach in honor of the old Madam Orcyval, a sort of aunt of Xenia's on her mother's side. Mrs. Bobočka herself drew Philip's attention and asked him to come so that they could meet there; it would be doing her a great service. Many people whom Philip did not know were invited, and by far the noisiest was Liepach's nephew, Tassillo von Pacak; there was also Liepach's sister Eleanor's daughter, Medika, the widow of an artillery major. With every other word Medika laid such stress on her family connection with the District High Commissioner, Liepach of Kostanjevec, her uncle on her mother's side, that it was half ridiculous, half embarrassing. In her mind the idea of the Liepach family was so imposing in every respect that it was as if some connection with that organization was at the very least a guarantee of indubitable security, as if under the protection of the name of Liepach, one could live as in the shade of heavy ironbound, double-lined steel safes, brimful of gold. Poorly endowed by nature, she still lived in the shade of her mother, Mrs. Eleanor, who even now thought of the Liepachs' position as it had been in the eighties, Everybody's digestion was in order—the gentlemen's, the cats', and the dogs', and it seemed as if there were no extraordinary problems at all; the vineyard would give a good yield, the chimneys were clean, and the inns were full. Turkish coffee was properly made in patent machines. Dominic would lay out the dominoes and the playing cards on the black table. All the time more children with the Liepach blue eyes would arrive. Soon there would be a wedding, and it was very likely that the District High Commissioner's young secretary, Silvius, would be made a baron. Could there be any pleasanter prospect?

The Countess Orcyval, who at the Liepachs'—heaven knows why—was called a cousin, née de la Fontaine-Orcyval et Doga-Ressza of the family of de la Fontaine of Žabokrek, was the center of this circle at Kostanjevec. She was an old lady of nearly seventy who still looked well and whom nobody would have put at over fifty. A former estate-owner at Galgócz-Tarján, Szöllösmonyor-Keretch, and Sárga-Somlovár; the proprietor of châteaux and land at Žabokrek, Resnik, and Grabar; heiress to the town of Kissasszony-Fabarany and Donji Varadin, this hysterical old lady today found herself dispossessed and wandered like a beggar from party to party, conversing with Steiner, the innkeeper, and Regina, the tobacconist, as with her equals, but nevertheless in her innermost heart maintaining her aristocratic isolation from all this plebeian filth, the isolation of the famous age-old coat of arms of de la Fontaine and Orcyval.

Having suddenly received some urgent letters from New Orleans, accepting some designs he had sent for the windows of a cathedral a year earlier, Philip had to answer immediately. He was therefore a little late for the party and so arrived just in the middle of an unbecoming and rather embarrassing scene.

For quite a while it had been whispered among the peasants of Kostanjevec that the old Count Uexhuell-Guillenband-Cranensteeg haunted the château, and had been seen lately in the vicinity of Liepach's residence. Yaga, a girl of nineteen, who worked in Liepach's garden, had seen him the night before near the greenhouse, and so was asked to come, at the request of Count Orcyval, to explain what had happened. The Countess was particularly interested in this because the ghost of the Count was her "uncle," and she was curious to hear something about the life beyond the grave of her dear departed "uncle." Philip arrived exactly at a moment when everybody had burst out laughing at Yaga, who, blushing, confused, ready to burst into tears of shame stood with a subconscious feeling of helpless shyness, in the center of the room surrounded by the guests. With her eyes cast down and crumpling her apron in both hands, Yaga kept repeating nervously that she knew nothing about it, but she certainly had seen the count and she knew nothing more than that she had seen him with her own eyes.

"We must ask her where she saw him. Let her tell us exactly where it happened," said the old niece of the ghostly Count in her shrill voice, like a dying chicken.

Tassillo von Pacak, the host's nephew, an excellent tennis player, winner of women's hearts, dancer and Radical, had assumed a sort of interpreter's role in the cheerful proceedings between the stammering and confused medium, Yaga, and this highly respectable company of distinguished people. He stood beside Yaga, holding her left hand to put her at her ease during the interrogation:

"Please, Yaga, be sensible! We should like to know where you saw His Late Excellency. Tell us where it happened. Near the greenhouse? The chapel? In the courtyard? In the corridor? Where?"

Yaga could not give a single exact detail. She stuck to her original statement:

"You see, Sir, I saw His Excellency with my own eyes just as I see you now, and I can say no more. How a person should look at a ghost, I don't know. How that should be done, well, wiser people than me can worry about that."

"What does she say, I can't understand a word she says," murmured the Countess, and her Adam's apple moved about under the black velvet ribbon, as if something alive and independent were moving there.

"She says that she doesn't know how one should look at ghosts. She has seen the dead Count, but how one should look at ghosts, let those who understand such things better, take care of that!"

"It might perhaps be a good thing if she described the clothes the dead Count was wearing," suggested the wife of the municipal physician, with her hundred and seven kilograms, all flushed with nervousness because she too was taking part in this brilliant incident.

"Yaga, listen, please, the ladies and gentlemen would like to know, and want you to tell us, how His Late Excellency was dressed?" said Tassillo von Pacak, leaning toward Yaga and condescendingly chucking her chin with his two fingers.

"He had a long jacket with sleeves, as red as a pomegranate," said Yaga, defending herself with shy and helpless gestures from Pacak's importunities, but not knowing how to get rid of him.

The Countess still could not understand a word of what she said. And she only added to Yaga's nervousness with her squealing voice, like that of a deaf person. One could see that Yaga was beginning to feel guilty that she did not know German.

"It seems he had a kind of red coat of pomegranate color, Countess," explained Tassillo, turning to the old lady with a subservient gesture worthy of a provincial dancing master. Philip, who had been watching the proceedings in a rather detached way, felt like stepping out from behind the lilac bushes and slapping the idiot. Even old Liepach became irritated.

"Well, Yaga, that's fine, but you've told us that already. Now we should like to find out just where this happened, where you saw His Deceased Lordship."

"I don't really know that, Sir. I saw His Lordship with my own eyes, but all of a sudden it grew so dark that it was as if a little angel had flown by or a dragon, but it seems to me it happened near the cucumber beds."

"If we could only understand her," said Medika Liepach von Rekettye de Retyezát, rolling her eyes, as if she had never heard of and had not been brought up among those same cucumber beds.

"A silly goose! We are not going to get anything out of her," said the chief speaker and interpreter of this spiritualist séance, Tassillo von Pacak.

"Yaga, do you know what you are; you are a simpleton and a stupid goose, devil take you! We have already heard that he was red and little and that he flew, but where, that's what Her Ladyship the Countess would like to know, do you understand?"

"Near the cucumbers, if you please, Sir!"

Philip could no longer control himself; he felt it was really out of place for him to interfere among those simple-minded parrots, but a real sympathy for the girl, who was blushing and perspiring with shame, moved him to interfere both decisively and directly in the ridiculous affair. As he suddenly and unexpectedly stepped out from behind the lilacs, his intervention appeared sharper and more resolute than he had meant it to be.

"I think, gentlemen, there is no sense in troubling this poor girl any further. After all, it isn't her fault that the gentry still believe in ghosts. It is difficult to give any information for police record about phenomena in the world beyond the grave and what you are subjecting her to is an extremely unpleasant interrogation!"

First amazement, then commotion, pleased gesticulation, surprise and bows, introductions and shaking of hands followed, and everybody agreed with old Liepach that there had really been enough of this ill treatment, and that the best thing would be to send the girl away!

"I am really pleased, Sir, that you have got me out of this situation! You have rendered me a great service," said old Liepach, taking Philip by both hands, introducing him to the ladies he did not know, and leading him up to Madam Xenia, "his godchild and his favorite," whom he had held in his arms at her christening, and whom he loved like "his own daughter"; and so Philip found himself next to Xenia, and everything was very embarrassing for him.

"My dear Yaga, we haven't learned anything from you. Dominic will drive you home. Thank you very much, but nobody can get anything out of you. You may go with Dominic now!"

"Thank you kindly, Your Excellency, and thank you humbly. You know how it is! I have told you everything as I saw and know it. My humble respects to you!"

Watching Yaga as she disappeared behind the lilacs accompanied by Dominic, old Liepach could not forget that frightful October night when concealed among the bushes, in his underpants and nightshirt, he had listened to the peasants demolishing his dwelling, heard the clatter of breaking glass, and seen the smoky flames pouring out from under his roof. Not a day passed when he did not several times recall that frightful sight.

"Yes, yes, that's what our 'dear,' 'good-natured,' 'intelligent' masses are like! And when they attack people with scythes and axes, it is called 'freedom' and 'democracy'! Too ridiculous, really, where one has to live nowadays!"

His nephew Tassillo von Pacak, from the very instant of Philip's arrival, had felt that his liberalism was in jeopardy. He was regarded in this circle as an adventurous social revolutionary and left-wing politician, and so he felt the need to define his "social position" before this stranger.

"Of course, it is rather difficult to talk about such things in an academic way, my dear uncle, isn't it? To tell the truth, within the framework of her own outlook on life, Yaga is not so silly as she seemed to be. Certainly, without any doubt one thing should be understood: she talked to us as to foreigners. In fact, two worlds, and two languages, which have nothing at all in common!"

"You are quite right! Two worlds and two languages! And that, you see, gentlemen, is what I can't grasp and won't be able to as long as I live; that I, for instance, can be of the same world as that wretched peasant girl! What foolish phrases about equality! What a demagogic deception!"

108

The Countess Orcyval, too, thought it necessary to say something after the silence.

"I think that she has made all that up about my late uncle!"

"But, on the other hand, the common people, the plebs, can see ghosts! They live in the fifteenth century! At that time people were still on very intimate terms with ghosts! I'm absolutely certain that she did see the dead Count. Only she couldn't find words to describe it to us! A gap of at least four hundred years separates us, and apparently it is rather far from one shore to the other."

Listening to the way this snob at his side spoke of the people and to his special emphasis on the word "plebs," Philip felt the blood rise to his head.

After all! He himself thought about these same "plebs" in the same aristocratic way, and he himself every day felt the distance between him and them, even wider than four hundrd years, but now he suddenly felt ashamed. Hell, how was it possible that he should think about such things in the same way as this snob? He did not, incidentally, feel separated from Yaga by a social distinction, he attributed no social secondary meaning to the word "plebs"; but perhaps they were only two kinds of snobbishness, and unfortunately, two extremely similar kinds! He felt the blood rise to his head and beads of sweat coming out on his fingertips. An abyss began to open under his feet.

The doctor, the foolish shortsighted doctor, said in his deep throaty baritone that it was of course natural that Yaga had seen nothing. "The day before yesterday they celebrated the anniversary of the Count's death, and of course the servants talked about it; a typical association and nothing more! Finally, Yaga could not say anything definite, either where it happened, or what the ghost looked like."

Unlike the doctor, Tassillo von Pacak was convinced that Yaga had really seen the Count—either as an association or materially, that did not matter. It was simply that she had not dared to look the Count in the face. He could perfectly well understand that; when a common mortal sees a dead Count walking through the park, it is natural for him to shut his eyes and run away! Common mortals cannot talk to dead Counts! To be able to talk to a dead Count, one should at least be a subscriber to the *Almanach de Gotha.*

"Mr. Pacak, you are always making silly, stupid jokes," said the Countess, feeling the need to intervene, and hearing Pacak mention the *Almanach de Gotha.*

"This is no silly joke, Countess, quite honestly! I believe that Yaga saw the dead Count! For Yaga, Count Uexhuell was no ordinary citizen from whom one could buy some thirty-five acres of plowland; when someone like Yaga sees a Uexhuell, she pulls her scarf over her head for fear of her life. For the Yagas, unfortunately, Count Uexhuells are no jokes at all! For five hundred years Uexhuells cut off the ears of such Yagas! Dear ladies and gentlemen, this must be understood!"

"So you are responsible for defending these Yagas in the light of history, then?" excitedly exclaimed His Excellency the District High Commissioner and host, Mr. Liepach, the blood rushing to his head and beating like hammers in his temples.

"Has history set you up as Yaga's defender? Is that it? Are you the only one who understands the wretched girl? In that case you are more arrogant to her than anybody else. The girl spoke quite naturally, until you confused her. In conversation here you always shine with your piffling democracy, but in practice you humiliate people of the lower class so that often I myself feel uncomfortable. Leave me alone! For instance, Dominic has been complaining to me for quite a while that you have been calling him Doctor! And that is, most likely, also in accordance with your democratic principles?"

"Excuse me, sir, Dominic calls *me* Doctor, although I have begged him a thousand times to drop it. I am no 'doctor,' I'm just an ordinary citizen. This way of calling a doctor by his title actually belongs to the eighteenth century; it is just as foolish as if one greeted one's shoemaker with 'My respects, Mr. Shoemaker,' and so Adolf Loos has very properly remarked. All that goes with the old rubbish, ladies and gentlemen!"

"Loos is a crazy fellow," protested Countess de la Fontaine et Orcyval, and she was probably the only one in the whole circle who had heard of Loos.

"Dominic is right to protest against your behavior, my dear! The servants are not here to be an object of people's ridicule!"

"I dislike Dominic precisely because he is such a perfect servant! I can't help it, my dear uncle; please forgive me, but I don't like servants at all! It's not in keeping with my character."

"Dominic is no servant, he is a good friend of mine, and I like him very much. He is a good and honest man!" Countess Orcyval came decisively to Dominic's defense.

In the center of this loud duel of words in front of the entire élite of Kostanjevec, Doctor Tassillo von Pacak felt like a hidalgo on the operatic stage, illuminated on all sides by footlights, armed with the sharp rapier of his superior wit. So he began to explain to the Countess, in a loud voice, that between herself and Dominic the valet stood the *Almanach de Gotha,* and when she, the Countess de la Fontaine et Orcyval, came down to Dominic's level as his well-intentioned friend, it was certainly a mark of honor. When a Countess of Orcyval holds out her hand to the friendly kiss of a servant wearing livery, it was likewise a symbolic event, as if the heraldic lioness in the blue field of her Orcyval coat of arms should extend her lioness's paw to be kissed by a common plebeian passerby. But we, we ordinary mortals, who are not so lucky and in whose veins there is no champagne instead of blood as with the nobility, we have the right to be insulted by people whose nature it is to be extremely servile, because by nature we are closer to servility than are genuine counts!

Having thus disposed of the Countess, Mr. Tassillo von Pacak devoted his attention to Philip, saying that he had heard of him from a friend of his, a sculptor, who particularly admired Philip's unusual and, one might say, extraordinary talent, high above the average. Such rare and, in every sense of the word, extraordinary, European figures as Philip were very important for the general cultural development of the country; especially in view of the deplorably low cultural, and particularly artistic, level, and he rejoiced that he was so honored and fortunate as to have this opportunity to meet so prominent a personality.

With a facile, seemingly genuine and spontaneous eloquence, Tassillo von Pacak poured out a mass of names, quotations, dates, facts; he produced there in front of Philip, within the space of two minutes, a whole store of proofs of his exceptional culture and good breeding, like a shop assistant displaying textiles on the counter before his customers. He recalled Plekhanov and Rolland Holst, and mentioned that recently, under the influence of a good American woman, he had become conversant with the most up-to-date literature on psychoanalysis, about the problems of the afterlife and the other world. Theosophy, anthroposophy, Hodgson, William Crookes, William James, Sir Oliver Lodge; the survival of man! Mediums in trance!

Looking at this babbler in front of him with his gray spats and monocle, Philip had one feeling: that there in front of him stood a sort of Levantine barbarian bothering him with solicitations to buy the cheapest kind of toys and mirrors; but he had not come here to buy colored glass trifles from a barbarian, he had not come to talk at a fair with shop assistants. Why was this fellow annoying him? Why could he not see in his eyes that he was boring him, and leave him in peace? Exhaling one puff of smoke after another, Philip looked at Tassillo von Pacak without moving either his lips or his eyebrows, while the former continued to talk about the internal logic of form, Negro art, contemporary expressionism in connection with the modern activistic trend, and collectivism in the field of art, with further references to Rolland Holst and Zamiatin, and this went on for a long time, growing more and more embarrassing. Everybody was staring at Philip, expecting him to say something in reply. But Philip did not say a word; he inhaled, exhaled, and now and then looked Madam Xenia straight in the eyes. All those people in front of him looked like plump painted dolls, and only her eyes glittered clearly like aquamarines, and her eyelashes were so thick, and black, and sweeping, that it seemed to Philip they were false. Those thick sooty eyelashes lifted, and behind them glittered a blueness, as if somewhere deep down the dawn was just breaking, while all the other eyes around her were dim and blind as those of hens.

"People are mere dolls, and they sit in their various civilizations as in showcases," thought Philip, watching this high society on Liepach's terrace. These dolls sit like mannequins in showcases, and from behind, in the background, some invisible window-dressers change their dresses, always different ones, different styles and different customs, and this—although nobody really knows why—is called " progress"! If one of the old ladies present were to appear in her prewar nest of lace, pasteboard, lacquered cherries, fruit, grapes, peaches, with ribbons and hair pads, full skirts and frills, everybody would laugh. And if in ten or fifteen years' time some of these slaves of fashion, the Kostanjevec girls, reappeared at a tea party wearing today's latest Hollywood fashion in hats, everybody would burst out laughing again. These human she-apes make fun of themselves when they see how they looked fifteen years ago! All this was really incomprehensible. Among multitudes of dolls, one doll is found from time to time who by mere accident is not one of them. That woman in mourning, for instance, with her silvering hair and light blue eyes, was no doll. She was certainly a living and warm-blooded person! She smoked like a man, and her gestures were human. She had been a Minister's wife, and had caused the failure of several banks! They said that she was a nymphomaniac, and that she had been the cause of one man's going to prison! When someone was not a doll in a shop window, the other dolls in the window never had a good opinion of her! Prison, murder, lechery, safe-breaking, suicide, adultery, infidelity, what a lot of foolish petty-bourgeois prejudices! That woman had the courage to sit behind the cash desk as the cashier in a dark café in this stuffy provincial backwater, and a released convict, a paralytic, an invalid, a man of the past, dogged her like a shadow. If she had not been a Minister's wife, none of these civil servants' ladies would have looked at the woman cashier, and now everyone had his own private opinion of her, but nevertheless sat in her company, because she used to be the wife of an active Minister!

Watching old Dominic dragging his tired flat feet like a penguin, the doctor's wife greedily mouthing a large spoonful of cream, and the old civil councilor's wife, Madam Eleanor, pestering the veterinary surgeon's wife with her incredibly boring cancer, Philip felt that it was all unbearable. He felt he must go. The surveyor's children were chasing a peacock along the front of the terrace, and Philip, talking and shouting to the vet's children, on the pretext that he was going to catch the peacock for them, slipped behind the lilac bushes and started off through the park in the direction of the old oak forest overlooking the castle.

In a glade of newly cleared land in the forest, he sat down on a felled tree and remained for a long while absorbed in his thoughts. At his feet lay an anthill which had been trampled upon by cows' hoofs. Under a dead oak tree charred by lightning, the deserted anthill lay before him, like something rotten, soft, and spongy, and the deathly quiet of that forsaken black tenement filled Philip with a gentle melancholy. This had once been Cranensteeg's orchard, and an old knotty apple tree survived alone in the glade, worm-eaten, gray, its heavy green branches laden with red apples like symbols of early autumn. In between the leaves, the separate apples showed up red on the branches, red as Regina's old-fashioned coffee cups. On an old bramble a spider was busy spinning his web, and kept letting himself down on a long thread at regular intervals like the needle of an invisible sewing machine; everything was wrapped in silence. Beyond the forest could be heard the clear voice of a shepherdess and the tinkle of a cowbell. In the valley below the glade, the Blatnja wound between vineyards and meadows in its deep-cut bed; and in the distance, in the ash-gray mist of the summer dusk, one could discern the contours of the hills increasingly clear, blue and transparent as in a Japanese drawing. In the changing shades of evening color, a line of willows stood out plainly in the distance, each one distinct, plastic as if put in with charcoal, while the colors merged into a monochrome horizontal bar above the haystacks and distant dark green cornfields. The glade was filled with the bitter evening beauty of solitude. Philip was not thinking of anything save how good and wise it was to think of nothing and quietly inhale the moist evening air in the forest. Everything came to that; to steep one's body as deeply as possible in such evenings and early mornings. To feel around one the chuckling of streams and the scents of plants and to think of nothing. To breathe.

Bending over the dead anthill, with his head in his hands, he felt a warm breath on his skin. Beside him, in full mourning, pale, with her silvering hair, stood Xenia. And as if it were quite natural, she sat there beside him, and they remained so for a long time without saying a word.

When Philip met Xenia Raday, most of her life was already in the past, her two completely unhappy, stupid marriages, and the tragedy with Vladimir Baločanski, a man for whom she had never really felt anything. Toward Baločanski she had behaved quite indifferently, feeling only a certain pity for him which she could not explain even to herself; but that vague sympathy had played a destructive role in the life of that confused and unhappy man. Xenia had married her first husband, Dr. Pavlinić, a lawyer and minister, quite cold-bloodedly, for his position, calculatingly, as many middle-class girls do marry. But unlike most middle-class girls of her age, who succeed in reconciling themselves to their married life for years by lying, she with her wild temperament, could not persist in the false compromise and tore up her marriage certificate without any concrete reason, more from caprice than from any real necessity. As her divorce coincided with the failure of the cooperative bank of which her husband was chairman and one of the chief creditors, there were many rumors that she was the main cause of the failure and, having foreseen the catastrophe, had withdrawn in time. There was no concrete evidence against her, and everything consisted in rumors that were spread at tea and dinner parties, and then disappeared like stains from old rags.

The lawyer, Vladimir Baločanski, the son of a former head of an Administrative District, had fallen in love with her like a boy, naïvely and quite innocently. From the first he bored rather than interested her, but in rejecting this weakling and keeping him very often at an unbelievably cruel distance, she dealt him a fatal blow; it might be said—indeed, in the town it commonly was said —that she ruined him. Because of her, Baločanski became involved in grave monetary difficulties, embezzled funds on a large scale, and forged signatures on bills of exchange. When he landed in prison and his wife in a rather cowardly and melodramatic way threw herself from a window, he remained in Xenia Raday's memory like the aftermath of a drama; then one day he came back to her like a dispatch from prison. A sick, broken man, he had rung her door bell; shortsighted, without his glasses, he was half paralyzed, had a graying beard, and was wearing a creased overcoat and a greasy bowler hat. She did not know what to do with him. Should she take him in and give him food and lodging? Should she hide from him? Should she not answer the door? Should she throw him out into the street, as they had thrown out all his things because of her? And so Baločanski came to live with her, and afterward, when there was no money left, they retired to Kostanjevec, where she still had a vineyard with a brick cottage; and when even this vineyard and its cottage became Steiner's property, she sublet the café in the municipal square from Steiner, stayed behind the cash desk as cashier, and now lived in the cottage with the paralyzed Baločanski, dependent on the good will of Steiner, the Kostanjevec café-proprietor.

During the three years when Baločanski was in jail at Lepoglava, Xenia Raday had lived hectically and concluded a civil marriage with a political speculator who had made his fortune during the war; scattering the money of this big industrialist like confetti, she had seemed already at that time, in her completely senseless and ruinous pace, to display something of that suicidal, insatiable, demented craze for dangerous pleasures which would one day finish her off.

At the time when Baločanski had felt that this woman was his destiny, Xenia, who was then called BoboČka by everybody, was twenty-seven years old. She had the sleek long head of a Borzoi on a fragile, slender body. Fair-haired, with deep shining eyes, she used her delicate, sharply cut lips shrewdly and sensitively; from those pale, moist lips flagrant and poisonous lies flowed like sheer poetry. Her body, a vessel of deep and obscure passions, was hermaphrodite, yet appeared the pure body of a girl on the threshold of her first spring. She blossomed like a cankered flower; her perfumes of wet decaying hay, her opium-sprinkled cigarettes, and her broken contralto voice clouded in thick smoke floated around the heads of the first and second generations of our newly established gentry like some mysterious incense. To turn something diseased and ugly into the charm of a love experience, to clothe perverse and obscure phenomena with the magic of blue blood, to deceive upstart gentlemen, bankers, and parvenus, with that blue-blooded nonsense, and at the same time empty their massive iron safes, was Bobočka's secret.

Bobočka was of noble descent. In her fragile porcelain body flowed clear blue blood, as clear as the aquamarines of her necklace. That wild blood, violet as the ink with which she wrote her fatal letters, that strange temperament of hers and that restlessness of her flesh, all made a picture framed in real gold and, according to what was rumored in the town, two banks, Minister Pavlinić's credit cooperative, and the Yugoslav-Dutch Bank, Ltd., had wound up their operations and paid their creditors less than thirty percent, largely on account of Bobočka and her blue-blooded demands.

After her divorce from Minister Pavlinić, Bobočka had at first a nine-room flat on the first floor of a large building in the center of the lower part of the city, where the green of a row of trees in the park was reflected on the curtains, and through the open balcony could be heard the murmur of a fountain and the chatter of evening promenaders. The nine rooms were furnished in unobtrusive Empire style furniture which Bobočka used to say came from the house of her Raday ancestors, whereas in fact it had been bought cheap in Vienna by Minister Pavlinić, at the auction of the effects of a Viennese gentleman. In the days of the Verböczy, the Radays had fought according to a family tradition for "The Rights of the Kingdom," but a truer picture of the Radays' patriotism was given when Bobočka's great-grandfather, Ambrose Raday, together with the people of Turopolje, had played the czardas and Rakoczy's March in exultation over the defeat of Illyria at the restoration of 1847. According to family tradition, the Radays always opposed their own people; from Rauch, the first compromiser, to Count Khuen, and to ordinary gentry like Czuvaj and Tomassich and Rakodzay and Szkerlecz, a Raday was always playing the same role as that first collaborator with Hungary. Human flesh was cut up and sold to foreigners, but the Radays were always good patriots, officials, and servants of the foreign nobility, and, according to family tradition, "they were defending the Interests and Rights of the State of Croatia, Slavonia, and Dalmatia. . . ."

Bobočka had a complete gilded baroque altar in her flat— "from the private chapel of her Raday ancestors"—turned into a cupboard, and from that baroque altar she served her guests with whisky and sparkling wines. Above her bed hung a portrait of a Raday in the robes of a metropolitan bishop, while in the drawing room was Makart's portrait of a mysterious lady in yellow silk, said to be a Viennese dancer, on whose account a von Raday had committed suicide. All this was arranged in Bobočka's flat as in a theater, where the flames of Ragusan candelabra were reflected in Empire polished wood, and the furniture was covered with Indian shawls; where by the decorative light of candles they smoked, drank, and told lies for whole days and nights together. They lied about music, from Schumann to Honegger and Milhaud; and all names were vulgarized to suit empty and foolish conversation over tea and champagne. They lied about books, they lied about lyric poetry, they lied about taste and fashion; they talked about Beauty, as if Beauty were the cover of a women's fashion journal printed in three colors, and they lied and babbled to such an extent that they spent about seventy thousand dinars a month, and three marriages were ruined, and two banks failed, and all through innocent conversations about Beauty, about Taste, about Eternity, and about God.

Already at Buda, before she was thirteen, and when she fought with boys who had curly hair and healthy teeth, the meaning of sex was revealed to Bobočka, a momentous revelation.

It was during the summer holidays, and Bobočka was staying at her aunt's. It was a Sunday. There was a scent of pine trees, and the Buda bells were ringing. Bobočka, tender, fair-haired, slight, barelegged, with firm kneecaps, and delicate, soft joints, lay in the arms of Baron Remény, her aunt's uncle. Her aunt, who was married to one of the von Radays, a high official of the Buda Praesidium, lived in the city of Buda, above Krvava Poljana. It was a beautiful sunny morning. After a heavy stormy night, the air was transparent; there were shadows, pigeons, and bells ringing. There was no one in the house. Everybody had gone to mass except Bobočka and the uncle. She was swinging on the swing in the garden, and the Baron, an old *bon vivant* and card sharp, was reading the paper. How it happened that the chain of the swing broke and Bobočka fell on a glass which somebody had forgotten under the swing, and cut herself and began to bleed profusely, remained vague in her mind; she had forgotten the details; she had fallen, cut her knee on the broken glass, and lost a lot of blood. The old Baron had carried her up to the flat all bleeding, laid her on the divan, and cleaned off the blood with cotton wool and alcohol, and then everything was lost in the delirium of a strange indescribable sensation about which Bobočka had read; but that this sensation spread like smoke and that the body was raised like a balloon, above everything material and physical, she had had no idea until that intense experience. The subsequent, almost unearthly, transport of the flesh carried away by rapture and all the mysterious intoxication of childish sensuality on that sunny Sunday morning remained Bobočka's most intense recollection of her early youth—the lowered blinds, the twilight in the room, the distant ringing of bells in the city, the smell of alcohol and warm child's blood on her knee, the sweating hands, the flame in her brain and her joints, a not unpleasant half-faintness from crying, the closeness of the uncle, and the way he had lifted her and carried her to the divan, stroking her bleeding leg with thin fingers and smelling of tobacco and alcohol.

In the seventh form she had a serious attack of bronchitis and traveled with her mother to Taormina. It was a warm spring night aboard the ship, and a Berlin *bel esprit,* the son of a banker from the big city, an idler and artist in love affairs, was explaining to Bobočka the Gothic style, and porcelain, and talking to her about his collection of glass and about the stars. Surrounded by ropes, high up in the prow of the white ship, on a warm starry night off Taormina, Bobočka gave herself to the unknown young man and caught from him a kind of tropical tubercular fever. The young Berliner was a doctor, a decadent type from the big city, who dyed his eyebrows, and for two whole days walked about the deck carrying leatherbound books with gilt tooling. He talked to Bobočka very sensibly and in an experienced manner all the way from Genoa, about the special technique of copper-engraving, about precious glass, and how boring life was unless one lived freely and intelligently, like monkeys in tropical jungles. So two kindred souls found themselves on the prow of the ship, talking about the symposium and about love in Bang's novels. All the vague, false, deeply concealed and intense feelings that had been accumulating in Bobočka for three or four years burst from her that night finally and elementally. The false decadent shadow, full of mystery and insipid timidity, that had dimmed Bobočka's imagination like a veil of fear and anxiety, disappeared from her mind that night and she went back to her cabin as someone who had discarded "the last burden of foolish, medieval upbringing and prejudice." Passing through the brightly lit saloon where her mother was playing bridge, the wild idea crossed Bobočka's mind to go to her mother and confess to her everything that had happened. But her feet seemed to be made of lead, and the idea so bizarre, so unhealthy, that she went on her way to her cabin on the first deck.

"But that's morbid!"

"And what is there that is healthy in life? All mere phrases! And that young sybarite from Berlin might be right! The monkeys in tropical forests live the most sensible life!" Among the ropes of the ship the south wind whistled; and the ship began to roll slowly, monotonously and tediously, and as if reluctantly. Bobočka was sick. She was seasick all the way to Taormina. Her mother went on playing cards till dawn, and when she returned, Bobočka pretended to be asleep, with her mouth full of bitterness, her eyes red and misty. Through the open, brass-rimmed porthole one could feel the salt tang and the murmur of the sea. It was a June morning, and in the brass circle ash-gray islands passed and the lamps of lighthouses went out.

Vladimir Baločanski, or as his father used to sign his name, Ballocsanszky, was a polite, correct, well-bred mother's darling. His mother, the blue-blooded Patricia Ballocsanszky, wife of the Head of an Administrative District, was a woman who had devoted the whole of her life to the perfect education of her only son. This son—an excellent pupil who was always first at school and had at least five distinctions in his examination—was gifted by nature, bright, frank, good-natured, polite; in a word, the child of an important man, and described always in superlatives. His interest in painting was high above average dilettantism, and his perfect English pronunciation, his beautifully pressed trousers and impeccable tie, his written work, the tidiness of his writing desk and wardrobes, his studies abroad and his examinations, which he passed with exceptional ease, all foretold a brilliant career for this young gentleman of noble descent and obvious distinction.

Vladimir Ballocsanszky was twenty-four, when as Deputy District Commissioner at Križanovac, he became engaged to Miss Vanda Dvořak-Agramer, the daughter of a prominent surgeon, Dr. Dvořak-Agramer, a rich landlord with property in the main street of Zagreb. Born in 1881, Vladimir was Governmental Secretary to the Department of the Interior when on the first day of general mobilization in 1914 he left to join his cavalry regiment at Virovitica. Already the father of three children, he served in Galicia until mid-1917, when, a distinguished Captain of Horse, he returned to the civil service.

The influence of his mother, who had vigilantly watched over all his thoughts for a full thirty years, the ideal happiness of his marriage with Vanda Agramer, his career in the Administration, and the complete isolation of his family and social life, were all elements which had fenced off Vladimir Ballocsanszky, as with strange and incredible cardboard walls, from the realities of life.

It was as if he were wrapped in cotton wool and brought up according to all the rules for inculcating the ordered outlook on life of a civil service administrator. With controlled nerves, inclinations, and temperament, he went his way through the world as the epitome of a distinguished gentleman and public servant who thought and acted in accordance with the clockwork machine of tradition and so-called conviction.

After the war he opened a lawyer's office, invested his wife's capital in industry, sat at the green conference tables of administrative councils, and so continued to live a comfortable life, ordered and clearly defined. Vladimir Ballocsanszky and his wife Vanda were ideally happy people. They had their children, the eldest Vladimir, and two girls, Dagmar and Alice, their eleven-room flat, with three maids and a manservant, the visits of his high-born mother, Patricia, the summer vacations at Lovran and Bohinj that were *"de rigueur,"* the customary trip to Vienna together "to freshen themselves up a bit after the provinces," solid, industrial clients and a well-run household—"only 18,000 dinars a month"—and all this went on silently and smoothly from day to day, from year to year, according to a program as regular as a railway timetable. In that polished, properly arranged box, all the toys were in their places. One knew where the music of Beethoven's sonatas stood, where receipted accounts were kept, what the child's nurse had said when Granny Patricia sent a postcard from Salzburg; one knew what was needed to complete the household medicine chest, and the children's wardrobe, how Alice's tooth was, and what progress in Greek prose the father's favorite child and namesake was making. The classics had a place in that life as well; these dear people found them boring but respectable, like plaster figures and copper engravings under glass; music also had its place, and tickets were booked in advance at the theater or concert agency. They bought paintings of Vanda's choice, showing tempestuous seas and storms, the only storms that wise and cautious lady ever envisaged, when after 11 P.M., her evening piano playing over, she waited to hear the sound of her husband's key opening the front door, when he returned from a late evening conference or business talk.

And then a gust of wind broke the silence. Into that polished

124

life of ticking clocks, warm carpets, and closed rooms, lies began to creep, at first slight and hardly discernible, which by their dangerous, antlike persistence, gradually undermined the idyllic existence built of cardboard and shining lacquer. Vladimir Ballocsanszky was introduced to Bobočka, and for the first time in his life gave his body to a woman, without reason or logic, simply according to the laws of the flesh, as boys not yet seventeen give themselves; unconditionally, come what may!

For quite a while Xenia Raday was a conventional figure in the background—a customer, a lawyer's client—and then she began to appear as an invited guest, as a partner at card parties, as a visitor in the box at the theater, as a close acquaintance at an evening entertainment at the restaurant, as a name which began to buzz along all the telephone extensions of Vladimir's private and business life. Vladimir Ballocsanszky began as Bobočka's lawyer in the very complicated business of her divorce, because the Right Honorable Minister threatened her with some letters as evidence of adultery, which subsequently turned out to be a mere lawyer's trick.

"Mrs. Boba rang you up at about five o'clock today!"

"Right! Thank you! She rang me at the office!"

"Has her case not been settled yet? Thecla told me that it was all over."

"Yes! But it's a matter for higher jurisdiction. These matters of church law and the marriage law are very much entangled! The procedure is all out of date, simply made to obstruct. Things which seem to be already settled, are returned for quite trifling reasons to their preliminary stage. It is all very complicated!"

"Well, I can't judge! That woman just gets on my nerves. She is not a nice person!"

Silence. Cigarette smoke. A silent movement from the window to the piano. Pause. Schumann's Fantasia.

Or: "Where are you going?"

"I have a conference at the Palace. The Yugoslav-Dutch Company! Preliminary conference!"

"I thought Doctor Klanfar had rung up to say that the meeting was at his house. You are not going there?"

"That was a misunderstanding. Tonight there is a conference

on Amsterdam. And anyway, these are business matters. Klanfar may have rung up, but this doesn't concern him at all! Klanfar is only a name here. Good-bye, Bibi! I'm going. Good night. You just go to bed; no need for you to wait for me."

"But won't you come back after the conference?"

"I don't know, my child! If I have to go on somewhere with the gentlemen, perhaps I shan't. Good night!"

And so one misunderstanding followed another.

"I have ordered the car and now you brush aside this one treat for the children as if it were a trifling matter! The children haven't seen anything of you lately. Really, you just pretend that you are busy all the time! I can't help saying it!"

"Sorry! I did say that excursion was only on condition. Is it my fault I have to work? All this is exaggerated! It is just superfluous fuss on your part, my dear!"

"Yes, yes, I control myself as well as I can, but when it is a question of the children . . ."

"Good-bye!"

And so followed disagreements and arguments about whether the box at the theater had been booked as agreed or not, whether it was all the same whether he should meet Vanda and the children after *Tosca* or yawn during the performance, whether he had fixed something else for that date because he did not know . . . because he had forgotten . . . because he had thought . . . because he could not know. . . . He was a busy man, worked the whole day for others, he too was entitled to his amusements and his Turkish coffee; that was the minimum. And so petty jealousy grew, in words, suspicion, smoke, and alcohol. A lot of smoke and a lot of cognac and whisky and something else which had not been there before; drunkenness and coarse drunken violence. Rumors spread about the town, rumors about Bobočka, rumors about Vladimir. That he had been at Bobočka's at a *soirée*, that he had danced on a table in the costume of a Spanish dancing girl! That he had been seen with Bobočka and her "suite" at the cabaret the very evening when he had refused to take Vanda to a concert by a French pianist! That he had not gone to Vienna on business, but to Opatija, where Bobočka had bought a luxuriously furnished villa! That he lost at cards and was wasting money. That he was spending wildly and getting into financial difficulties. That things were not as they should be with him. Anxiety and distrust! Ever greater anxiety and deeper distrust, and new, unknown complexes, and thoughts logical and pessimistic, something that had never happened to him before.

About this time, Vanda began to discover in her husband a man who was completely unknown to her. A man without will power, a man who lied, to whom nothing mattered but external, conventional form; about whom everything was shallow, unreliable, and egotistical, indeed cruel. She saw faults in him only, of course. She herself was a mother; she lived for her children, for the idea of the superior purity of her own family, and only in the last place for him. She was a martyr and she was neglected as if she were not a human being but an inanimate object. She was simply disregarded.

I n Vladimir von Ballocsanszky physical and carnal needs made themselves more and more strongly felt. He had actually lived the whole of his life as if in a mental home, where in the patients' own interest no one was allowed to do anything. It was forbidden to smoke, to drink, to play cards, to make love, to do anything instinctively, to enjoy life, to think! Everything was forbidden and everything was strictly prescribed, as in a private asylum. Apart from the morbid monotony of his fixed program of daily occupations for so many years, and the desperate, clinical, patientlike subjugation to habit, regulations, principles, what had he ever really experienced? An apathy of the will, a daily resignation for years, an appearance of vague, imaginary happiness, which was really not happiness but a slow, pernicious, Philistine wasting away of everything positive within him.

What had he actually experienced in life, frankly speaking and taking a comprehensive view? He had had bronchitis and tonsilitis, and drunk a concoction of mallow. He had twisted his ankle on Whitsunday when he was in the fifth form, and had had his leg in plaster for four weeks. That was all that had ever happened to him! The only real, genuine impression of his childhood was a night drive with his father in a cab to the vineyard at Božjak. That mysterious flickering of the cab lamps on the horses' shining hairy flanks and hindquarters had been the only great experience of his childhood. Bobočka was right in asserting that the greatest curse of our contemporary life is the systematic destruction of the natural, the deep, the imaginative within us. "One should live an uninhibited life, like monkeys in tropical jungles!" Altogether independent of all our European intellectual ballast, we should really live somehow like that. It was shameful, but true, that the first woman he had had, other than his wife, was a prostitute, and that had been at Rožnjat in Galicia in '16. It was during the World War, and he was a thirty-three-year-old cavalry officer and had been fighting for two years.

And now this extraordinary woman, this Bobočka, was a revelation to him! Here one could find an escape from everything annoying, tedious, habitual and commonplace; bright colors had been revealed to him, and a completely unknown intensity of emotion.

And what was the meaning of those foolish phrases about the duties of "a husband and father of a family"? They had kept repeating such foolish phrases about "duties" to him all his life. His governess when he was a child, with her unbearable *"occupation quotidienne,"* and his mamma who had tyrannized over him with her pathetic love for thirty years, and his school, and examinations, and his profession, all were mere restraints! A man runs in shafts like a cabman's horse, so why should they keep on shouting to him from the cab that it was the duty of a husband, the father of a family, and a well-bred only son to continue to run at a regular trot, right into the first-class grave that was already bought and kept ready for any untoward event. But he was not going to do anything to upset that arrangement in its entirety. Let them just allow him to stop and take breath for once! He wanted nothing but a moment's pause in this futile martyrdom.

He is as soft as putty, he lacks will power, he is a gambler who stakes the happiness of his own children on a throw of the dice!

That is ridiculous. What is will power? An apelike imitation of the customary gestures. He had the will to want something out of the ordinary for once! So far he had lacked will power, yes, and now for the first time in his life the essence of the common phrase was revealed to him—what it really meant "to have the will." And what he had a will to do was against nobody's interests. It only meant that he wanted one brighter interlude for himself in this gray boredom, a single unescorted, unsupervised excursion. But he would come back. Why was everyone so upset, as if he were not going to come back any more? Why all this exaggerated care about his person? His personal affairs did not concern anybody else! People were unreasonably intrusive and inconsiderate.

Especially society ladies, and particularly if they were mothers! He worked, he earned his own living, entertained those intrusive and inconsiderate people at his own table, so what was the reason for all this unnecessary anxiety and nervousness?

So Vladimir von Ballocsanszky sat in a bar and watched the kaleidoscope of colors and materials and female flesh. Naked female shoulders passed him, skirts and draperies swirled about, faces moved among the noise, the crowd swayed to a Negro rhythm, muted, primitive; and Ballocsanszky sat in a box, drinking one cocktail after another, and watched Boba moving about the floor with some people he did not know.

Who were those unpleasant young creatures, with the shoulders of their dinner jackets cut so brutally square, as if the black cloth and starched shirt fronts hid some great athletic strength? Who were those people nobody knew, with their thick, coarse hair smoothed back with brilliantine, their strong teeth, and their English way of shaking hands? Athletes who talked about foolish novels, traveled in winter to the Bernese Oberland, drank liters of tea, and, surrounded by flowers and shaded lights, talked about books and music and made love to Boba. They danced with her for nights on end, while he sat in his box, drained one cocktail after another, and waited for the time of weariness and the dawn to come. Just to sit with her in a car and take her home. It was all irregular and unbecoming and dissipated, and in fact revolting and meaningless and expensive—to torment oneself so hopelessly, to wait long nights through, to be subjected to torment, humiliation, physical exhaustion, but to sense one female body above all others and let oneself be tormented by that body and yet be happy. That crowd pulling Boba about down there on the dance floor! Women of the lowest kind, shouting and laughing; drunken musicians driveling over the piano keys or their saxophones; shop assistants with swollen, sweating hands and lead rings jostling one other; dances which verged on the punishably indecent and scandalous, and in the midst it all Boba was dancing as pleased and innocent as a little girl! The atmosphere was hot and fuggy and smelled of common soap and rancid cocoa butter;

the waiters moved about as stiff as dummies in their tailcoats; the chief waiter had a gold bracelet and a topaz ring, transparent as old wine. In patent-leather shoes, with powdered faces, waiters were serving these drunken profligates on silver plates to the sound of guitars, and every such gallant night as Boba's escort cost at least a thousand dinars.

And was Boba really a nymphomaniac?

No, Boba was the sincerest and the most innocent woman in the world! She had not concealed from him a single detail of her life! Not even the young Hungarian Hussar officer, a philanderer and a young sinner, into whose arms she fell when she was eighteen. He was a cavalier and a nobody, an adventurer and a blackmailer, a lover and a brute, and finally he had abandoned her like his other mistresses and married another girl. His name was Németh; von Németh. And then there was her marriage with that unpleasant careerist Pavlinić and all those moral wounds which remained unhealed. She had not concealed from him a single detail. And the mass of flirtations and debauched nights in filthy inns, under the beastly eyes of drunken rascals, men smelling of dirt and sweat, with bits of straw and hay in their curly hair, showing where they had spent the night before. With one such fellow whose trousers were held up with string, and who wore torn galoshes instead of shoes, she spent the night, drunk, in some sort of a carriage in a locked barn somewhere in the suburbs. But that was the despair of loneliness, that could be understood!

But there were some unpleasant facts, too. The face of Muki, the little old dwarf who, with his monkey called Bobby moved about Boba's rooms like a sort of court jester: ninety-eight centimeters tall, with tiny wrinkled hands, like the wrinkled skin of a foetus preserved in alcohol, little Muki used to hop round Bobočka's flat like a bizarre poet. He jingled his bells, played with Bibby, the chameleon, wore a dinner jacket and a red Harlequin cap, and got drunk on champagne. Baločanski had finally succeeded in getting rid of Muki, but that little cellist, the hunchbacked Eleanor, a child prodigy, a pale, tubercular, sickly girl, who was in lasting and continuous favor with Boba—there was something very disturbing and mysterious about that!

And all those people at Bobočka's dinner and tea parties! They were all sinister and mysterious figures! Eccentrics, who drank wine from human skulls, gourmets, whose only worry was about lobsters and asparagus, and precisely when both lobsters and asparagus were out of season. People who babbled for whole days about ties and face creams. And finally all this was very expensive, and all the asparagus, artichokes, and lobsters were put on his bill. There was a Siamese dinner given by Boba in honor of a close friend of her childhood, Lorrie, a singer, who arrived in town in his own Rolls Royce. That Siamese dinner party had indeed been expensive. Chinese wax candles, Malayan pottery, rotten eggs, bad fish, overripe melons with mayonnaise, heady spices, smoke—and all of it, ultimately, paid for by Baločanski, and everything so boring and unnecessary!

There was nobody in Boba's circle whom he really liked and esteemed. The crazy countess of Orcyval was about Boba too much. Why did she come so often on a visit from Szent-Miklos, and stay several weeks? As for Mrs. Angelica Benito-Benitzka, a woman with a boy's body, the wife of a notorious and confirmed cardsharp, she was a person too compromised in every sense for a distinguished lady to appear in public in her company. And Boba sat ostentatiously with that Angelica in a box at the theater every evening! Mysterious Paris and London wholesale agents for perfumes and stockings constantly paraded through Boba's salon, and played poker for whole nights, or *chemin de fer,* and lost, and then won; mysterious visitors with high titles and the prominent position of commercial attachés. Only unattractive figures! Who was that sinister Georgian, that charlatan, Dr. Kyriales? That two-faced von Križovec, Klanfar's lawyer, who was bent only on edging him out of the Amsterdam combination? And then her cousin on her mother's side, Baron Urban, counselor at the Legation at Petersburg, who had sunk so low as to sign newspaper articles with his own name! The other day a conjuror from Cairo, called Muharem-Abi-bey, had come to supper at Boba's place, and something had happened that had puzzled Baločanski ever since. A pearl necklace belonging to Boba had disappeared. Next day, when this was found out and the only possible suspect was the Cairo conjuror, Boba would not allow this only logical solution to be considered. She began to scream hysterically when Baločanski declared that he was going to ring up the police. And last night, he had quite by chance found on her dressing table a pawn ticket from a Vienna pawnshop for the same pearl necklace. What kind of secrets were these? He had bought Boba that necklace for 320,000 lire at Milan last Easter! A villa at Opatija, too, for 842,000. Last month's grocer's bill for champagne, caviar, and other trifles alone amounted to 27,000! And he had forgotten 11,000 for Boba's box at the theater for the second quarter. (At home he had a deficit brought forward from last month amounting to some 18 or 20 thousand, while for the current month he had paid nothing as yet. Vanda had not said a word to him about that!) And there was the trip to Vienna, and the new dress, and the school fees for little Eleanor, who in Boba's opinion showed great talent, a child prodigy, with an exceptional gift for music?

And Boba was really not a nice person. She talked about a lot of things very affectedly, as if she were acting. She very often showed the most elementary lack of education! Toward people with whom she had for one reason or another broken off relations she was completely indifferent, and the distance between herself and people who were physically unattractive to her was just not human; the distance was positively interplanetary! The other night they had gone together to the opera, and Dr. Pavlinić, who had a seat in the pit, had looked with interest at his former wife, appearing in public with a new zealous admirer. That was indiscreet on the part of Pavlinić, and a proof of his poor breeding, but the hatred against Pavlinić with which Boba had reacted was quite inhuman.

And how did such an obscure person come to be looking like that in her direction? Her tone was like a razor, and quite possibly the man in the pit was not so indiscreet as it appeared. No, Boba did not suffer from too large a heart!

But what did she feel for that little consumptive Eleanor if not compassion? The girl lay ill for days and Boba nursed her like an angel, sitting up with the little hunchbacked musician for nights on end, making lemonade for her, playing with her, accompanying her on the piano, taking care of the girl, as if she were her mother. What else could this be if not good-heartedness?

Dr. von Ballocsanszky sat in the bar and watched Boba dancing. Women's shoulders swayed past, skirts and bare feet, faces moved to the accompaniment of the music, bodies rocked to the Negro rhythm, but Vladimir von Ballocsanszky sat on in his box, drinking one cocktail after another, and watching Boba moving about the floor.

Vladimir Baločanski melted
in Boba's fingers like a wax flower, and of the sad crumbling mess
there remained the two or three seals with which the police sealed
up his things, his cashbox, his desk, his office, and with them the
whole of his famous career, which so many had envied. When
things began to look black, Vladimir's wife, Vanda, tried to talk
to that haughty old lady. Madam Ballocsanszky, her distinguished
and glacial mother-in-law, about Bobočka, "that criminal wretch
of a woman who had undermined Vanda's and her children's existence." Something definite ought to be done about it, and Vanda
thought "that it should be the duty of her noble mother-in-law, as
Vladimir's mother"!

Unabridgable distances separated Vanda from old Madam Ballocsanszky, and in those crucial conversations, when she could
still have done a great deal in the interest of her son, the old lady,
who had never loved anybody and had never been able to tolerate
her daughter-in-law, remained frigidly cold, completely and con-
sistently passive—*par distance.* During those quietly spoken
scenes, when Vanda accused Baločanski and had so many reasons
for doing so, the old lady played the role of the dignified mother-
in-law, protecting the reputation of her son in relation to this
woman, so different from herself in birth and upbringing.

"Here, my dear child, tears can be of no avail! He is at the
same age as his father was when he too began to show a liking for
light women, something I had never noticed before in my husband! You just have to wait. That is the only remedy in the situation!"

"But this has been going on for too long, Mamma, for heaven's
sake! I myself thought that the best thing would be to leave
everything to time, but this has lasted two years now. If it weren't
for Dagmar, I should know what to do, but with things as they
are, my hands are tied, and so I thought that it might be your

place to take the initiative. Last night Theresa was here and she assured me in all seriousness that there are rumors in the town of Vladimir's financial ruin as something very likely. But he refuses in principle to tell me anything about it!"

"All men are like that. . . . Nothing can be done about it! One just has to drink one's tea quietly and wait."

"But if these rumors about his going bankrupt are true, then he is going to cause my ruin and that of the children too!"

And so these low-pitched tragic scenes would go on, between half-past seven and eight o'clock in the evening, over the cold tea, in a few words' conversation.

He was out again; he had telephoned that he had been prevented from coming because he was busy . . . This morning, she had helped him to tie his tie; he had been so nervous that he just could not make the knot himself; and when she, on seeing this, had burst into tears, he had stroked her hair and called her his boring old nanny.

Baločanski himself, in the fever of the last few days, could not feel the ground beneath his feet; he had an undefined but intense feeling that he was lost. Boboička's coming into his life had revealed to him with undeniable force that he had been living a foolish, artificial, mistaken life, in a series of absurd deceptions and theatrical settings, and that he had failed to penetrate to his own innermost self. But this woman seemed to break through, like an elemental force, into his very self, his most essential, secret self. For the whole of his life he had wandered among objects and phantoms, like a shy, restless, trembling child, and now, when for the first time he stood upright and wanted to begin to act as a rational being, he came into conflict with material things. With the penal code. He had never dared to confess to himself certain fundamental truths about the falseness of his intimate physical life, but now, when he was beginning, half audibly, half in a dream, to admit the errors he had committed, avalanches and catastrophes were already upon him. He had passed his last two years in drunkenness, with dwarfs and hunchbacked girls, in the softness of a woman's warm arms, with men who in their drunkenness kissed women's gold shoes, ate rotten fish and bad eggs, smoked opium, took cocaine; and that slimy, flatulent, rotting,

137

monstrous animal within him felt the need to stretch itself like an enormous antediluvian beast, to live, to forget, to bite into somebody's throat with its teeth, and even before anything had happened, everything was finished. A warrant for his arrest had been issued, but he explained to Vanda, with a broad, altogether too natural smile, that it was a very trifling matter, that he was preparing to go on an urgent business trip to Holland, and that all these trifles would be settled quite simply, by some timely transactions. He was surprised in the disorder of his room by plain-clothes policemen, amid scattered papers, torn-up letters, and half-packed suitcases; he had opened the door of a large, old-fashioned wardrobe, and was sitting in it as if on the threshold of his own house and staring at the disorder on the floor in front of him. He was holding a silver garter of Boba's in his hand, and smiling a silent superior smile. The wardrobe into which he had crept was one in which his grandmother had committed suicide. She had gone into it and shut the door behind her, and there they had found her the next morning, although none had heard the shot. Right from his earliest childhood, this wardrobe had attracted Baločanski like a deep, closed sepulcher.

Then he was dragged through law courts, hospitals, asylums, prisons, and finally he had come back to Bobočka, and now sat every evening at the Crown next to the cash desk, reading the paper. He played chess, wrote poetry, and talked to Philip about painting and artistic creation.

A hot, sunny August was approaching its last days. Tired and sleepy, Philip sat in the garden under the walnut tree in the twilight and could not drive away an unpleasant feeling of emptiness, which had lately begun to grow gloomier and gloomier within him. The summer was drawing to its close, autumn was on the way, the ripe pears were falling from the trees; yet another dropped and rebounded from the roof of the summerhouse, rolling down onto the red currant bushes and breaking two or three stalks; a dry cracking of dead leaves marked the fall of the heavy fruit. Pigs were grunting behind the fence. Little Ann, the pig-girl, had been crying quietly, continually, half audibly, all the afternoon; a wasp had stung her leg and it was all swollen; she was crying, but there was no one to help her. Now and then the murmur of human voices and the clatter of machinery were brought by the wind; the people at Kostanjevec were harvesting their wheat. Through the branches of the fruit trees appeared the undulating stretches of plowed fields below the vineyards, all veiled in the heat haze, deaf and dumb, a vast landscape in the ash-gray cloak of twilight. The chickens had taken fright in the courtyard behind the house; there was a cackling and a clucking, loud and perturbed, a nervous fluttering of wings, and then again silence. The smell of smoke under the mossy roofs hung about among the fruit trees under the weight of the warm, heavy August clouds, and the penetratingly sharp, acrid smell of the damp smoke seemed to emphasize the heavy stolidity of the village and the dark village roofs. Philip lay in an armchair, with his head thrown back, holding in his hand a little bronze Europa on the humped back of a bull, a child's toy or a grave ornament from the dead and long-decayed Pannonian past. The deaf-and-dumb cowherd, Mike, had found it in a pasture and given it to Philip, an unusually valuable bit of filigree work, wrought in the most refined decadent taste of miniature plastic art, and yet quite simple, or rather monumental, in the lines of its composition.

Imperial Pannonia had once stood where these plowed fields were now—imperial Pannonia, with its marble towns, its foundries, and its artists' workshops, where talented sculptors created such wonderful works of art with their own hands. Life overflowed in the towns, torches flamed in the theaters; there was applause, wine, cheers, delight. There actors had played Plautus and Greek tragedies, and now little Ann was crying above their graves and pigs were grunting. Only pigs grunting and twilight falling and everything lying in the half-darkness, like the dead anthill up there in the glade; arches, buildings, aqueducts, signposts, statues, and now this twilight, in which no man living could create with his own hands such a perfect toy as that with which those decadent dead Pannonians, down there underneath one's feet, had once played.

Romantic with regard to the idea of the continuity of European culture, Philip grew pensive under the impression of this tiny bronze figure with which his fingers had been playing all the afternoon.

Warm seas once glittered here, golden oranges ripened on century-old trees; the silver silence of a clear sky and the calm of a golden age that was ended. Ships from the rich harbors with spread sails sped over the blue waters to all four winds: sailing ships creaked under their freight of cinnamon, wheat, bananas, pineapples, currants; a wonderfully painted still life in the lap of a Roman Europe which bathed in quiet bays and sped around the world on the back of a bronze bull, with all the colors sparkling fresh as on the frescos of Pompeii. Now muddy, pastoral, bovine Kostanjevo stood above these graves, and the only event in this wretched Kostanjevec for the last thirty years had been the planting of a pear tree by the sacristan. They had bored a new well at Martinmas, and bought a basin and a kerosene lamp at the fair. Beyond Kostanjevec thundered the tall red iron foundries, the great black forges of Europe with their anvils and hammers, traverses, rails, flaming wheels, burning spindles, evening fires; and Kostanjevec was lost in twilight, with its pigs grunting, and everything decaying like that trampled anthill!

For quite a while Philip had been feeling again the attraction of sooty towns; his nostrils longed for the smell of metal, his ears yearned for the thunder of machines; in those dark western streets there was nevertheless intense movement and as if in a laboratory everything was bathed in the greenish light of the modern philosopher's stone. Piles of leather accumulated in those towns, game, fabrics, clothes, silk, soap, the gold shoes of velvety theaters glittered in the semidarkness, the entranced silence; there the human voice resounded like a musical instrument, and over everything thundered the grimy ironworks and blackened driving-belts slid around. Why had he got stuck in this Pannonian mud? What was he expecting and why did he not move on somewhere?

Philip was seized with a restlessness which grew more and more intense. He had always felt isolated in the circle of his own emotions, and he knew very well from long experience how difficult it is to rouse the people around one to the intensity of one's own feelings. Man lives in his own closed world, has his own beauties, his own nervous excitements, intense and often rapturous and genuinely beautiful—but to inspire others with this beauty, with the genuineness of one's own rapture, is hard, and very often impossible of achievement. Impossible indeed!

People are warm, stubborn, selfish animals! People in the main live amid the smell of their own perspiration, but while they enjoy their own rottenness, they think everything that is rotten about their neighbor stinks.

To knock, to approach, to visit, to offer, to give oneself, constantly, and at the same time to be happy that there is someone willing to appreciate the sincerity of one's conception of beauty, such had been the history of Philip's associations with women. How many foolish women there had been, shortsighted dolls, impersonal passersby, whom Philip had approached at one time or another with his abundance, and afterward found that nothing was left behind but an unpleasant memory of wretched, perspiring bodies, as irrelevant as the noise of pots and pans behind a closed door. In his aloofness, lack of confidence, and indifference, he had wandered for years as an intellectual adventurer, without any particular aim, driven only by his own sincere desire to discover concealed and exceptional beauties, and at last had grown tired and rather bored by it all. But when he met Xenia, she knew, as none of the multitude of other women up to now had known, that precisely those most ephemeral, trifling, elusive, seemingly quite insignificant inner experiences were the only valuable phenomena in life! She could feel this deeply, sincerely, genuinely, directly, and this understanding of his agitated, nervous states of mind was the secret of her intense attraction for him. Having herself been deeply wounded, beaten, left bleeding and scarred inside, she felt that kind of catharsis which is concealed in beauty, and she entered into his conception of beauty with deep understanding from the first day of their association.

Philip's idea, for instance, that within us other beings live as in old graves, and that all of us are mere dwellings full of unknown dead occupants, was extremely acceptable and attractive to Bobočka. She herself had often felt how through the misty glass of her gaze others looked out, faces unknown to her; and waking in the early morning, before dawn when the floorboards creak, and over the deserted streets hover heavy, rain-filled autumn clouds, she had always had a fresh sense of waking again to a sort of unpleasant dream, which was the dream of some other peson unknown and alien to her. Baločanski lay snoring there next to her, pale, with his sunken cheeks and thick, bristling mustache like a brush; two of his front teeth were missing, so that he looked like a toothless corpse. And she lived with this toothless dead man in a low ground-floor room, with a trellis of rotten grapes and caterpillar-eaten leaves in front of the window; the rain beat on the small panes, a peasant with a blanket over his head was driving his cow along the road; it was morning and she had to get up—to get up and go into a green-painted kitchen paved with red bricks, to make the fire, boil coffee, wash the dishes in tepid greasy water, and then go and sit in Steiner's café behind the marble cash desk, and count out the lumps of sugar for the first Turkish coffees to be served in the afternoon.

Intensely troubled by the uncertainty of his own origin, all beginnings were inscrutable mysteries for Philip, and for him all contacts with reality had from the first remained enigmatic: the half-heard ticking of clocks, the heavy scent of jessamine, the gray surfaces of walls reflecting misty dawns, the touch of cold glass on his feverish lips, the bitter taste of water that flowed in luke-warm gulps down his aching throat, wet door handles and his tired body—all were for Philip the subject of long meditations on the fundamental cause of things.

He lay in bed like a child in a fever and thought of processions of dead servants, bishops, canons, chamberlains, unknown chance customers of the tobacconist's, all passing through him as through a tunnel. He told Xenia of these early delirious fancies in one of their first conversations by the café cash desk, and she had lis-tened to him with unusual interest. He talked about scents in a man's warm nostrils, about the intimacy of shy touches, about forgotten, dead sounds that disintegrate within us like cheese under the glass cover of our sense of hearing; and she listened to the stranger there talking to her about bizarre, hidden places, about distances, about mysterious dawns, and it opened up within her her own perspectives, her own distances, and her own strange dawns. Indeed, when looking at the portraits of her grandmothers and great-grandmothers in the rooms at Buda, she had often con-sidered the idea that she herself was merely one of the many Raday portraits; that she was, it was true, moving about, alive, but that she really belonged in one of those dark brown rooms with yellow armchairs, and that her place was there above the cupboard in a golden frame!

The dead, the unknown hypothetical dead, in Philip, were all made up of endless complexes of the most impossible hypotheses and obsessions: bishops, servants, old women with jays in dark rooms, faces from the velvet album, Polish civil servants in fur-trimmed leather coats—all of them had shouted within him and had moved about his child's bed like living creatures. Even later, as an adult, he could feel his nails growing by themselves, like nails on dead hands in closed graves, and they were the nails of those unknown dead beings within him, and his was their hair too! Man is nothing but a vessel full of other people's tastes and experiences. There were times in his life when he was convinced that it was not he, personally, subjectively, who was seeing the things he saw, but some distant and unknown being within him who had been looking at things of his own, in his own way. Lis-tening to the ringing of bells dying away in flat circles over the

Krajina, like ripples on the shining surface of water at the touch of a bird, Philip often thought of that unknown and alien, wax-like, dead ear which through his own, was now listening to those bells ringing. Suddenly, without reason, he was oppressed by a painful and unutterable sadness; some forsaken being within him was grieving for someone. He, Philip, was not forsaken, but he felt sad as he listened to the humming of the telephone wires on the roofs, and thought how everything was a dark space full of strange movements in the branches and of distant thunder in the night.

Bobočka was not a drunkard by nature. She personally felt a constant aversion to alcohol, but she had drunk so much in her life that she could go on drinking for three successive nights, feeling a vague but real and irresistible need to drink herself into a stupor and to die somewhere in a muddy ditch on the road to Kostanjevec.

God knew where some Raday before her had lain in a ditch of rainwater, and his warm bleeding tongue was now touching her glass, and everything in her life seemed drunken.

Thinking about himself and his own existence in time, about his beginnings, and about the limits of his own personality, Philip lost himself in vague pictures, and could not find his bearings.

Really, it seemed as if somebody else's life streamed through our hands and made itself felt in chance touches, and all those fragments of old toys, those chipped porcelain handles, those cracks we feel with our tongues on the rims of old glasses, the letters, the kneeling, the sudden starts, were all nothing but replies to old letters read long ago, echoes of forgotten words, memories of old guilt, suffering for somebody else's helplessness.

For more than twenty years, Philip had felt himself stirred by women, by beauty, by the things of the imagination; but he classified his feelings for women and femininity in accordance with other people's complexes, with a sense of bitterness and painful loneliness; he always felt as if it were somebody else in him who was standing and waiting before the various women, while he himself was quite helpless and wretched in the face of those experiences. The womb, which in his eyes seemed to symbolize female nature and motherhood, would subsequently appear merely warm flesh, of which it was futile to dream. He had no developed sense of life's reality, no sense of touch for things and objects, no feeling of equilibrium among things. Fluttering and fading like an iris in the wind, Philip in his dreams was afraid of fish, of the teeth of corpses, and especially of the dull gleam of black silk hats. Others before him had touched things and objects with gloved hands, and so in his fingers the sense of touch for life's reality was lost. For his fear of shining black silk hats, he found, quite by chance, an explanation; his mother told him how all the Valentis' property in Poland was auctioned off; how her father as a child had seen the auctioneers beating a drum in front of the parental home, and they had worn tall hairy black silk hats!

In his contact with Bobočka the feeling of subjective uncertainty as to his own identity was at first only slight. It was in the silent green moonlight that he felt for the first time the need to forget his own sense of disharmony and strain in that woman's arms.

Dense green moonlight, and all sounds were muffled as if swathed in cloth. Frogs were croaking in the semidarkness and he waited for her at the end of a row of trees, near a tiny fountain on the promenade in front of the druggist's. On his way there he had plucked—he himself did not know where and when—a convolvulus bell, and was crushing the faded flower in his sweating fingers; she arrived smelling of hay, and was as warm as a young girl. She talked to him that night about her childhood, at length and in great detail: how she used to comb her hair with thick combs, how she had worn it tightly braided, how at boarding school she had knelt at early morning mass, played in the moonlight in the shade of chestnut trees, and as a child had been particularly afraid of waxen saints in glass coffins under an altar. There had been one such effigy at Buda of a female saint dressed in brocade woven with a gold thread, on whose hands and legs thick, greasy, black blood had coagulated!

In the excitement of a tempestuous and frenzied St. Rock's Eve, their dream caught fire like some fantastic firework. St. Rock of Kostanjevec had been for more than a hundred years the patron saint of all lepers and epileptics, all injured, insane, and crippled persons from Bikovo and Kravoder to Jama and Turčinovo, and farther down below the Blatna as far as the vineyards at Žabokrek. On his feast day crowds of people came by cart and on foot, through forests and ravines, to pray on their knees before the wooden miracle worker who was known to have raised a young girl from the dead twenty-two years earlier at Jalžabet in Vidovec, when she had lain dead for two days from snakebite. St. Rock of Kostanjevec was in every sense a miraculous saint. From time to time he would move his eyes, and flowers on his altar never faded; a well under a lime tree on the mound near the chapel had never run dry in the memory of even the oldest people in the district. This well cured the foulest wounds and was miraculous for rheumatism and for the worst cases of paralysis. Around the well three crutches were always stuck in the ground, in honor of the saintly miracle worker, a tribute paid to his honor and glory by those who had begun to walk again.

St. Rock's Day was sunny and clear, with poppies flowering and ripe crops waving. Bright colors lit up the oak forests and vineyards; everything quivered dreamily in the rich light, and Bobočka and Philip decided to go to the festival at St. Rock's Church. It was more than two hours' walk through the quiet, green oak forest, where the old trees stood silent in a greenish twilight; the summer wind carried seed above the tops of the trees and a woodpecker could be heard rapping on the trunks, now here, now there, as if discreetly following from one oak to another those who passed through the forest, giving them from time to time his mysterious sign.

Having started rather late from the vineyard at Kostanjevec, they arrived at St. Rock's Church toward evening, when the fires of the meat roasters were smoking thickly, and roasting pork hissed and crackled on the spits. Night was drawing on. The shadows fell deeper and darker, and the faces of the goitrous ostlers and cattleherds from the Drava valley, who had arrived with their well-fed, fattened mares in calf and were now busy with buckets, shafts, and axles or carrying armfuls of hay to their horses—these pilgrims' faces in the ash-gray light looked like red masks. A drunken woman, her pockmarked face crimson with erysipelas, was shrieking and crying with a lighted wax candle in her hand, while drums, bagpipes, clarinets, the Kostanjevec firemen's brass band and exploding fireworks, the burning clouds of sunset and the sound of hurdy-gurdies, all mingled and swelled in an infernal furioso. At the gingerbread stalls and in the bar tents, wine flowed, iced mead gurgled, new barrels of fresh beer were tapped, so that in the welter of fried sausages and gingerbread rosaries, amid the drunken pagan uproar around the church, a wild and primitive force seemed to howl, hairy as a gorilla, with a cabman's pawlike hand and a picture of St. Rock in three colors stuck in its hat. The drunkards around the church were inspired with this sullen, floodlike strength, and in that maddening, demoniacal din of trumpets, lemonade and soda-water bottles, fireworks and litanies, bleated the voice of a pagan festival. Around the small baroque chapel of the poor injured saint, one could hear hoofs of centaurs and the hairy foot of the Evil One; in the sound of the blind men's hurdy-gurdies, in the children's screams, in the cracking of whips and the gestures of girls, in the gay, foolish laughter everywhere, there was something wild and triumphant, which contrasted strangely with the sorrowful, resigned figures above the altar.

Some hilarious young men with hoarse voices had surrounded a drunken old beggar-woman and were kicking her with their nailed boots, while she rolled on the ground and swore by Almighty God that it was not true that she had slept with the Black One the night before in Šimun's fields!

"Yes, yes, you did, you old hag; you gave yourself to the devil!" shouted the fat young Christians around the gray-haired, hunchbacked old drunkard; these God-fearing pilgrims in black suits, greased boots, and scarlet waistcoats could kick an old woman with their nailed boots and spit on her as on dirt. The atmosphere in the church was Shakespearean; above the thick gray cloud of incense and the smoke of the altar candles, a poor, naked, dilettantish figure of Christ, with a transparent, pale pink Easter banner in His hand, blessed the beggars and the poor in spirit from the main altar, and at Christ's feet knelt a small curly white lamb.

Returning home through the forest in the dusk, Philip talked to Bobočka about his painting; he had long had in mind the idea of painting a Christ, and he had been carrying that picture within him for years. In the loud riot of flesh, heated bodies, and tainted pork, the greasy clouds of smoke from the roasting meat and the incense, Philip, standing among the packed sweating crowds under the vaults of the church, amid starched petticoats and the belchings of overloaded stomachs, had conceived a feverish vision. None of his artistic conceptions had ever appeared to him with such clarity or such irresistible persistency; never had he talked about any other of his artistic ideas with such excitement as he did that evening, walking arm in arm with Bobočka through the forest where it grew darker and darker as they went.

As he spoke, the mists in his mind dispersed as if someone had lifted a veil, and it grew increasingly clear to him in detail how this subject should be treated so as to feel under the brush the first basic outlines and then open up perspectives of endless vertical lines above it.

The stench of those drunken herdsmen and the hairy rumps of their fat mares, those streams of brandy and beer, those mounds of meat and that hysterical noise of voices, that whirlpool of hairy buttocks and calves and thighs, fat women's legs, ankles, joints, skirts, neighing horses, the lascivious movement of breasts and hips, flesh on flesh—this should be the furious orchestration of the maddened Pannonian wedding feast that howled on the hill in drunken transports around a wounded Roman miracle worker. A mass of trumpets, a mass of lights, a mass of colors, as on the walls of the Sistine Chapel the crucified Christ rises above the multitude of naked bellies, muddy chins, trodden breasts, and drunken hags! A symphony of something diabolical, licentious, Flemish kermislike, both around and within us; it should be brown like a Brueghel, a vast, troglodyte flood, flowing below the central figure like a stormy accompaniment under the melody of the main theme. All this mass—devilish, monstrous, dragonlike, primeval, and diluvian, issuing from the mud and slime under our own feet—was to be merely the ground of the painting, which was to be spread like an enormous, monumental Gobelin tapestry! What a sorrowful, miserable Christ stood there on the altar, risen with his magenta banner above those drunken hunchbacked old hags, cabmen, and cattleherds! A Christ who would really step into Pannonian uproar, that stinking turmoil of a country fair, should be felt above all things as a metaphysical shock to all that is physical, lascivious, carnal, pagan within us! That Christ should be a rock rolled down from the starry heights, and not a provincial, poorly colored drawing, painted in a dilettantish tempera technique!

Standing amid the drunken throng that evening, Philip had experienced Christ above the altar as an armed, marble, Michelangelo-like naked Titan, with legs like huge dark basalt pillars, and the swinging movement of Christ's fists had roared above the rabble like a howling wind as keen as a razor. Those hands, those divine, unearthly clenched fists, should rise above all that is earthly within us, moved by the furious rage which appears in dark heavy clouds toward evening in summer when one can hear distant thunder before a storm, when the earth itself shakes under our feet, and this titanic, starlike, marmoreal, naked body of Christ is the only bridge across which man could escape from the mud and stench. A day of wrath with shining fanfares like the alarm of war trumpets on the eve of battle, when banners wave amid whistling bullets, the movement of bows on cellos and the ringing notes of harps; a lot of gray color, a lot of inky shades, to make that white marble body of Christ stand out in its supernatural light, and not as in a Styrian four-colored prayer book for the use of silly maidservants. Christ is not and should not be an eighty-year-old blond Biedermeier daydreamer with fair curls and a beard, à la Alfred de Musset; Christ is no Raphaelized hermaphrodite of whom old spinsters dream on church benches; a real Christ should be put on canvas for once to break forever with the falsity of all such pseudoreligious playing with the paintbrush and turning great painters' conceptions into oleographs for sale at village fairs. This clash between the pagan, Pannonian environment and that pale Man who was hanged like a thief, but who has remained a living symbol of this day—the visionary hatred of that higher Man who realizes from His Cross, from that fantastic height from which all the hanged look down upon us, that the dirt under our feet can be dominated only by the clash of granite —this should be put on canvas for once! The empty balance sheet of these two thousand years of effort to turn such barbarians into real people, while His popish priests in their parishes were rather winegrowers and herdsmen and closer to their smelly old women in striped feather beds than to Him who remained hanging on the Cross. Above those drunken hags, above the muddy roads where even today the Evil One bleats among the auctioneers, meat roasters, and red umbrellas, someone should put on canvas all the corpses raised from their graves, raised from that dunghill, from that foul, muddy pit of our times! Above the waves of poison, among the agitated throng of excited flesh, where all the faces are stiff and silly as wooden figures, among the drunken, devilish confusion, dissipation, and darkness, like that which surrounded the little church on the hill tonight, a stroke of the artist's brush should portray the wind rushing triumphantly over men's heads in the angelic heights; a dance above the clouds, above the opened graves! The howling of drunken wedding guests, the fluttering of ribbons, the stampede of frightened horses, the breaking of glasses, the dancing on the edge of bloody, atrocious crime—all this should roll across the picture like a moving, swollen ocean, and above it all a mass of naked female bellies, clammy white female bellies, huge as millstones, a mass of such enormous female bellies that they would look like swollen devils' carcasses, dead men's bellies, clouds of drunken Saturnalians who devour their own flesh, and have turned their stinking backs on all that is starlike above us, and everything reeks and smokes and flings itself into the abyss!

Out of the sooty darkness full of the smell of melting wax candles, from the flickering, dark orange candle flames on the altars; from the warm twilight in front of the church, where above the naked thigh of a young girl who was being sick in a ditch rose a vague loathsome Eros; from the scabby matter and festering wounds in front of St. Rock came Philip's suffocating impressions like smoke from the sooty flame of a cheap candle. As he talked, his impressions developed until they seemed to hover over him and the woman like ghosts in the dark forest. He explained how in this picture, as in old votive pictures, one should leave at the bottom the baroque tower of the little church on the hill with its lime trees and meadows as scenery, and above it, in the windswept open space, in blazing fiery spirals, should whirl a mad drunken crowd of goitered men and foolish women, drunkards and monkeys, with barrels and flasks, and mutton, and pork, and sausages!

"How to paint that smell of roasted pork, the noise of the fair, the horses' neighing, the cracking of whips; how to depict that barbaric, Pannonian, Scythian, Illyrian instinct for dynamic movement which urges drunken cabmen to drive their horses and coaches across a rotting bridge so that everything is dashed down into the mud among bleeding heads and broken bones is a matter for inspiration. This self-destructive impulse of ours for the breaking of bones has not yet found its painter. One should deliberately set to work, tackle the problem, take the risk!"

It had grown increasingly dark as Philip continued talking, and to the sound of distant thunder in the ravines and valleys, the ominous stirring of leaves in the tops of the trees began to be evident. He talked about a vortexlike, wild, restless, infernal roaring, which ought to resound like demoniacal laughter above the wooden saints as a negation of our secular backwardness; and around him and his feverish words in the dark forest, between the mighty old trunks, there began to howl the rumbling laughter of a summer storm, bursting through the clouds like an overheavy burden which tore the celestial canvas, and slit it up into ragged curtains in an instant. Philip spoke about the seething kettle of the passions and the flesh; of how the deep, fetid breath of the flesh waits for the awakening of its pulse; of how unseen and unpainted pictures hover like smoke around us, and it is only necessary to grasp them, exactly, in their grotesque simultaneity;

of how everything is unbridgable, scattered, simultaneous. There is no duration in the causal sense of the word, and there are no explained motives, but everything is one incomprehensible movement, simultaneous, convulsive, the clash of instinct and passion manifested through the flesh. And around Philip, around his words, around Bobočka's blouse, a whirlwind began to howl and seemed as if it would uproot the entire forest and hurl all its vegetation down into the bottom of the ravine, where the stream could be heard roaring like some huge, dark torrent. Then came the furious downpour of a cloudburst, in thick black sheets, with broken branches, and flying black leaves and moss, and the frightened chirping of birds; everything was lit up by lightning, which struck with tremendous crashes, as if all the rocks from the quarries and dark wooded cliffs were falling; in the green vertical thunderbolts it really seemed as if dark, basalt Titans had arisen to uproot the forest, break the oak trees, and trample underfoot the two small human beings who had taken shelter under a young beech tree, as the only shelter available.

"Look for a beech tree," old Liepach had said to Philip the night before at supper, while relating his boring hunter's adventures and experiences: how he had been caught by a storm one night while out hunting, and how he had taken shelter under a beech tree, remembering the advice of his grandfather, an experienced mountaineer and hunter.

"Lightning strikes oaks and pine trees, but no lightning ever struck a beech tree!" is what old Liepach, Pressburg Councilor and first nobleman of the family of Liepachs of Kostanjevec, had said to his grandson Silvius, the District High Commissioner.

Pressed close to each other, drenched through, like a single naked body, they stood cheek to cheek below a beech tree and waited for the storm to pass. Philip talked of the numberless multitudes of gods, who from the Congo to these inane variations in tempera over our altars work with the same instruments: rolling the drums of thunder and striking terror into the faithful with lightning. And thus whole series of gods die like animal species in natural history; but man, epileptic, bescabbed, leprous, dances shaggy and drunken, and swills drink from barrels and staggers away bleeding, and no one had yet been able to paint his portrait;

152

but all this will be engulfed in darkness, and no one will know how to paint it all!

Quite composed and quiet during the cloudburst, the roaring of the thunder, without so much as the movement of an eyelid, Bobočka stood close to Philip and listened attentively and with great interest to what he was saying, as if they were sitting in a warm room at tea. She was quite sincere, it seemed, when she said, as the lightning split a tree trunk only a few steps away from them, that it did not matter to her whether she died that night or the next day.

And that was exactly what was marvelous in such a catastrophic situation; to stand next to someone who was quite fearless and had left everything behind and squared accounts with everyone! Together with such a strength, which was inspired by his own strength, it would really be possible to create!

All was feverish that night and insane, truly catastrophic, but that intensity of feeling did not return again. Everything slowly turned gray and faded, like leaves after a day of sweltering heat. Philip put nothing of all that overwhelming flood of ideas on canvas; he sketched several cartoons for copper engravings, but everything remained unfinished on the sketch pad on the cupboard. And he did nothing, read nothing, but lay about, beginning to feel silent remorse within himself because of his inertness, and futile boredom.

And now he would be called to dinner, and would have to be bored by old Liepach. Then he would wander across to the café and read the newspaper there and wait for Boba, and all without any real purpose! He would drag himself along the dusty road back to the vineyard, tired, with his eyelids heavy with sleep, but with a long and weary sleepless night before him.

At Šimunek the innkeeper's the windows still showed lights. The orange light fell through two squares into the thick darkness; on the light green wall, in the yellow light of a kerosene lamp, through the barred ground-floor windows, could be seen a gold-framed picture of a scene from Rossini's *Barber of Seville*—Figaro with Don Basilio. Green walls, and on the table red, juicy slices of watermelon; bottles of beer, bacon, dirty dishes, the clatter of dishes from the kitchen, and lame Šimunek sitting with his back bent over a drawer and counting his money—there had been a party in his inn that night. The fluttering of wings in the hen coop, the distant noise of an owl in the forest, the wind in the branches, and then a long, uneasy silence. From the direction of Kostanjevec, down by the watermill, came a muffled shot, and then again everything fell silent. The old thatched roofs, the rats, and the ducks in the coops—all lay asleep. The moist smell of cornbread from the warm ovens merged with the smell of cattle and dung; the maize-fields rustled in the wind; here and there a heavy drop of rain fell. Autumn was slowly approaching, and Philip was wasting time with a strange unhealthy woman.

Why had she been so nervy this evening? She had kept him at a cold incomprehensible distance ever since that mysterious man had made his appearance. Who was this Kyriales? Where had he come from? He chewed his English pipe, sat in a cloud of sweet-scented smoke, and had such a strange way of looking at one, as if he knew something more than ordinary mortals. He was an old friend of Boba's, but where had the perverse woman met this Georgian? A Greek from the Caucasus, a doctor of medicine, an adventurer? Who was this man with his long, thin, cold, tobacco-stained fingers? Why had he come? What was he doing here and where was he going? What was all this leading to?

Sergei Kirilovitch Kyriales, a Greek from the Caucasus, a graduate of the Sorbonne in Paris, with doctorates in dermatology and philosophy, who was to play such a decisive role in the drama of these morbid weaklings and confused decadents in Kostanjevec, was a prewar Russian emigrant, and when he had made his appearance in Boba's circle in the Baločanski era, he had arrived from Riga, where he had been working for the *Rigaer Tagblatt* as a storywriter. His mother was supposed to have been a Greek Jewess, from an island off Asia Minor; his father, Kiril Pavlovitch, a Russian staff lieutenant in a Guards Regiment.

This rather elderly man, cold and reserved in every respect, was certainly over fifty, but on his face there were absolutely no traces of those unknown fifty years of his life. Morose and phlegmatic, dark-skinned, with thick, jet-black, curly hair, Dr. Serge, as he was called by Boba's crowd at that time, spoke all the European and Levantine languages, had roamed all the five continents, and held himself incredibly coldly aloof from the events of the world and its problems, as if he had been watching life from a glassy, starry distance. This Kyriales showed an unapproachably lofty superiority toward Philip, and had the strange and unusually dangerous power of being able to destroy all Philip's ideas, to crush his beliefs and enthusiasms, and to reduce his physical and intellectual powers to dust and worthless ashes.

From his earliest childhood Philip had had obscure, subconscious, painful complexes in relation to various people whom he met during his life; various morbid natures, by their very nature inferior beings, hysterical, mentally decadent, morally unbalanced people, exercised a decisive and inhibiting influence upon him. For all those phantoms, parrots, and ghosts—who, Philip knew, were only ghosts and phantoms—he would feel a morbid affinity, though in the presence of such beings he had a special kind of physical uneasiness that often made them almost unbearable to him. He would feel an icy hatred emanating from them and an infernal, furious antipathy toward everything that belonged to him personally; yet in spite of all that, he could not shake off the insidious approach of those destructive influences; absorbed their mysterious poisons like a sponge.

Such a man was this Sergei Kirilovitch Kyriales. The father of Sergei Kirilovitch, Kiril Pavlovitch, had had water on the brain, was an imbecile, a thick-necked staff lieutenant, the son of a Kiev merchant dealing in textiles and ready-made clothes; he had a swollen face like a drowned corpse, and an unhealthy, pale complexion like a cultivated mushroom; he slept in the Guards on the back of his fat white mare like rotting yeast. Kyriales' grandfather had spent his whole lifetime in a small dark back street in Kiev, in the poor light of an acetylene lamp, surrounded by ready-made clothes as if by hanged bodies, in such a dreadful green light that everyone's face among those smelly textiles looked slimy like flesh of the drowned. From such a dull, bald, unhealthy, inert family there had suddenly surged up within the young Sergei Kyriales his Levantine Jewish blood; but who knows whether he himself would not have finished his days as a drunken staff lieutenant or a half-witted ready-made-clothes dealer, had it not happened that one night events hurled him from St. Petersburg to Tibet, and from Tibet across all the five continents to Bobočka Raday and Kostanjevec, where one rainy night he disappeared in the mist, just as stormily as he had come. It would be hard to say whether the qualities through which he had such a destructive effect on Philip were really magical, or whether their relationship was conditioned by Philip's own weak and undefined inclinations. Throughout his life, Philip had often subordinated himself to inferior and morbid men and women, and in such a dependent, subordinate condition had usually experienced his severest conflicts and shocks.

Toward Kyriales, Philip had a feeling of deep, organic uneasiness, almost of fear. While still a schoolboy at the grammar school he had been inexplicably afraid of certain phenomena and objects which could exert an unpleasant, almost serpentlike, influence upon him; he was far more afraid of the hat of his professor of mathematics, for instance, than of mathematics itself, or of that old, gray-haired fool with Virginia cigarettes in his pocket. One of his schoolfellows, Andjelko, had shoes of which Philip was unaccountably afraid; many years after those boyish fights at the orphanage, he would shudder with fright on recalling Andjelko's shoes; those hobnailed, clumsy, muddy shoes, tongueless, tied with string, and worn with green socks! So from the very first day he had dreaded Kyriales' morose, dark face; the gaze of his ash-gray, bloodshot eyes; the touch of his clammy, cold, sweating hand. In that man's presence he would at once begin to stammer; he did not know how to express himself, and worst of all he would forget what he wanted to say, and begin to doubt his own arguments. And Kyriales did not in the least conceal his sense of superiority to Philip. He would express his intellectual contempt indirectly and directly in various unpleasant ways, often in a very rude, it might almost be said coarse, manner.

Kyriales had no belief at all in any special human talent or ability, and of Philip, as an artist, his opinion was crushing. He was not only certain that Philip had no talent at all, that he was a common babbler, who deceived himself with high-sounding words and would never produce anything; but, in speaking of topics in various spheres, he surprised Philip with his immense erudition, which was varied and genuine, exposing to the nervous person in front of him the very often vast lacunae in his pitiful artistic mind. The word "artist" as used by this strange Greek sounded like an insult of the highest intellectual category, and as a dermatologist by profession, he began, the first evening that they met, to speak about the state of Philip's nerves, about his deficient and obstructed internal secretions, with the cold certainty of a physician making a subcutaneous and entirely gloomy, hopeless diagnosis of a patient's incurability. He told him after a few preliminary sentences, which they had exchanged in front of Boba's cash desk at Steiner's café, that he, Philip, had a passive nature, inclined in every way to the overestimation of his own impulses; an unbalanced nature with unsteady nerves, with very poor prospects of any improvement, and with completely ruined centers of volition. He said that Philip's future would be a futile, insectlike life, a life deprived of any prospects of any sort of success; one of sterile suffering, much talk, self-deceptions caused by sexual impulses, leading eventually to suicide. This last event however was not very probable because Philip was by nature a weak and cowardly organism, and weak and cowardly types in the animal world do not usually destroy themselves.

About all such intimate and poignant problems Kyriales spoke bitingly, like a raven tearing out human intestines and dragging other people's bowels through the mud in his black beak. Worst of all, he spoke in terms of a solid logic; every word was uttered in a simple and stony way, with the clarity of a code of law. Together with a certain prominent Japanese histologist, he allegedly had been working for years on important histological sections, and one such important section of a mouse-hair had been called after him the Kyrialic! No matter what the subject of their conversation, he could not help falling foul of some trifling detail in Philip's observations, and playing with him and his words, as with a confused, unstrung, hysterical, backward child. He had an extraordinary ability to extract from Philip in the space of two or three minutes all that was in him, as if he were emptying a glass of water; Philip would suddenly realize that he was drained and completely empty.

After such a night's conversation with this sinister fellow, Philip could neither sleep, nor think, nor read, nor speak, and as if he were deaf and dumb, he would feel himself then and for a long time afterward inextricably in the other's power. To rid himself of this vague and worrying hypnosis he had to strain all his mental strength, and only by a strong effort of his own will could he withstand those termitelike penetrating influences, which increased his natural negative tendencies to such a dangerous extent that under the influence of Kyriales' words he became ready to accept the most foolish, even insane, conclusions.

Conversations about painting, for instance! Philip, on the basis of his own observations and his long experience, was already inclined not to believe in the overgreat importance of painting as such, but Kyriales' statements about painting in general were like hydrochloric acid on all Philip's pictures. After listening to the Greek's words, Philip could see nothing but charred, foul-smelling canvases; the smell of burned rags!

"What is happening in painting today? It is a half-literate, half-maniacal, rather limited and completely unrealistic consideration of such questions as: Did so-and-so become a Fauvist at the right time? Did X adopt Matisse's coloring eight years late, as compared with Y, who had done so five years earlier? Was one for the Courbet-Manet line, or neoclassicism, colorism, neocolorism, formalism, objectivism?—all this was a mere classification into the categories a, b, c, d, e, f, g—schools alpha, beta, gamma, delta! The gamma school, class 'c,' with a delay of five years, Pannonian variation of the mid-thirties, as compared with the delta school, class 'f,' a Central European variation, with such and such spheres of influence! Cézanne, Van Gogh, yes; but Cézannism, Van Goghism? What is painting for you? Biological morphology teaches us that in nature too there are styles and repetitions *à la mode,* but it does not matter whether a canvas shows the influence of Hieronymus Bosch or Toulouse-Lautrec, of Callot or Dufy, but whether the person who is painting has an internal physiognomy. Painters' skulls today took like watermelons without flesh; an internal nonentity is quite naturally subordinate to alien influences. That is the reason we have an unintelligible chaos of painting today, devoid of any sense and purpose!"

Philip had brought on this conversation about painting by saying that for a long while he had been trying to paint a street in movement. All those dirty, sorrowful, drab-looking people passing in the street, with their bad teeth and their debts; thin, easily hurt, weary as they drag themselves along the grimy streets.

"But excuse me, my dear sir! You watch people as they pass in the street and then in a completely futile way pile up your own bizarre observations; and those observations, strictly speaking, are not really your own; they are trifling things you have read and picked up without any particular system, here and there, by mere chance. And so, playing with words, you believe you have mastered the matter around you. But in fact you have mastered nothing, and it is impossible to accomplish anything in life by such methods, least of all to paint a good picture! What a foolish idea to paint people passing in the street—people with bad teeth and debts! That is pseudoliterary raving, not painting! What does painting mean today? I won't say that at the time of Philip II or some other such dead mannequin, painting was not still tolerable as a court decoration, as a Gobelin tapestry, but today . . . ? A self-respecting cosmopolitan civilization should have its windows open on reality, it should have parks and fountains, but real parks and real fountains; for the civilized people of tomorrow there will be no need of baroque scene-painting! From the beginning painting has been only a sort of substitute for reality! What do I want today with your pictures of people with bad teeth and debts? What is the purpose of such paintings? They are absolutely useless! Even if you were a genuine artist, and really knew how to paint. Debts and bad teeth are boring and superfluous things in reality, and even more so as substitutes!"

Philip listened to Kyriales speak of painting as if he had been listening to the voice of his own most secret self, speaking to him from within. He felt that this unpleasant man was telling the truth, that things in reality were like that, and that it was foolish to paint pictures today, all the more if one were not talented and wished to paint substitutes like a maniac. Nothing save contradictions and mists from which an unpleasant voice emerged and formulated his own secret convictions! Philip was aware of a fatal process of disintegration recommencing within him, of falling back into an inferior state as if dreaming of being drowned in muddy water. This man was stripping his clothes from him. He was systematically extracting everything from him: his observations, his impulses, his sense of beauty, his feeling of life's fullness, and describing life to him as it really is and as Philip himself really saw it. Doll-like, he was stripped of his clothes by this man. He remained completely empty, like a room from which everything has been taken, one article of furniture after another, and nothing left behind but one minute article of belief, which still spluttered on the table, like a candle about to burn out.

K yriales' notion of man was that he was one of the lowest kinds of animal.

"Man is an animal who, in individual isolation, is a melancholy object and, it might be said, quite out of place in nature. Having lived for a long time now in herds, man is crueller than any other kind of beast. A shameless, false, stupid, malicious, apelike beast. The funniest of all animals is certainly the monkey, and how much closer is the monkey to direct and logical life than is man! After the monkeys, which in every way are inferior to other kinds of animals, man is the most apelike species of all. He is a beast greedier than the hyena, for the hyena when gorged with carrion can fall asleep next to it; whereas man, when he has overgorged himself to such an extent that his stomach revolts, still goes on eating, and, looking around him at other hungry animals of his species, licks his lips with satisfaction. All is dark in my mind. There was some light, but it has gone out. I do not believe in Krapotkin's social instinct within us, nor in the goodness of man. That goodness reveals itself far too slowly in man and in his deeds! I do not believe that man is an animal capable of development into some nobler species of animal. Or perhaps the rate of progress is so slow that I have lost my patience. I have therefore, in a word, become a misanthropist, and a somewhat bad-tempered one!"

Of what kind was that light which had existed within him, and which he so frequently said had gone out? "It did exist, and intensely," but long ago. How had this stranger, this unknown traveler and chance passerby, this fugitive and emigrant, settled down into such an obscure system of logical hatred, always ready to ridicule the most positive manifestations of everything that raised man above the animals? Was his hatred for all that was human his real nature, or a sort of resentment for old injuries? Where could that already elderly man have been so hurt that hatred

161

could be felt behind him as unmistakably as the gnashing of teeth?

Bobočka had told Philip what was supposed to be the story of Kyriales' tragedy as a boy; how twenty years earlier, the Cossacks at St. Petersburg had shot his sweetheart. He had been waiting for her to meet him near an advertisement pillar, and she had arrived, and fallen down before him covered with blood! They took her to a hospital, and she died the same night from internal bleeding. Of all that dream there remained to him only her kimono embroidered with swallows and wisteria flowers, and afterward, half mad, he had spent several sleepless nights over that kimono, continually tapping the polished table with his forefinger.

This tale was just the thing for Bobočka's fancy. A bleeding girl and a kimono embroidered with swallows! Could this be the reason for such a destructive misanthropy in a man with a lifetime behind him? Without doubt, Kyriales had joined the radical movement while he was still a student, and in his twenty-third year had been exiled from Semipalatinsk and sent to the taiga in Transbaikal and had never returned to Russia. He had fought his way across Tibet to Western Europe, and somewhere in Belgium or Alsace, was again sentenced to several years' imprisonment in a fortress.

One night when Baločanski, Philip, and Kyriales had drunk almost a liter of *rakija,* the Greek spoke in a very lively and striking way of that far-off night in Belgium, when he had been waiting for them to come for him. That night his aim in life had definitely swerved away from the notion of "man."

Restless from being unable to get to sleep, he had tossed and turned in his bed, and worried for a long time. He just could not fall asleep. He lit a candle, took a drink of water, and listened to the ticking of the clock on the table. Time was passing, one minute perishing after another. His fate was at hand. The heavy, nailed door of the fortress would be closed behind him, and those officials, his comrades, would pass over it in the agenda as if nothing had happened! These petty-bourgeois servants of the revolution would continue to meet in pubs in the suburbs, in those yellow smoky rooms where the wine-stained tablecloths looked as if they were stained with blood. A blood-smeared brutal picture of a smoky inn in a dim yellow light with those familiar faces. One had a protruding, oval lower jaw; another the pointed teeth of a nasty-tempered rodent; a third behind his glasses had the vague cloudy eyes of an idiot; a fourth had purple lips; the fifth was a hunchback with a gaping toothless mouth—all that would remain behind him. The bleating of dry uninteresting voices beneath kerosene lamps at tables with red cloths; one of these people was called Bloom and had a curled mustache and the gestures of a waiter—always one of them was called Bloom—and they would pass over his case in their talk and he would remain lying in the beer cellar of the fortress, listening to the rats scratching in the walls. The separation of his ideas from the reality of those physiognomies had been decisive for him; there were certain ideas about love for one's fellow men, and that one should love one's neighbor as oneself, and many resolutions have been passed in the last two thousand years on the basis of those fundamental ideas, but human physiognomies have not changed, not even by a millimeter; the oval lower jaws, the sharp pointed teeth, the red sensual lips of hunchbacks, the trembling fingers of consumptive idiots—all these manifestations of life bleat and chew dull resolutions in their jaws and pass on to their agendas, and under these their agendas, as in graves, lie buried the fates of living individuals.

Kyriales had spent many years lying under the gravestone of one such dull resolution, and he refused to allow himself to be deceived by any sort of medieval scholastic tricks! He had long been contemplating the idea of writing a seventeenth-century comedy about the Jesuits, in which he would expound his individualistic outlook on life, but he was so intellectually honest that he realized the idea was too big, and certainly exceeded his capabilities. He saw the Jesuits with extraordinary clarity, both those of the past and those of the present. Jesuits in socialism, what an infernal invention! A man sells trousers and mirrors, and one day he gets bored with work, and becomes a worker for the revolution. He sits in smoky inns, votes on agendas, works in a new type of commercial business with political dividends, and maintains his point of view that one must love one's neighbors as oneself!

"Human beings are human beings, and everything human is

only human, unfortunately! And if this last movement leads to nothing, then there is nothing left. You as a misanthropist, therefore, are for universal and inevitable nihilism," argued Philip, though he himself was quite passive in relation to every social movement.

"No, I am not in favor of nihilism! On the contrary! I make a distinction only between believing and not believing. The stage of believing is the lowest stage in human thinking; it stands below knowledge, far closer to the animal world than is thought. And all those fine phrases about man always develop into complexes of the believers' beliefs! Union officials with their agendas and Jesuits in the pulpits of provincial churches represent one and the same thing, and that is, human insides and stomachs exist unchanging and identical, and above these insatiable, two-legged trunks men like parrots, mumble some sort of resolution! Man is born to live as an individual only once. And irrespective of the fact that reality outside us is objective and of such long duration, that it seems to us to be eternity, nevertheless, my dear sir, everything is experienced in itself only once. And those who fail to realize this had better not have been born. I do not mind those individuals who by some sort of suicidal self-denial bring about their own destruction for the sake of certain truths, but those little parrots on altars, in pulpits, in leading articles, who mumble something about resolutions, they indeed are odious! That silly, birdlike imitation of other people's voices is revolting to me! Thirty thousand revolutions take place daily in nature. When the monkey lit a fire, that was certainly a great revolution on earth; cause and effect were born. The sowing of the first seed, the taming of the horse, the lifting of a stone by means of a lever—all these were great revolutions within the complex framework of ignorance and suffering! To develop from an orangutan into an impressionist painter, from a fish gill into a biped, from a slave into a Christian—all these were revolutions, only they take too long, and finally, how much of this can be believed? The earth is without doubt round, and revolves around the sun, but to lie in prison for three years because of that would be too foolish! And, as you see, I lost the whole of my youth for such Copernican idiocies about certain evident but uninteresting truths!"

Philip listened to this expert talker chatter about difficult and serious things with as much ease as if they were a matter of the dominoes which the curate was moving about on a marble tabletop behind his back. This Sergei Kirilovitch Kyriales talked of things that were in fact old and well known, but his speech was impressive and, however far from the final truths, essentially correct. Boba listened to him with the greatest interest. One could see that she enjoyed his every word; he was an old friend of hers and had probably been her lover too! And that emphatically expressed negative attitude of the stranger toward Philip's painting had in it the seeds of secret jealousy! What he had said about painting was in the main correct, as far as Philip was concerned, in the main. But all the rest about social problems was rather confused. They had, of course, drunk a liter of *rakija* by then, and then another half-liter had been brought in. They had each smoked thirty cigarettes, and yet others were smoking between their fingers, but what Kyriales had said earlier about the immature psychosis of a delayed puberty, that was a challenge! That the whole of Philip's imagination should be nothing but a belated adolescent's restlessness combined with the last flaring-up of sex? That his physical constitution was already showing the first signs of old age, and that this made the conflict appear even more grotesque? But why should everything that the Greek said be so highly intelligent that there was no answer to it? Because he was a dermatologist and a Doctor of Philosophy? Because he had been in prison for three years? For that matter, who knew whether he had really been in prison? And who was he anyway, and where had he came from? And that old paralytic Baločanski nodded approval of every word Kyriales uttered, while he, Philip, looked like a weak fool, with whom the stranger played as with a toy! The Greek talked about art, but he really had no conception of it. He talked in the most general terms and used the most commonplace phrases and lies, like those very Jesuits of his! He too was a mysterious Jesuit-like shadow, only how in his roving life had he come to this inn?

The smoke in the inn was thick and swirled about, enveloping everything in gray clouds. The mold green room with its Biedermeier windows under deep arches, the kerosene lamps, paper flowers, and gold-framed pictures of the death of Carmen floated in a yellowish foul-smelling mist; on the green cloth the billiard balls cannoned against one another, and the click of the pure ivory mingled with the tinkle of glasses, the shuffling of playing cards, the rattle of dominoes on the marble table in the old, stale, drunken song of a provincial inn. The curate, a physician from the municipal hospital—Dr. Mitternacht—and the surveyor were playing dominoes; someone was talking loudly about the curate's enviable strength, how the other night he had satisfied and exhausted three well-known temperamental mistresses: the doctor's wife, immediately afterward the wife of the chief engineer, then the postman's wife—even the reverend curate's Rezika had not been left out of this nocturnal adventure. Through the smoke and sourish wine came the bleating of hoarse, barbaric laughter, the same sort of laughter as can be heard in all the inns of these marshy forests; yet there, at a table immediately next to the cash desk, Philip was talking about "the sublimation of matter."

Philip was not completely drunk, but he was stimulated by the *rakija*. He was excited. His internal vibrations were disturbed, and he felt the quivering of his nerves; his restlessness, overcoming his strength, was gradually increasing and becoming stronger than any reasoned resistance. This could be seen by the smoke of his cigarette and the way he nervously rolled one cigarette after another. It could be seen by the way he more and more rapidly and eagerly drained one glass after another; by his restless movements and the agitation of his fingers, which moved from his cigarette case to his holder, from the marble table to his glass, from the buttons of his coat to his eyebrows, touching and tapping things, twisting and clutching and clenching in increasing agitation. From this nervousness slowly awoke the passion of a man who felt injured by an impertinent and provocative stranger, one who had come here and had been insulting and tormenting him in his intimate circle of friends for days.

Bobočka sat at the cash desk, poured vanilla into punch, distributed white lumps of sugar, poured out a Bohne Campa for someone, and then, overhearing the conversation, moved across to Philip's table; from time to time she got up, gave glasses and orders to the waiter, and again returned to the table and joined the three men at their third half-liter of *šljivovica*. This evening she felt particularly tired, as if she were going to be ill. It was the sort of weariness that comes before the breakdown of all strength and passes slowly into dizziness and a helpless faint. She had had enough of the smoke and the smell, of the conversations and the *šljivovica*. And of her customer in his celluloid collar, who was nodding like an imbecile and delighting in every telling phrase of the Greek's, because he heartily disliked the painter and rejoiced that someone had turned up who could take the painter down a peg! Kyriales was the more intelligent of the two, his nerves were not affected; but he could feel the *šljivovica* in his head, and had an increasing craving for it. He, too, was tired and in shabby clothes; he also had a deep secret need to drink himself into a stupor and to lie in a muddy ditch; he had had enough of traveling, and now this neurasthenic was worrying him with his "sublimation of matter"! To hell with the "sublimation of matter"!

"Leave me alone, and the devil take your worn-out plagiarisms!"

"You don't let me finish a sentence; you interrupt every single word I say, so that it's becoming intolerable! Will you, please, allow me to explain things! To say what I think! As I have said, there exists in the creative process a sublimated state without which it is unthinkable——"

"I beg your pardon! The soul is merely an indication of a certain state of the body! The soul is bound up with the body, that is evident, it's clear in itself."

"You see, you systematically won't let me speak! Surely you didn't gather all the wisdom in the world during your studies in

Tibet! You will, however, I humbly hope, be kind enough to allow me to say that if someone paints a picture, if he sits down and loses himself and is inspired by a sort of rapture to paint a picture—for example Rembrandt's 'Night Watch' or 'The Encounter at Emmaus'—it is after all, God knows, something abnormal, isn't it? It is not quite exclusively determined by the body; it is not merely 'a certain bodily state.' It is, after all, an extraordinary and extremely rare phenomenon in nature! Rembrandt was an unnatural phenomenon, and has nothing in common with your theory of the physical!"

"Yes, that's quite correct, an unnatural phenomenon! Rembrandt was an unnatural phenomenon, I allow that! An unnatural phenomenon, but not a supernatual one by any means! In the whole of painting—allow me to include in that your own—I see nothing that is supernatural! It is no more unnatural to walk on one's hind legs—that is, I beg your pardon, I wanted to say just the opposite—to walk on one's hind legs is just as unnatural as to be a Rembrandt! In fact, it is even more unnatural! And a billion and a half bipeds walk on their hind legs. Do you find any supernatural revelation in that? I, personally, do not! And our so-called civilization is nothing more than a deviation from the natural, since everything we call our civilization is simply a by-product of the fact that certain quadrupeds, quite contrary to nature, reared themselves up on their hind legs. It was unnatural merely because it was up to then the only known case in nature, but it was by no means supernatural. In this I at least see no nonphysical elements. Everything in us is physical and everything is related to the physical, and a painting like Rembrandt's 'Encounter at Emmaus' (which by the way is not called that), can be nothing else but an expression of the physical within us and around us."

"But only read, please read, what artists themselves have written about the problem! The poets and philosophers of all ages agree that from a genuine work of art stems a kind of suggestive force incomprehensible to our ordinary reason. That effect of the work of art which our reason cannot explain, that which brings a kind of immediate conviction, is not of a material nature, or is not exclusively of a material nature, and cannot be so easily explained away as prosaic materialists imagine!"

"Excuse me, do you include your own artistic productions under the term 'a genuine work of art' from which, according to you, some rationally inexplicable force of 'supernatural origin' is transmitted?"

Philip felt the insolent insistence like the prick of a needle, as if he had received a poisonous sting in a damaged nerve center; he began to feel in his brain the current of some obscure restlessness, such as snakes exhibit at the sound of the snake charmer's pipe.

At this he should unhesitatingly have risen in his own defense, fought to the death with this ignorant man! But, contemplating the vague, misty circle of his own miserable creations, wearily reviewing his own futile efforts, he could only—his tongue stiff and his eyes glassy—ask the Greek very quietly, politely, almost timidly—it might indeed be said servilely—what he meant by that?

"Do you think that your own paintings serve as a proof of the emanation of a supernatural force from artistic productions? Do you regard yourself as a madman who maintains a link with the supernatural world, while to us more commonplace materialists and commoner mortals this is not given?"

This was uttered insultingly over the Greek's shoulder, as if a legal interpreter were talking to Philip over the green cloth of the courtroom, translating concepts that were unintelligible to him into his illiterate "idealistic" idiom.

Yet Philip had not spoken of himself, but of Rembrandt, and this showed his personal delicacy; whereas this man turned everything upside down against him in a way which showed his lack of taste. It was impossible to speak about such psychological imponderabilities in terms of the logic of a lawyer or of a boy at a secondary school. Aesthetic emotions are of a metalogical nature; that is the first presumption of all aesthetics. How otherwise could it be explained that very often just a single patch of color, a single stroke of the brush, or a single word, is sufficient to evoke in man a feeling of pleasure, a feeling of beauty, sorrow, or strength; of time and space, and of all life's potentialities and happiness? Let Kyriales explain to him, if he could, that intensity of the metalogical impulse in terms of the logic of his "physical" causes!

"Logic! You say that, my friend, in a very dry way like a genuine born artist! But what, if you please, do you think logic is? You think that logic means a book in stiff covers, a boring hour spent in front of the black pedestal of a crucifix, when the windows are open and outside sparrows are twittering cheerfully in the leaves and rejoicing in the May sun? Logic means a cycle of bright, transparent, crystal systems which are perhaps more valuable and are certainly a million times more important than your various artistic worlds and constructions. And, why, if you please, should not the differences which existed between Plato and the Eleatics until Kant raised the brilliant question, 'What is truth?' be at least as valuable as the foolish naïveness of a Benvenuto Cellini? You see, there is an enormous difference between pure and empirical knowledge; an enormous and, without logic, incomprehensible clash between the *a priori* and the *a posteriori*, the vague mass of Kant's 'basic matter' and the mathematical transcendence of the notion of God. These are no lessons given in secondary schools, my dear sir! Dante's discipline is most transparent when it amounts to pure Thomist logic. Neither the Albigenses, nor the Lutherans, nor the Jacobin mediocrities, could, without other people's logic—like ridiculous followers-on—have taken a single step forward in their so-called movements! Have you ever held a human brain in your hand? Have you ever felt the weight of fourteen hundred grams of gray matter in your fingers? Do you know what the human cerebrum is? If you had dissected this human cerebral tissue twenty-seven thousand times with your own hand as I have, you would have thought about the other functions of the brain too, and not only about the intuitive!"

Philip felt how big words, vast conceptions slid from this unpleasant man's mouth like endless tapeworms, how they crept toward him, hovered above him, swathed his head like leaden compresses, until he was beginning to feel sick, as if from poisonous fumes. And that sinister man in front of him sat in a thick cloud of smoke, his swollen crimson lips moving like two red leeches, talking between his teeth about transcendental deduction and the play of concepts between Euler and Newton and Huyghens, flirting as ironically with Kant's old-fashioned metaphors "On the wings of thoughts" as if Kant as Kyriales' apprentice had written serials for the *Rigaer Tagblatt.* He talked of how the analysis of concepts, the transcendence of Space and Time in conflict with physiological possibilities, and the baroque philosophical schemes toward the end of the eighteenth century constituted quite intelligent forms of thought, but at the same time were not such; they were an interesting, rather musical baroque conception, an infinitesimal musical theme which hovered between all spheres, all feelings, and all conceptions, so that everything that passed from the sphere of one logical category into another moved through this musical medium of the "logical" baroque scheme as the vibrations of a musical instrument hover in the air, losing their material volume, but still retaining the quality of the sound which slowly fades and disappears like smoke. "But, of course, for all this one must possess a sense of tone, and *messieurs les artistes* usually imagine that such complexes do not exist because they are deaf to them from birth!"

As the flood of words rolled on toward Philip, he became aware of a deep, in fact, an organic need to withstand this wordy insistence, which was obviously artificial and without any real foundation. At the same time he felt incapable of mastering those vague masses of data, which were not clear, or which were only vaguely known to him, but which were superficially convincing, so that they clogged his mind like glue, and he was already beginning to feel like a fly on a flypaper.

And this mystifying Russo-Levantine was saying that when a man develops and matures to a point where he can feel all the stages of vertebrate development in his spine, he can sense within himself the process which raised his species from that of the dumb quadruped to that of the upright biped, and to a stage at which he can consider the human cerebrum as a cosmic dominant —when he detects in the metamorphosis of his own embryo all the stages through which all organisms have passed from the elementary cell to the gill, and from the gill to the fish and on to his own cerebral tissue—he has then the right not to allow himself to be mystified by anything, not even by the mystery of art. The fact that art still, unfortunately, existed as a metaphysical factor, was only a sign of backwardness. To keep a record of data about life in this age of behaviorism, using primitive picture-symbols from mythology and allegory, was as out of date as archaic Egyptian hieroglyphs compared with any modern infinitesimal formula. And now here was an artist with only an average talent and knowledge, who sought from Kyriales an explanation of the mystery of the aesthetic emotion based on "the logic of physical causes"! Poems and pictures could in general be enjoyed only in a state of extreme cultural backwardness, and when someone was so underdeveloped that he could still derive pleasure from such primitive hieroglyphs, it would be difficult to say what might cause the aesthetic emotion in him or any other emotion, but that it certainly was not anything "nonphysical" or "supernatural"!

"First of all, there exists within us an immeasurably large amount of what we have learned—discipline, tradition, education, trained retrospection awake within us the memory of various states experienced in our own personality. Under such examination we unwind like a ball of wool. To look into one's own open abdomen is an experience which is always a little sentimental. The viewing of things retrogressively gives rise to a sorrowful resignation of the transitory and the fragile. Our self-satisfied and conceited Ego is very glad to remember itself, from its earliest days. The classics. Ovid: *Forsan et haec olim meminisse iuvabit* (It may be a pleasure to remember this one day). Which of us has not seen Dante in some poorly illustrated copy dreaming for the first time of Beatrice, and which of us has not then thought of himself? The laurels! The marble busts! There is not a single living human being who has not at the same time imagined himself as a marble bust. In the main, these are romantic complexes, usually connected with the experience of love. Recollections. Our Ego becomes sentimental. Our Ego very often dissolves in soft soap and lemonade, without always realizing that it is only soft soap and lemonade. In the life of all human beings there exist moments of weakness when everybody, even the harshest, feels womanish, and takes pleasure in swallowing tears! This is true, I allow: verse can have a certain effect. The effect of poetry and painting is charming, intimately personal. All of us have dreamed in green twilights, and all of us have kept an unforgettable memory of the dear, gentle gestures of dear, gentle women. To find such a gesture described somewhere is a pleasant experience, and so it should be! If this effect did not exist, it would be impossible to experience beauty at all. Those lyrical enthusiasms of yours would not exist; neither would poetry and painting! But I definitely assert that within the complex of that effect there is nothing that is not physical, much less supernatural. We reflect other people's recorded experiences by the echoes of our own memories. Our physical, physiological, or if you like, in a metaphorical sense, our spiritual being, is turned into a 'musical instrument.' Man has created for himself an extremely flattering concept of the supernatural fineness of that 'musical instrument,' neglecting the fact that the instrument in question is nothing but an unusually entangled and rather long mobile tube equipped with various apertures and appendages!"

"Oh, if you're going to be coarse——"

"Am I responsible for life's reality which to you as a layman seems coarse? What is more, I have made a truly transcendental concession to you in proclaiming our physical body to be a musical instrument! I am not so amusical with regard to your complexes as you are with regard to mine. I agree that it is possible for an aesthetic concept to have an effect on us like the strokes of a bow drawn across an instrument, to which we respond. But to call this response sublime, incomprehensible, or even supernatural, seems to me to be a conceited overrating of our own physical significance and of all the other functions connected with our trivial personality!"

When Philip had interrupted Kyriales for the first time, he had been aware that his remark was out of place. Tonight this man had uttered hundreds of sentences. Although one disagreed with his arguments, the actual way in which he expounded his viewpoints was not so commonplace that one could confront him with

173

such a trifling phrase as the accusation of "coarseness"! In his endeavor to rectify the error Philip felt that he was blushing, and he began to stammer.

"Your conclusions are intentionally coarse, and the whole of your play with certain truths of life is playing with paradoxes. It is all an unusual way of talking nonsense! It is very simple. With your system, which on the surface is not unconvincing, you turn the meaning of things upside down. It is a very shallow sort of playing with words, a kind of nihilism, where nothingness and emptiness are almost synonyms! For you nothing in the world has any higher meaning!"

I am not expressing it properly, thought Philip to himself, I haven't given any concrete answer to it all! His views should be undermined in a completely different way! But how? Where? In what way? This Georgian's argument is no empty nihilism! Behind all this something obscure is hidden. This is not mere amusing talk!

Sergei Kirilovitch Kyriales looked at the confused, unstrung man in front of him, and thought of his own ruined nerves. If only this insane painter knew how weak the man talking to him was, the ruins of a man, an old rotten rag, which no one would use even to clean their shoes! He knew from his own shrewd experience as an old dialectical polemicist that in a struggle of words the great art is to use one's opponent's own arguments against him. To be able to spot the weaknesses in other people's way of thinking, and to put these weaknesses to them so that they hear their own words, is the first principle in any kind of dialectics. And if only someone could read *his* thoughts, how wretched all this would turn out to be! From the first he had noticed that the painter who stood before him lacked self-confidence, and especially confidence in his abilities as a painter. And he had seized him as a dog seizes a quail! Now through a mist of *rakija,* he was rather sorry for him. He had unnerved Philip, and there had been no particular point in doing so.

"Everything in life, and even in art, has certainly no special, and absolutely no supernatural meaning! In our life everything is arranged so that the most valuable moments are perfectly meaningless. The pleasure of a certain nervous vibration has not necessarily a higher meaning, but it is no less pleasant because of that! A warm woman, for instance, a glass of wine, a cigarette, smoke, autumn, *rakija*—your health, my dear sir. Let us touch glasses and drink this glass to the health of Madam Bobočka!"

Philip clinked glasses morosely and drained his to Bobočka's health. He remained morose and ill-tempered.

"To you all things look dirty, like skin diseases! It is a kind of dermatological outlook on life! I am not, unfortunately, a dermatologist!"

Sergei Kirilovitch gave a quiet, hardly noticeable smile, directed within, at his own weaknesses.

The fact that he was a dermatologist was his least weak point! He was just such another hopeless castaway as this painter in front of him, another such wreck of a man as this, who seemed to have no aim at all in life, but deceived himself with aesthetic Philistinism in the same way as for the whole of his life he had systematically deceived himself about his hypothetical artistic talent, and who sat there, turning gray, growing older, with black rings under his eyes, exhausted, unable to see himself in the mirror, yet deluding himself with the notion of abstract vision and thinking himself exceptionally clear-sighted. How sad it really was! He sat there with this woman cashier in a stuffy inn and babbled for whole nights about the effect of something invisible, about magic currents, about the miraculous meaning of the sacred flame within us, and he had attached himself to this passionate and unhappy woman, so that all three of them were in a stupid and helpless entanglement. That was approximately the diagnosis: *Status praesens.*

Like torn rags, the fragments of the drunken Georgian's muddled sentences fluttered in Philip's mind, and he felt the need to say something in reply, but he could not get a grip on the entangled problems or find appropriate expressions.

What foolish things this ignoramus had said about the inferiority of the Egyptian alphabet! Had he any notion of Egyptian painting? Had this charlatan ever seen a single Egyptian bronze? Or those pale green Egyptian grave-lamps with their transparent plates of limestone and bas-reliefs symbolizing the afterlife? How could anyone talk like that, just in the air? He, Philip, was perhaps a belated romantic, and the whole of his outlook on life was perhaps romantic, but this was just empty talk, with worn-out materialistic phrases which incidentally had long since been refuted by science, and in which only such old-fashioned, intellectually decadent dermatologists could believe!

Philip felt that with one wave of his hand he ought to sweep off the table all those loud, clinking, worn-out intellectual counters, but he could not pull himself together. Parallel with his wish to offer resistance, a quiet mood of resignation was growing within him. Why should one explain music to those who are deaf? There is no sense in explaining Orphic raptures to barbarians, and what in fact are Orphic raptures? The sublime, the deep, in every sense of the word problematic, the unknown, the mysterious, the supernatural, the most intimate within us, that glassy gleam of the last silver toy that has remained as our last joy and comfort in this mud—it was all too foolish! How could one explain this, like eight-sided figures of cardboard, to minds which had no idea of the mysterious nature of that kaleidoscope? Why? The fascination of this mysterious play with beauty is so irresistible that entire continents have been playing with it for centuries, races, cultures, epochs, ages, and here this nobody with a pipe in his mouth had to emerge from his stinking smoke and reduce it all to a despicable joke! This unknown "someone" had to come here and reduce all these most strenuous aspirations of the mind to a mechanical movement of the "exclusively physical" within us, as if the incorporeal did not exist in our works of art, as if it did not still appear in the same way and with the same vividness as it did in an Egyptian bronze seven thousand years ago, when that bronze was still warm from the foundry! So Philip only brushed it all aside with his hand, and said that, in his opinion, one could achieve absolutely nothing with such vulgar materialistic phrases.

In no respect, in no sense! They were mere dead words, but life went on underneath, springing up in endless variations of the beautiful, the incomprehensibly and mysteriously wonderful. Whereas everything that Kyriales was talking about, was impertinent journalistic nonsense!

"I have, it's true, got a living out of journalism, but I have never boasted of having been a journalist! But you schizophrenically proclaim your 'painting' of romantic fictions to be a transcendentally, incomprehensible phenomenon. You believe that such 'painting' of second-rate fantasies in colored oils is of supernatural origin!"

"I speak with respect about fields of knowledge which are unknown and not clear to me! I would never venture to speak in front of you about any problem in the field of skin diseases with such superiority as that with which you speak about painting. I am not intellectually impertinent because I do not reduce everything to the simplicity of mediocrity, as you do. I still leave certain concepts intact. I am no verbal materialist, nor a cynic, nor a dermatologist. If you have held some trifling cross section of the cerebral tissue in your hands twenty-seven thousand times, I have twenty-seven thousand times trembled in front of my canvases! I believe in the purity of artistic intuition as the only purity which has remained in this animal world around us. Do you understand me? And I do not let anybody insult me, do you understand?"

"And you think that your present outcry represents such a pure artistic intuition?"

"Oh, hell!" cried Philip, pushing the table with such violence that the sugar scattered from its dish and a stream of *rakija* poured down onto Baločanski.

What tasteless stupidities! A mere wasting of time with the deaf and dumb, with fools and maniacs! What did such barbarians know about direct intuition? What did they know about the necessity of looking forward instead of backward? Directly, purely, cleanly, without thought or premeditation. Just to observe for oneself, not as one had been taught, not through someone else's glasses, but through the lens of one's own emotional powers, unlimited by space, or time, or intellect, or reason! And he had not yet lost his strength of feeling; he still felt vividly that art was not what those barbarians imagined it to be: a bird's footprint in mud, or a wax cast. Art was talent, and that was something beyond the comprehension of those without talent. And talent was a force that was inexplicable in terms of anything

177

physical, and the functions of talent were clairvoyant and immeasurably higher than the ordinary functions of brain and body, beyond the reach of the human mind!

There was a sudden excited shouting outside. For some time the loud, drunken shouts of a coachman had been audible, the stamping of boots, the slamming of doors, the cracking of whips. Then suddenly there was a scream and a fearful cry of "Murder! Murder!" They rushed out into the darkness. In front of the inn a coachman in a scarlet waistcoat was lying on the ground with his stomach ripped open. His bowels had fallen out into the mud, and the hot, bright red blood gushed out in the light of a lamp, which someone was swinging agitatedly just above the injured man's head. The bloodstained mass, the bright red color of the open wound, the bleeding twisted intestines, and the hot flood staining the scarlet waistcoat and the boots, and forming a dark, smoking pool on the ground—everything was confused and ghastly. The horses were neighing in fright. The smell of the warm blood had alarmed them, and one, maddened, tried to jump the shafts and break away, rattling his chains and stamping his hoofs.

"Well done," said Baločanski, bending over the injured man, who was groaning in his death agony like a slaughtered beast. "Well done! Why so many words! Just a kitchen knife, and straight in the stomach! That's the simplest way! Who cares?"

"What does he mean about a kitchen knife," thought Philip mechanically. "What kitchen knife?"

The man in front of him, in the flickering light of the lamp, was as pale as drained meat. His lower jaw gaped open senselessly, and he frothed at the mouth like an epileptic.

This is what came to the wretched fellow from drinking *rakija*, thought Philip, himself quite sober now, as if he had not drunk a drop. He should be taken home and laid down, and not left somewhere in a ditch. "Who cares?" Strange!

For two days after this nocturnal drinking bout, Bobočka did not appear behind the cash desk; they said she had tonsilitis. It was raining; the somber, yellow autumn was drawing on; the third evening Philip went to visit her. He took a short cut, but someone had removed the tree trunk from across the pool where the cows were watered, so Philip went back and, walking round by the brick kiln, climbed up from the back to the small house in the vineyard where Bobočka lived. There was a light in the uncurtained window of her small room, and he went up to the window; a candle flame flickered on the table. He could see Baločanski sitting at the table reading a newspaper, and something was moving on the bed. A black shape and the white gleam of a naked woman's body; legs, thighs, and the red quilt, all lit by the flame of the candle, dimly, undistinguishably, but beyond any doubt; there on the red quilt, an incredible scene was being enacted. A shape in black and a naked woman in a tangle of limbs, a scene which might have been taken from the gallery of a medieval belltower. One of the seven most deadly sins; a woman in the lustful embrace of the Evil One.

He tapped on the window.

At the sound he started as if from a dream, and realized that it might have been wiser to have gone away unheard, but it was already too late; by then Baločanski had come to the window and very pleasantly, with almost studied politeness, invited him to come in. During the time it took Philip to walk around the house and to talk absent-mindedly and impatiently to Bobočka's little black Pekinese which stood in front of the door, there had been no great change in the scene in the room: Bobočka was still in bed, only she had covered herself with the quilt. Next to her, on a small stool, was a basin for gargling, and her neck was swathed in a towel. At her feet, in black silk pajamas, sat the Caucasian dermatologist, sullen and unapproachable, rolling a cigarette; Baločanski continued to read his newspaper, completely composed and indifferent.

Boboćka greeted Philip rather coldly; if all her friends were like him, she might die, and such friends would show absolutely no interest at all in her.

Philip did not know whether it had been a dream, or whether the whole mad scene in the light of the wax candle had been a morbid hallucination—but anyone who had that sort of hallucination was already a madman, God knows, in the most literal sense of the word. He shook hands with Boboćka, feeling a wave of warm perspiration pass over him, as if from a Turkish bath. His fingers were so wet that they stuck to the poilsh of the chair that he took from the table and set beside Boboćka's bed. He felt cramps in his joints, in his fingers, in his knees, and he was dizzy; if he had not sat down, his knees would have given way under him.

And this Greek or Russian, or whatever he was, sat quietly at Boboćka's feet and rolled his cigarette, talking about his impressions of his last year's tour of Sicily, as if he were carrying on with what he had been saying when he was interrupted by the arrival of Boboćka's unexpected and in every sense unnecessary visitor.

The sea was actually just a huge puddle, and it was inconceivable to him what sort of elemental force people could find in it. The sea was just a rather large quantity, humanly speaking, of oxygen and hydrogen, on which people were carried about on ridiculous rafts; and in the restaurants on those rafts they paid far more for mineral water and hash than in any ordinary restaurant on dry land. People traveled on these rafts, drank pineapple juice through straws, rattled cutlery and china, with a phonograph playing "Sonny Boy" somewhere, and in human phraseology it was said "that the sea has an elemental force." On those tubs of theirs people hung funny multicolored rags, and such decorated rafts represented the "mastery of the sea," and all this took place on a large quantity of liquid gases spread over a muddy ball. Sergei Kyriales had sat on the deck of a ship last year between Taormina and a little ruined town in Sicily, and next to him had stood a Jesuit. An enormous, bronzed, sunburned colossus, more

like a butcher than a Jesuit, with thick, swollen hands, so that in
his clumsy Jesuit paws his breviary disappeared like a small note-
book. The fleshy Jesuit had stood next to Kyriales and the red silk
ribbon of the black breviary fluttered like a tiny banner in the
wind. The smell of sweat could be noticed from beneath the Jesuit's heavy habit, and that butcher, with his breviary in his hand,
had stretched out his arms in admiration of the majestic wisdom
of the Lord, who had created the elements, as for instance "this
majestic sea." As if "this majestic wisdom of the Lord" were that
of the advertising chief in some wretched provincial travel agency
for foreigners! And afterward, when they had drunk plenty of
chianti, it appeared that the Jesuit knew how to retell as fine
Calabrian coachmen's jokes as if he had read Balzac.

Kyriales had roved about Sicily during the autumn, but had
not done anything of interest. The only thing he saw was a white
kid with a white beard like Garibaldi and red eyes like a hare.
And a little boy that he had thrown into a cauldron of boiling hot
bronze in a bell foundry.

It had been late one afternoon. The old Norman bell foundry
stood in the shade of a stone quarry, overgrown with ancient ivy
and evergreen; it had huge Norman windows, all heavily barred.
Inside the foundry the light was pleasantly dim, and there was a
not disagreeable smell of wet clay. The mold of wet clay for the
bell was ready lined with wax; and in the furnace next to it the
mass of molten bronze, a sulphury green, with a dazzling flicker
of shimmering orange, illuminated the old church with a strange
green phosphorescent light. The bell founder's son was standing
there, a little boy of nine, extremely timid and delicate, as fragile
as a little girl; he was watching the furnace nervously, with
sweating fingers. His father wanted some more wax, and said he
would return at once. Kyriales went up to the boy and began to
talk to him about his secrets. He took him by the hand and asked
him whether at his latest confession he had confessed His Secret?
The little boy's hand was all wet with sweat, and he stammered
sweetly and pleasantly; the mysteriously false relationship of that
child's warm flesh with God was as delicate as a warm silky but-
terfly held between one's fingers, so that one could feel on one's
palm the wriggling of the tiny stupid worm, yet would not set

free the soft powdery wings. All this teasing lasted for quite a time, and then Kyriales was seized with an incomprehensible black moment of physical disgust; he had snatched up the little boy and thrown him into the furnace! A foul-smelling cloud of smoke had hovered over the glowing bronze and risen to the dark arched ceiling of the bell foundry in a ball; and the cicadas under the cypresses, the quiet Sicilian early autumn afternoon . . . cicadas . . . nothing. . . .

Philip listened to the vile Georgian telling his lies, and watched the tired woman with her neck swathed in a towel. It was as hot as an inferno in this ground-floor hovel, and the imbecile sitting at the table only rustled his paper. What was all this? What if this man here were not lying, which was quite possible? And everything on and around the bed . . . was this a madhouse? And this creature was talking about the need to look at everything human from a distance of thirty-five centuries, retrospectively. At least thirty-five centuries, because he who cannot see from such a distance is blind from birth. What were fifteen centuries? A quite insignificant moment of time, as insignificant as the flutter of a fly's wing! And all the rolling about in beds, the wretched movements of our bellies, everything that goes on between man and woman, everything that can take place between the sexes, all this vanishes before the melancholy of anyone standing in front of a grave!

"Standing by the graves of strangers, we are completely indifferent to all that has happened between those men and women who lie there. And at a distance of fifteen centuries from all the actual, the present, the human, man's heart must be as cold as a dog's nose! If someone could cast a glance at this room from fifteen centuries away, it would be quite irrelevant to him whether somebody had thrown someone else into boiling bronze, or whether this woman had slept with one man or the other!"

"Are you speaking about me?" asked Philip, in a flash of temper.

"About you, about myself, and everyone, my dear sir! I don't know whether you believe me, but I view things from the forty-fifth century, I give you my word of honor. And now, I am going to make for you such a Caucasian punch as you have never drunk in your life!"

Philip wanted to take his leave, but they would not let him go, especially Boba.

What an unpleasant way of behaving; first of all not to come for two whole days, and now to want to go away after a few minutes as if it were a polite call!

Baločanski, as soon as he heard that they were going to make Caucasian punch, folded his newspaper and visibly cheered up. He began to fuss around Kyriales as cheerfully as a kitchen boy; he cut up lemons, opened the old worm-eaten cupboard, rummaged about among crumpled packets and paper bags, brought various bottles and spices from the kitchen; in fact, he bustled about singing to himself like a child.

Philip stayed by Boba, but they did not exchange a word, So he got to his feet, crossed to the table, and picked up Baločanski's paper; the paper was old, several years old, dirty, greasy, pencil-marked, and the letters were worn and faded.

What could Baločanski have been reading in such a greasy, foul, dirty paper? And for so long and with such interest?

At the very bottom of one column among local news items, the following four lines were underlined in red pencil: "Last night on a warrant from the State Prosecutor's Office the prominent lawyer, Dr. Vladimir von Ballocsanszky, was arrested in his own flat and placed in custody in the court's precincts on the basis of a complaint lodged by certain banks for whom Dr. B. was previously representative. Investigations are in progress."

The Lermontov arrack made by the dermatologist was really excellent. They finished the first bowl in a few minutes, and while boiling the second, Kyriales began to talk about death. The bluish flames of the burning alcohol flickered up to his gloomy face. It was quite dark in the room, and everything trembled in the bluish glow of the flame in the glass bowl on the table. Baločanski gazed at the serpentine flickering of the flame quite vacantly, without moving. The Greek's voice sounded tired; in the dark corners and around Bobočka lying in bed it hovered like some strange tired bird, which flew down and fluttered around her red

183

kimono, around the dusty boxes on the wardrobe, wrapping everything in its black webs so that all the room grew darker and gloomier; only the spluttering of the candle could still be heard, and from time to time the Greek's pipe would glow red below his chin.

Kyriales spoke of death and of what the dead in their graves think about returning to this world.

"It must be a favourite and engrossing occupation for those who lie among the rotten boards and ribbons and paper cushions to think what it would be like to go back and begin all over again. Such ideas come into the decaying heads of the dead like the bubbles of drunken dreams rolling over the graves like transparent glass balls; and in each ball's greenish glow is a puff of something mysterious, warm, intense; something that can be sipped with delight like warm punch; that can be felt like a warm bed and is pleasant like a newly bathed body, like the only true leisure in life, a drop of that elixir of life that circulates so warmly in our veins. And under the ground everything is so strange. About the graves a mass of glassy smoke freezes around the dead in strange lines, and thoughts swirl up like blazing tongues of punch flames in the glass; how to realize again the feel of wounds, movements, and breath in the situations in which we lived, but from which we were removed in polished boxes like wax dolls, like birthday cakes decorated with lace paper, and everything around us left open like an open wound; to feel again those wounds on which the blood has hardened would be so sweet! Only our fingers have grown incomprehensibly icy, as if from camphor; our fingers are cold and everything is as cold as ice and transparent as calcite and empty as the place left by an aching tooth, which we lick with our tongues, and it feels cold after the novocaine, and the hole bleeds and the wound festers; but then there is nothing; and all that remains is a decayed tooth no longer there, and a cold, marble, alien tongue. But there was a tooth there once, and a swelling and a pulse in the veins; there an illegitimate child spent his childhood crying for shame, and now many other children cry like that and all goes forever in infinite concatenations. A naïve little girl has become a prostitute; someone else has killed his wife and burned his own home over his head; others do not know what they want and so rove about the world, and this subjective agitation continues; mornings are misty, steamships arrive, death must come, and when everything is as quiet as a foul, trampled rag on the rails, dreams reappear in the graves and in the minds of the dead, who surely dream of lighted windows and warm rooms and how pleasant it is to have an umbrella and galoshes when it rains and not to be in debt!

"Have you ever been on the verge of committing suicide?"

The drunken Greek asked Philip this question so abruptly that he did not know how to answer. But the Greek did not wait for an answer from anyone. He was under the influence of the thoughts he himself had expressed and as he stirred the glowing drink in front of him with a glass spoon, he was becoming more and more deeply involved in the dark, maddening labyrinth of his own ideas.

"The mind of a suicide, in that second when he passes out of life, is flooded with the pictures, memories, and impulses that are in and around him at the moment when he decides to throw himself under the engine—as an example I take the case of a rather unintelligent suicide who throws himself under the wheels of an engine—the wet autumn mist, the clattering of a grimy steam engine across the bridge, whistling mournfully, and down below, the muddy water flowing under the bridge, the darkness, the dawn just breaking.

"That concentration of vital forces which drives all of us across this world, which moves within us, which forces us irresistibly to move with the dangerous motion of the universe—that mass of intestines, flesh, warmth, memories, impulses, beauty, fear is all packed tightly together in a brain like a shell, and bursts open like a wound. In that opening, in the last breath as the eyes close forever, in that last instant before the curtain falls over everything, before that last break in the presence of the irrevocable, in those two or three seconds' experience, spaces open out that must be as vast and as full as the whole life of the person who is about to throw himself out of reality into that from which there is no return. Even so the break must be painful! Excruciating! A moment of excited delirium, fever and fear of the—after all—unknown; an agonizing panic at the loss of all that has been warm, familiar, and dear: home, food, childhood; in short, all the pleasures of body and mind, bowels and skin, flesh and blood. And beyond all this is death: a cold insensibility, like a camphor compress; a cold, level, mysterious mist over the railway line, the engine, the telephone wires humming in the wind. The umbilical cord is broken; the cold muddy water gapes; the silent, irrevocable, monotonous darkness. So first of all the jump in front of the engine, then there is no return; the eyes are closed, there is the last tremendously intense, convulsive revolt of the body against the loss of experience, but the irrevocability of this last act has already carried us away, the subjective temperature ceases to exist, everything seems cold, aimless, exhausted, one more last thought —what would you be thinking of in that moment?"

"I should think about my wife Bibi, who jumped from the second floor, and killed herself. And when I was at her funeral, walking behind her coffin, I could smell Bobočka's perfume on my handkerchief, and I thought about Bobočka naked!"

Baločanski's voice disturbed Philip. He searched his memory to find what he might think of in such a moment. So he did not answer, but asked the Greek what his thoughts would be.

"Mine? Of nothing! Quite certainly, nothing! If I thought at all, certainly it would all seem stupid that it had not happened long, long before!"

"Ah, yes! All this is very well, very interesting," said Baločanski again, loudly and aggressively. "But who will give me satisfaction?"

"What kind of satisfaction?" asked the Greek, pouring himself a glass of hot punch and draining it to the last drop.

"What kind of satisfaction? It's quite obvious: satisfaction!"

Bobočka, who during the whole of this conversation had lain silent and motionless under her quilt like a cat, suddenly sat up in bed, so suddenly that it seemed as if the unsteady bedstead would collapse. Her eyes were fixed on Baločanski.

Baločanski rose and went toward the Greek: "My satisfaction!"

"What kind of satisfaction?" asked the Greek in a very forceful, almost insulting, tone, turning to Baločanski.

Baločanski approached the Greek with a gesture as if he

wanted to explain something that was of particular importance to him, and especially to Bobočka and Philip. He stopped with his hand in the air, and remained motionless for a moment before making a gesture of futility as if it were all too wearisome for him. Then, stretching his hand toward the wardrobe, he took down from it his old ivorybound prayer book and went back to his place on the divan near the lamp. He opened the prayer book at one of the pages marked by the picture of a saint, and with a deep sigh crossed himself piously. "We do not know either the hour or the day," he muttered in a low melancholy voice, and then went on reading his prayers as if he were quite alone in the room.

Wretched and helpless in his present state of mind, Philip looked on with the nervous impatience of someone powerless, yet desperate, ceaselessly digging in his own darknesses with a lamp in his hand, like a miner buried under the thick layers of a collapsed mine, when on all sides everybody is feverishly tunneling to get out. He knew perfectly well that Kostanjevec was a backwater for him and that it would be a good thing to move on as soon as possible, but at the same time he felt that he lacked the strength to make a sudden break and leave in twenty-four hours. It was simple. He had just to take a cab and drive over to the Kaptol railway station and there get on the first train.

It was becoming increasingly clear to Philip that this hesitation was fatal in every sense; if any one of the persons involved in it had felt the fatality of every insignificant event from the very beginning of this passionately dangerous game, it had been himself. The excitement of flesh, loins, and nerves had never left him feeling so tired and weak, so weak-willed and without resistance, as this time. Bobočka had excited him physically to a very high degree, and his fear at the day-to-day uncertainty of her fate, his incessant mistrust of everything in his complete exhaustion, the presence of the mysterious Greek, who had further aroused and intensified his vague fears—everything flared up within Philip in the abnormal temperature of his agitated state of mind. Cracks were appearing in his bliss, and above the cracks appeared more and more unhealthy signs: the raw decay of the flesh, the fire of sensual ecstasy, the weakness and frequent blankness of his mind, his preoccupation with dreams, dreams with strong tendencies toward animal self-indulgence—all this fermented and seethed within him like inflamed, tainted blood.

In the midst of this wretched weakness and uneasiness of the flesh, a calmer but more and more intense dislike of Baločanski

188

was developing within him. Watching that thing that had once been a man as he sat at table and greedily cleaned up the plates like a dog, and talked about his only comfort, "the Holy Sacrament"; listening to him expressing himself in the most commonplace pseudointelligent *clichés,* Philip was overcome by an unreasonable repugnance, full of animal hatred. He had never known that he could think coldly about the death of anyone near to him, no matter who he might be, but considering all the possibilities of a way out, the idea of Baločanski's death continually recurred to him as the best solution. If by some chance the madman should die, or if they could put the wretch into an asylum, that would be the only salvation for Boba! He thought about it quite soberly, he sniffed at that death rapaciously, with a cold wolflike muzzle, feeling that he had canine teeth and at any given moment could tear the living human flesh.

This idea came to him, of course, only occasionally, and at once disintegrated into numberless combinations inspired by his loneliness, the feeble deceptions of his imagination constantly turning in a closed circle without any exit. On the one hand all this restlessness seemed to him something strange and unusual, the first signs of senility; yet on the other, his creative power was coming back to him. In the last twenty or thirty days he had painted a whole series of canvases, made several hundred sketches, prints, and watercolors; images had crystallized and poured from him as from a fountain. It was altogether unimportant to Philip that his emotion stemmed from a sensuous source, that his blood had been excited within him by the sensuality of the flesh, that the lucidity of his conception was largely due to factors that were probably of an exclusively physical nature. It did not matter how or why, only that after a long, depressed, and futile rumination, he had again begun to react to life creatively, with a new power of observation, of imaginatively reproducing what he saw in all its vivid picturesqueness. He had painted a number of green sunsets in deserted forest glades, with the distant ash-gray chains of mountain sides, pale as old seventeenth-century Japanese lithographs. He had painted a series of watercolors of the winegrowers he had seen in the twilight with their copper-green shoes and the glow of their smouldering pipes, countless masklike faces in the twilight with the red fiery light on them, like people standing over graves and lighting candles. His mother, old Liepach, fat Carolina, Mike the cowherd, Bobočka, and Baločanski—he painted them all as they sat drinking tea, in the full glare of the sun round a samovar in the summerhouse; old Regina with His Excellency, like two ridiculous parrots; fat Carolina in the center of the composition with her swollen stomach and red butcher's hands; the deaf-and-dumb Mike, and the imbecile Baločanski; two epileptic, demoniac, grimacing masks; Bobočka pale, in black silk, was pouring tea for him, Philip, into a bright red cup. He painted himself in front of the circle with his palette and a cigarette in his hand, and on the summerhouse, on the green ivy he set an old, secular raven. Everything was oily with the heavy strokes of the brush, too wet and too rich in color, lapidary, ponderous; possibly a shade too Nordic, the motif a little too problematic, though not the execution; it had been put on canvas in a single sweep, almost modeled in a single stroke.

Just lately he had turned everything around him into pictures and with his every breath he had a vivid feeling of how much progress he had made; of how he had broken through his inertia of the last years, his futile gazing through gray rainwashed window panes, and reached a new, regenerated, abundant power of painting. Space hung with the gray veils of futile weakness; empty rooms filled with stinking cigarette smoke; northern, misty, sooty distances—all this was slowly left behind him. He felt he had shed his old skin like a snake in the spring sunshine, throwing off everything unorganic within him, everything he had outlived; the scabs of the old wounds had fallen off, and his health was restored; the young, living, healthy tissue was growing underneath the scars.

For Philip, Bobočka and everything around her were vaguely and troublingly mysterious, and after having lived with her and near her for several months, Philip had still no idea who she really was, and what was going on in her and around her. In the beginning everything had seemed clear and simple: a woman, about forty, who had been ruined, who probably was rather unhappy; a cashier in a stuffy provincial inn, who dragged along with her a paralyzed lover, a man ruined like herself. All in itself

190

quite dull and uninteresting! The stammering, shortsighted, paralyzed man at her side had, because of her, broken the social framework of his own life, had come under an influence far beyond his power to resist, and now was dragging himself about the world like a corpse that was not yet dead. At first Philip had been indifferent and even suspicious of them. And even in the most conventional phase of his own early intimacy with Boba, he had known that nothing worthwhile or concrete could or would come of it. He himself, with his unstrung nerves, his lack of any strong or definite desires, his deep, almost pathological feeling of his own futility, with his excessive nervous sensibility and his overstrained intelligence, what could he experience with a woman cashier at Kostanjevec? True, he came every evening to the café, sat near the cash desk with its marbletopped table under the small glass cupboard with the torn lexicons, read the *Daily Mail,* drank *šljivovica* and cognac, smoked forty cigarettes, and watched the red balls on the green cloth of the billiard table. So the nights at Kostanjevec had passed, and Bobočka rattled the cutlery, counted sugar lumps, turned now and then toward the cupboard behind her back, poured out liqueurs and punch, and smiled discreetly at his witty remarks. Restless from sleeplessness, cognac, the disturbance of mind, flesh, and blood, in the presence of this woman whose slim snaky body could be discerned under her black silk dress, Philip puffed out smoke and said witty things about himself and the things around him, and Bobočka was clever enough not to talk nonsense, but Philip never noticed any other signs of particular intelligence about her. Two or three times, indeed, there were indications that she lacked ordinary education, but on the whole the cashier knew how to conceal her shortcomings very cunningly. He knew that she had gone to various Catholic boarding schools, that she spoke several languages, and knew how to pass judgments on things as if they were her own opinions. "Verdi, for instance, is in no way inferior to Wagner," or "Münch is more of a poet than a painter," and all this combined with the charm of her throaty contralto voice, the prettiness of her graying hair, and the quick glance of her eyes, clear as that of a young girl, which shone intently in the smoky atmosphere like a concealed green flame.

In the company of this unhappy lady, Philip unconsciously fell more and more under her influence; she had not always been what she was now. Judging by a large number of photographs she scattered around him, of her travels, the interior of her flats, her dogs and horses and cars, one could tell she had not always been only a cashier; numbers of carpets and books had passed through her hands, sculptures and paintings, and heavy metal cages with tropical birds. She had sailed in Greek waters, watched the setting of the midnight sun, millions, literally millions had slipped through her fingers, and much moral, resistant, inner strength must have been needed not to give way completely under the burden of such a fate as had fallen upon her now.

Philip had conceived a liking for the woman because of her misfortune and her helplessness. In her most intimate confessions, in her complete lack of any further resistance, her admission of the realization that she had reached her limit—in that weak and helpless state of one who sweats blood because of his inability to surmount his difficulties—Philip had begun to feel for her a sympathy that gradually became stronger and deeper. But even at this stage, from the very beginning, the most incredible things used to happen. One very hot day, immediately after lunch, when there was no one in the café, Philip discovered a small busboy sitting in her lap. They said he had got a splinter in his finger coming down a ladder, and she was taking it out with a needle, but there was no trace of either the needle or the ladder, and holding the boy's head in both her hands she had been so absorbed in kissing him on the lips that she failed to notice Philip had come in. On another occasion she was late in coming to meet him in the glade in the forest near the old anthill, where they had met for the first time after that stupid supper party at Liepach's. She arrived all confused and muddy—the night before there had been a mild shower—and explained to him that she had fallen down at the crossing above the head roadman's fields. Later on he heard in the Liepach circle—his mother was pleased to pass on the information—that Bobočka had been seen at night in the head roadman's fields with the new gamekeeper.

And what about that business of old Korngold? Korngold was a prominent Viennese industrialist, a huge man, like an asthmatic rhinoceros, weighing a hundred and twenty-nine kilograms. He owned fourteen steam sawmills in the vicinity of Kostanjevec and used to come to these forests every other year to a hunting lodge he had bought from the manager of the estate of the bishop of Turčin immediately after the agrarian reform. One night he had found himself in Bobočka's company. He was supposed to have known her in the prewar days of the Radays at Buda, and afterward her first husband, the minister, had had business relations with him—a lot of champagne had been spilled in those nights, and one Saturday he invited Philip and Bobočka to supper at the hunting lodge in the forest at Turčin. Piles of fish, cold meat, and mayonnaise disappeared into Kornbold's jaws, as if into the jaws of a hungry hippopotamus; red as a lobster, sweating in his silk shirt, breathing heavily and loudly, like an enormous marine mammal, the old man cut thick pieces of meat, crushed ice, sipped wine, smoked, puffed, spat, and told witty stories about excessive eating and drinking. This was his forty-third cigarette of the night, and he had been troubled by laryngitis for the last seventeen years; those gentlemen who were specialists in throat diseases, who had glittering mirrors on their foreheads and treated his throat with lapis and other foul liquids could do absolutely nothing about it, either for him or for so many other people who smoke some fifty cigarettes a day. But in fact smoking had a bad effect on him, and it smelled, and the smell was revolting in every respect, and it was not even pleasant. Why indeed one should burn grass under one's nose? No one could explain— nor, by the way, could they explain so many questions around as well as inside us! For instance, asparagus or trout, or Turkish coffee, or cognac, or toothpicks—all this confusion of things around us, which was known as a comfortable middle-class life with various kinds of soap, dentists, motor bicycles, cars, and tedious meetings of administrative committees at tables covered with green cloth, in offices where as a rule the most modern stupidities are hung on the walls as pictures.

"I don't like modern art, it is all nonsense and rubbish! You are a modern painter, too, aren't you? Have you any paintings for sale, by any chance? I'll buy them from you! You just write to me, please; I don't need to see the stuff at all! . . . Two thousand shillings? Yes, all right? Do you accept? . . . It's settled!"

Smoking his forty-third cigarette and gnawing a toothpick, old, fat, thick-necked Korngold spoke about his fatness, his irregular functions due to his fatness; about asparagus, about meat, about fish, about his forestry business; of how he really could not understand why he could not discard the habit of gnawing toothpicks, those unnecessary bits of wood that so-called well-bred people say it is not polite to use in public. And, finally, toothpicks were not such innocent things as they seemed to be! The consumption of toothpicks was immense! There was no bar, no inn, no wagon-restaurant without these silly sticks, so that it was hard to believe what vast millions lie in such apparently trifling splinters of wood! In Canada and in Finland whole industries existed, water-falls and sawmills, which daily rolled thousands of tons of fragrant wood, and everything working at full speed—and it was difficult to get shares in firms dealing in toothpicks, and over here the business was pretty safe. All Europe had bad teeth and her consumption of this commodity compared with America was high, and still higher since they had introduced dental clinics in American primary schools with compulsory free treatment for every child in the United States; that had brought the consumption of toothpicks down by fully forty-seven percent. Ever since some nationalization of industry here, Director-General Korngold himself could claim to have made a great effort to bring about the nationalization of the toothpick industry. "Together with the husband of our charming guest, Madam Xenia, I have worked very hard in that field"—and the prospects were good— "in our country teeth are not being attended to in elementary schools"—but they had had no success.

"For the time being they are investing only in heavy industry! Our people, unfortunately, like genuine barbarians, still—*en masse*—use matches instead of toothpicks!"

Philip listened to this flood of oily, oversatisfied words, chewing his own toothpick automatically, irritably. The toothpick tasted of mint, and under the sharp flavor he felt on the gum between his teeth the bitterness of pine resin, which spread in his mouth and through his brain, as if the wind had brought in the

194

strong scent of mountain pine trees and distant blue horizons. Aware of the bitter taste of the pine wood, Philip took a deep breath and drained a full glass of Korngold's heavy wine, forgetting that this was already his twelfth or fifteenth glass, that he was sitting there in the company of a barbarian culture-bearer, a rhinoceros, and that he himself was drunk. He was completely drunk and everything round him swirled in giddy circles, both Bobočka and this unpleasant *parvenu!*

How was this potbelly behaving toward her? He caressed her upper arm with his fat fingers, he slid his arm round her shoulders; he had drawn his heavy-upholstered chair close to her, and she was flicking with the toe of her shoe the edge of his napkin which was spread over his senile knees. What was this—a drunken dream, a mental asylum, a brothel? The old man was moaning that all was up with him because the doctors had found a lot of sugar in his blood, and his kidneys were no longer as they should be: he had albumen! Around the old hippopotamus moved physicians in their mysterious burnouses like old-fashioned nightshirts and looked at this idiot, examining his throat, his intestines, his kidneys, his bladder; boiling his urine in glass tubes and smelling it to find out whether there was any sugar in it, drilling his teeth, measuring his blood pressure. And while he talked of all these foul, intimate details, he caressed Boba's shoulders, touched her thighs with his knees, and all of it was shameless and stupid, and completely drunken! This asthmatic old potbelly, with his stomach prone to indigestion, this asthmatic hairy creature in a cloud of Turkish coffee and tobacco, was frightful and enormous like a gorilla; yet Boba laughed at him as gaily as a young girl, measured his blood pressure with her palm against his temples, and called him Director-General. They talked about excursions they had made long ago to glaciers in the Dolomites, when this rhinoceros was still riding a bicycle, and before Boba's cure in Paris, when they had believed that she was pregnant and about to give her first son to her husband the Minister; but this, the Minister's one earthly ideal, had been destroyed by her Paris paraffin-oil cure.

Having realized that he was getting dizzy, Philip disappeared from the table. His room was on the second floor, right under the roof of the wooden villa, built in Swiss style, with colored glass and antlers. Philip tossed about all night and finally fell asleep, and then was awakened by someone giggling. It was Boba's voice. The Director-General's room was on the first floor, just below Philip's, and it was Boba's voice that he heard from the balcony. It was dawn.

"Where the hell could Boba be, laughing like that?" On the balcony below his room, on the wooden balustrade, Boba was sitting in her pajamas, smoking a cigarette and laughing while the Director-General rolled up the left leg of her trousers and stroked her naked calf.

On their way back through the forest that same morning Philip and Boba had a quarrel. She laughed in a superior way. Philip was furious; he had been seeing ghosts. The Director-General could have been her father! In a serious quarrel, still not quite sober, Philip struck her in the face and drew blood, and everything ended on the moist grass. In his embrace, lasciviously, Boba twisted his hair round her forefinger and told him intimately that men were fools and did not realize that the greatest pleasure of all for a woman was to be beaten by them.

Thus there had been many things even before the arrival of the Greek, but that medieval, gothic, obscene tableau on Bobočka's bed with Baločanski reading a newspaper by the faint light of a tallow candle remained engraved on Philip's memory. After that dreadful drinking party, after that flaming Caucasian Lermontov punch, Philip did not go to the café again, and three days elapsed without his receiving a word from Bobočka. After the night at Korngold's, they had not seen each other for nearly a week; she had gone to town and come back with a multitude of things; the finest English-made tennis racket, a small black Pekinese dog, several bottles of eau de cologne and genuine Benedictine. For Baločanski, she brought silk shirts and a tie; and for Philip, a box of the finest Dutch paints. He had thrown the paints on the floor at her feet in indignation; he was rude, he shouted at her, and told her some brutal truths, and she shrugged her shoulders, collected the scattered lead tubes from the floor, and told him quite calmly and without confusion that "it was very difficult to be friends with such inconsistent, bizarre people."

She was right. In the whole of that confused affair, she was perfectly innocent. There was no guilt on her side; it was he who was really "bizarre and inconsistent." If anyone was inconsistent in their relationship, it was only he. Why was he so alarmed because of the Georgian, as if Baločanski himself were not also a suspicious quantity? Who were all these men around that insane woman? A Caucasian Greek, whose mother came from Smyrna and whose father came from Kiev; a Georgian who had worked as a journalist at Riga, and was now roaming through the Pannonian forests, had black pajamas, and made punch like that Lermontov used to drink as a young man in love at Tiflis. As for Boboćka, she was a Hungarian, a Pannonian, from Medjumurje, with a mixture of German, Italian, and South Styrian aristocratic blood in her veins, so that she could hardly speak Croatian! And Philip, on his father's side, was no one; the Valentis had come to Cracow from Verona, and at Vilna had married Lithuanian girls; his father Philip, the chamberlain, was born at Ždala, and his mother was a Hungarian from Szekesfehervar. Lithuanians, Ukrainians, Veronese, Pannonians, Hungarians; what distant parts of the world had they come from? Out of what distant mists had their bodies reached this Danubian mud, to crawl about here in these narrow surroundings, with that blood still flowing in their veins? And who could remain consistent in all this movement and complication? That unpleasant Greek had been right the other night, in saying that "nationality was a petty-bourgeois prejudice." On another occasion—against his own innermost convictions—Philip had argued that nationality was a subjective factor, a psychological phenomenon, a notion of metaphysical origin. Just lately, he had been too much under the influence of such vague metaphysics! The last few futile years were to blame for that, those difficult cloudy years, when he had read such foolish books. That man buried him under a whole heap of names—he was well read, or pretended to be; he was always pretending—but he was often right! There is, and there can be, no consistency either in the behavior or in the evolution of individuals, and even less in the huge collections of people known as nations. And the man had listed a whole bibliography of skull measurement to prove that the concept of the nation was a mental fiction. "In human minds there is nothing save fictions. Morality is just one of these fictions."

"It is a difficult thing to be a friend of bizarre, inconsistent people," so Bobočka had told him. And at that moment she was certainly superior to him. He had gravely offended her, and she was picking up his tubes, like a well-brought up little girl. She was certainly superior to him and above his petty-bourgeois prejudices. And his not going to the café for three days after the scene with the Georgian was also "bizarre and inconsistent" on his part! What did he expect from the whole affair? Had he ever asked himself the question? And when? What did he want from Bobočka? And was not he, Philip Latinovicz, the person who had lowered this woman to the level of a prostitute?

One morning, near Turčinovo, where the Blatna flows under the railway bridge, the shepherds discovered a body. It was so mutilated and bloodstained that no one could recognize it. The dead man had no papers on him, and it was only possible to read on the inside of his black felt hat that the hat had been bought at Metropolis Ltd in London. Three days passed before the news reached Kostanjevec that someone had been killed by a train on the railway line to Turčinovo. . . .

When Bobočka arrived in Turčinovo, the unidentified person had already been buried. She recognized the pipe and the hat, the havelock and the tie, the only effects of the dead man: they were Sergei Kirilovitch Kyriales'. She asked for the grave to be opened. This was a ghastly job, because for the last few days it had been raining continuously; the heavy clay had become saturated with wet and it was difficult to dig in the rain. Bobočka remained standing in the cemetery, in the rain, the whole morning, with a gravedigger, a beardless young man with beautiful curly fair hair and moist, warm, shining eyes looking at her as at a holy image. He gave her hot soup to drink from a blue enamel can with a light blue enamel lid; the can was greasy, not properly washed, with a sour taste of milk, and smelt faintly of smoke. When the young gravedigger drank after her, his teeth clinked on the enamel.

The coffin covered with mud, the bloodstained clothes, it was all a revolting sight! Yes, indeed! There, amid the yellow mud, underneath a thin, broken, deal board, Kyriales' already decomposing hand projected from the cuff of a blue silk shirt that belonged to Baločanski. She had bought the shirt for Baločanski in the summer with Korngold's money, and Kyriales had left all his things with her, saying that he would come back in a few days; he had changed his clothes that morning before his departure.

Boba gave the authorities details as to the identity of S. K. Kyriales, Doctor of Philosophy and Medicine, former Professor of the University of Istanbul, after whom and to whose eternal memory international science had named a microscopic section of a hair and, worn out with the boring and pedantic interrogation and all the entries in the registers, she returned to Kostanjevec wet and exhausted.

She knocked at Philip's door. This was the time when they usually met, in the attic of his mother's house, when the forest was wet so that they could no longer meet in the glade or underneath the old oak tree where they had found shelter that stormy night on their way back from the pilgrimage to St. Rock's Church, when they had been caught in the cloudburst. "Shun an oak but seek refuge under a beech tree."

She asked Philip to forgive her for interrupting him and troubling him with her worries, but she had a favor to ask. She had made up her mind to leave that very night, and she needed money to take her to Hamburg.

Philip was so impressed by the news of the Greek's death on the railway line and the idea of opening his grave that he could not breathe. His diaphragm felt tight, his heart seemed to be beating in his knees and elbows. Holding his head in his hands, dizzy and shivering as if from an attack of fever, he told Boba that he had not so much on him, but that he would go with her to the town to see her off, and of course he would place at her disposal, without question, all he had.

Her face gray, but quite calm, Boba resolutely refused to allow him to accompany her. She was grateful for his kindness, but she was going on her own. She needed no one to accompany her. She needed the money tonight, not later than seven!

The municipal treasurer, Philip's school friend at the Kaptol Bishop's Orphanage, had been handling his financial affairs lately; going frequently to the banks at Kaptol, he was familiar with Philip's financial situation, and Philip had an open credit with him. Philip suggested this plan to her: that he should go to this friend and bring her as much as he could get that evening.

But even this she refused.

He need not trouble to come to her house. She was now on her way to Steiner's, where she would remain at the cash desk until seven, and at seven she would come over for the money herself. So they parted.

The treasurer, of course, was not at home: he was at a municipal committee meeting and was not expected back until late that night. Philip's contacts with the people of Kostanjevec were very slight; he hardly knew anyone. The thought of borrowing from his mother he rejected immediately on principle, so there was no one else to turn to but the surveyor. The surveyor had nine thousand dinars in his cashbox, and of that he had to deposit four thousand with the district authorities. So Philip took five thousand from the surveyor, and as he himself had two, he returned home, put the seven thousand in an envelope, and began restlessly pacing from the cupboard to the oval table, and back to the cupboard, like a jaguar, on the verge of madness. The grimy rafters above his head, the gilded kerosene lamp suspended above the table, the foolish Jelačić picture over there above the blue velvet chairs near the door, all began to get so much on his nerves that he felt he wanted to break everything about him.

Old Regina in her room downstairs realized from the footsteps of her son that something was going on up there. The whole wooden structure resounded with his strides, as he paced about up there above her head; his footsteps rang through the wooden house, the hanging lamp shook on the ceiling and the olive branch with its small gray buds from last Palm Sunday, fixed in the frame of the picture of the Virgin Mary, fell down; the holy-water vessel was shaken, and the plaster began falling like dust from the ceiling rafters. But the man in the attic continued to walk furiously up and down.

The old woman sat in her armchair, silent with fear, and had not the strength to climb the wooden stairs and ask him what was the matter. And Philip, with bent head, continued to pace from the cupboard to the table and from the table to the cupboard, and looked at his watch for perhaps the thirtieth time; time had stopped, had ceased to move; it was still a quarter past six. Mike had already come back with the cows; Carolina had locked the hens in the hen coop and had drawn water from the well, while he sat in the armchair and, holding his head in his hands, remained a whole eternity. And yet it was still not later than a quarter past six, not a minute more.

He buried his face in his palms, shut his eyes, plunged into dense darkness, and there, in the green and red circles of that darkness, where there was nothing at all save the blue tongue flame of the burning punch flickering on the edge of the glass bowl, he heard the voice of the Greek in the darkness saying that at the moment, at the very last moment, when he jumped under the engine, he would think of nothing! If he thought at all, it would certainly seem foolish to him that it had not happened long, long before!

And it had happened that muddy, rainy morning with a grimy old engine on a railway line wrapped in mist, and the telephone wires buzzing in the wind! Boba intended to leave that night; the seven thousand lay there in the blue envelope on the plush table-cloth . . . and the cows were back, and the hens gone to sleep . . . and it was still only a quarter past six, or rather sixteen minutes past six. Philip felt he must become blind or deaf, or hide in a deaf-and-dumb airless darkness, and it was so dark here, so suffocating, as close as in a box; everything was plastered with those stupid pictures, those hanging lamps; the ceiling was so low that one could break through it with one's head; there was no air, one's heart could beat only in one's elbows; everything was all intolerably, hermetically sealed!

He got up, went to the tiny square window and opened it wide. The quiet autumn rain was streaming down the mossy boards as if down old, worn fur. The glass was misty, outside wept the gray sorrowful autumn. On the muddy road a blind man in old-fashioned Austrian uniform was dragging himself along like a shadow. He carried an accordion on his shoulders and a beggar's cotton bag round his neck, and as he tapped with his stick through the puddles, barefoot in the mud, he sniffed the smell of warm smoke like a dog and listened to the murmur of human voices under warm roofs. For a long time Philip looked dully after the blind man. The cold dampness was pleasant to his enflamed bronchial tubes and he gulped in the rainy twilight, feeling drops of rain trickle down from the top of his head to his neck, and it refreshed him like a cold bath. He heard footsteps on the wooden staircase. It was probably Mike bringing him some sort of an old flute or broken piece of glass. He had spoiled Mike by giving him money for the tiny bronze Europa, so the deaf-and-dumb cowherd now believed that any old thing was worth keeping as a relic.

Someone knocked on the small narrow door.

Strange! Twenty-two past six! It couldn't be Boba. Those were heavy footsteps, yet Mike never knocked.

He went to the door and opened it curiously, nervously.

In the half-dark aperture, framed in boards, stood a man in black with derby hat; it was pitch-dark, it was impossible to recognize him.

"What do you want?"

"Good evening. Please forgive me if I am a nuisance. I have come to see you. You have not been to the café for the last three days, so we thought you might perhaps be ill?"

It was Baločanski. Shortsighted, toothless, without his pince-nez, and with his thick mustache soaked with moisture, he looked like a blind man. He stumbled over the threshold and dropped his hat, and as the felt dome-shaped object rolled down, they felt a momentary embarrassment standing in the dim light by the open door.

"Good evening. Do come in! You are not troubling me at all. Please, come in!"

Philip lit the candle. Baločanski sat down at the table without taking off his overcoat and looked round the small room with its low ceiling and old rafters; he had never been in Philip's room before.

"Everything seems very pleasant here, cosy somehow, I haven't been in a cosy room for a long while!"

"Yes, but it's a bit old-fashioned, though; petty-bourgeois—typical. Will you have a cigarette?"

"Thank you!"

They both lit cigarettes. Smoke circled round the candle. Silence. On the table stood Baločanski's wet derby hat and Philip's clock; every tick of the mechanism echoed loudly, metallically, on the polished surface. The minutes had now begun to pass feverishly quickly; it was two minutes off half-past six!

On the table, in the glow of the wax candle, stood the tiny bronze Europa riding a galloping bull. Baločanski took the tiny figurine in his hand, and began to examine it under the light holding it close to his eyes, so that he seemed to be sniffing at the little Europa like a dog. He looked worried, gray.

"A nice little thing! Unusual! At our grammar school we had antique plaster casts in the corridor in front of our classrooms. On one of the pedestals stood Scipio Africanus. I was impressed most of all by that Scipio Africanus! He had a head exactly like a burglar's. Later on I had the occasion as a lawyer to come into contact with real burglars and afterward I even ate soup with those gentlemen, but I have never come across such a well-modeled delinquent's skull as the cranium of Scipio Africanus. A fellow who slaughters whole nations becomes the ideal of a grammar school! And someone who kills just one person is sent to the gallows! The peculiar legal point of view! You know, professor, all we humanists had Rome as our ideal. That same Rome which created such wonderful things as this little Europa. But when someone in his own lifetime experiences for himself the barbarous, inquisitorial, imbecile baseness of the Roman code, he loses every respect for such cultural-historical toys! Rome was not this . . . it was this!"

In speaking the first part of his sentence "Rome was not this," he showed Philip the little Europa, holding it in his palm; then, placing it on the polished table, he pointed the forefinger of his left hand at himself, and began to tap his soaked overcoat:

"That was Rome, what I am now: a heap of trampled flyblown meat! I have watched those Caesaromaniacs, those patricians of ours; I have eaten at their tables! How many of these people must become what I have become myself, a rag, no longer a man, so that Scipio Africanus can remain standing on his pedestal! My dear sir! Art is a fine thing, but life is a serious matter!"

Philip watched Baločanski's dull, cocaine-addict's face and his long fingers with their dirty bluish nails, trembling and shaking on the edge of the ashtray, nervously flicking off the burning tobacco, and pulling threads of the frayed silk on the torn lapels of his shabby, greasy overcoat, and he could not understand what he had in mind in referring to this Scipio Africanus, or why he had come to see him, and just at a time when the hands of the clock were moving so quickly that it was already after half-past six, nearly a quarter to seven.

Philip began to talk about the distant, buried Pannonian ages when Roman chariots sped over these marshes along stone-paved roads, and men traveled from Rome to the warm baths of Pannonia in four days. And nowadays, if everything should perish in a catastrophe, we have our feeble threadlike strings of telephone wire and cardboard-covered cadastral books, so that if anyone digs up this mud in the distant future of history, the only thing of lasting value that future generations will inherit will be these excavated Roman stones: such little bronze Europas, little grave-toys and jugs and finely wrought pins. Measured by the aesthetic criterion, the whole of our civilization means absolutely nothing compared with these Roman works of art.

Baločanski paid not the slightest attention to what Philip was saying. He had come here himself from the café, driven by a strong impulse, to clear up certain fundamental things with this man. Now he was sitting here, concentrating on one thing that was on his mind and obsessed by the main reason of his visit, while this man in front of him was talking about "the hands of future generations," and it was obvious he would politely show his visitor out with some stupid phrases.

"It is not a question of the hands of future generations, professor, but——"

Baločanski had begun abruptly; he had started his sentence quite wildly, and then all of a sudden he felt that he was too weak to bring it to an end, and so he stopped.

Philip gave him a look of feigned surprise.

They sat silent for a longish time, and only the clock could be heard ticking on the polished table, loudly and quickly.

"You wanted to say something, doctor?"

"Yes, I had something to tell you: it concerns me personally in the first place. I have come to ask you something!"

"I am at your disposal."

"I have come to ask you to do me a service, me, personally."

205

"Please, what is it, if I can do anything, doctor!"

"That is to say . . . how shall I put it? It is a question of Boba!"

"Doctor, please———"

"The fact is: there are times in life when one . . ."

Baločanski fell silent again. He was not looking at Philip, but at the orange halo around the candle, the light green ring which radiated red light, like some strange rocket. This circle of light had attracted his attention, and he was aware that he had to talk about certain decisive matters here, but the light was something completely apart from everything else, as if placed above everything, and it sputtered loudly and flickered in a drop of molten tallow as if alive. This lasted for some time, and then as if awakened from sleep and stepping into a newly revealed space, Baločanski said in a very low voice, almost intimately: "I know everything that is going on between you and Boba!"

"I beg your pardon. What is going on between Boba and myself concerns us two! It does not affect you! You have just said that you were going to talk to me about a personal matter."

"Yes, between Boba and me a personal matter of mine has to be settled."

"Then you may settle it personally between yourself and her if you think it necessary! It doesn't interest me."

"What? It doesn't interest you? Well! All right! But, anyhow, I have come to tell you that I will not in any circumstances allow myself to be thrown over!"

"Thrown over? What do you mean by thrown over? What sort of fancies are these?"

"Look here, professor! Boba has made her mind up to leave me tonight. She wants to leave me and to escape from me!"

"Oh, you are imagining things!"

Baločanski smiled silently, raising the corners of his lips scarcely perceptibly, and began to smooth his mustache with all five fingers of his left hand. How stupid! He had been in the café and there was the surveyor telling everybody at the table that earlier in the evening Regina's son had come to see him and had borrowed five thousand from him. The money was lying there before him on the table in an envelope, and what Boba had told him about having to go to town for two days to see about the Russian's property was just a lie. She was not going to come back at all. And now this man was trying to tell him it was merely his fancy and that he was dreaming!

"Professor, please, do allow me to tell you that all this is no fancy. That's how things stand! I have come to ask you to explain to Boba, that on no condition whatsoever am I going to allow her to throw me over. Tell her that; that these are no fancies! Because of that woman I brought dishonor upon my name; because of her I left my children in the street; because of her I have been to prison!"

"Excuse me, doctor, with all respect for your personal situation, I still think that you were not under age and that you knew what you were doing——"

"Oh, that makes no difference now! Anyhow, I should like you too to know that I have decided to become an actor in this play."

"In what play?"

"In what play? What a funny question! Do you think that I have become simply what I am now, that I threw my own wife out of the window, that I have foolishly ruined myself only to start wandering about again, tonight or possibly tomorrow, along these muddy roads like that beggar with his accordion who passed a little while ago? I don't even know as much as that blind man knows, how to play the accordion! And to turn me, as I am now, out into the street is that human? Is that Christian? And now, when I have come to you, for the first time since we met, to ask you to render me a service, you are telling me lies. Is that human?"

"I beg your pardon——"

"No, no! After all this brothel business here between us, am I now going to mind my words? You have borrowed five thousand from the surveyor tonight and the money is here in this envelope!"

Baločanski jumped up like a man in deadly terror, and as if by some sort of higher intuition began to tap with his left forefinger the envelope containing the money, which lay next to the candlestick: "These are no fancies at all; it's just this: Boba is leaving for Hamburg! She has a friend who keeps a so-called bridge-room there. And I have come to beg you to explain to Boba——"

"I think, doctor, that after all that you have just said, any conversation between us is unnecessary! I have no intention whatever of explaining anything, either to Boba or to you. I am sorry, but——"

Philip rose and went to open the door. After a long silence Baločanski took his hat from the table, and then rather slowly, without any sign of perturbance, as if he had shaken off an unusually heavy burden, he bowed extremely politely: "Very well! I have explained my point of view to you. I have decided to become an actor! It is an old rule of physics that in life everything moves along the line of least resistance. I have begged you to warn Boba of this in her own interest."

At that moment someone knocked very discreetly at the door. With his hand already on the latch, Philip opened the door. It was Boba. Then followed an uneasy, irresolute pause and the door silently closed behind her. It had begun to rain heavily and water dripped from her umbrella. Taking in with a quick glance their two shadows under the low ceiling, she did not know what to say. This lasted for some time, when underneath the steep staircase a door opened on the ground floor. Someone climbed the old wooden stairs to Philip's door, hung a lamp on a nail in the pillar of the balustrade, then went back with loud steps. Baločanski twirled his derby hat in his fingers, and then waving the black object like a spoon, he showed Bobočka the door. "Come, let's go!"

"I am not going!"

"But this man has shown me the door! Come along!"

"You go! I'll come afterward!"

"We'll go together You have no business here! This man has insulted me. Come."

"I am not going!"

"You are not coming?"

"No, I won't come! Don't be a nuisance! You can wait for me downstairs for a minute."

"Not a minute. Do you hear me? You must come at once!"

"I will not——"

"You won't?"

Baločanski shouted the last words so that the windows shook in their frames. It was a shriek like the cry of someone mortally wounded, a sudden scream in the silence, like a falling shell.

On the ground floor a door opened. Someone had come to see Regina and she was calling loudly for Carolina. Philip stood by the table, leaning his right hand on it, and did not know what to do! Should he throw this madman out of the door, down the stairs? It was impossible; there would be a scandal. All the tenants of the house were listening to what was going on up there, and through the rotten timbers every word could be heard. Moreover, old Liepach was down there visiting. To get involved in any sort of argument with this excited man was unnecessary; the fool was out of his senses! Philip caught a nervous look from Boba. She stood motionless, biting her lower lip until it bled, her eyes cast down meekly, sullen and helpless. For the moment there was nothing else to do. Erect, with her head thrown back, she went up to Baločanski and said firmly, "All right! Let's go!" Then she turned toward Philip, waved, and said that she would come back before supper. "If not, I'll see you in the café as usual."

She took Baločanski's arm and disappeared with him through the door. Their footsteps could be heard descending the wooden stairs, and then everything sank back into silence. Rain on the window and silence. Philip dragged himself as far as the divan and collapsed there. He felt the cold linen of the pillowcase against his cheeks. His mind was a blank. He was completely beaten.

T he rain beat against the windows for a long time, the candle flickered, the clock ticked on the table, and Philip, dragging himself out of a half-sleep, thought it was dawn. He got up and went to the table. It was three minutes past seven.

"Before supper." That meant at the latest by eight! "If not, then in the café as usual!"

He lit a cigarette and threw it away immediately. He walked up and down the room several times, and then again sank down onto the divan. He heard footsteps on the stairs. There was a knock at the door.

It was Regina.

"Good evening, Philip! Are you asleep?"

"No. What do you want?"

"I came to ask you whether you'll be at home for supper. Dr. Liepach is downstairs. There is hare and dumplings."

"No, thank you very much! I shall be out for supper!"

"Can I light the lamp for you, then? It's quite dark here."

"It's not necessary, Mother. I am going out anyway in a few minutes. Thanks!"

"Even so, I'd better light it!"

So the old woman began to fuss about the lamp; she took off the milky-white globe and lit the wick, muttering something about Carolina's carelessness in cleaning the lamps, and that one had always to do everything for oneself. Philip was so irritated by the old woman's obstinate meddling that he could not control himself.

"Why must you light the lamp when I told you I was going out?"

"So that I can see you; otherwise I never see you. For the last two months you have never come home before dawn; then you sleep, and at night I sleep, and so we live one beside the other and never see each other, like two moles."

"Oh, Mother, Mother, how boring all this is with your lamps and your talk!" He got up and walked back and forth across the room several times. The old woman folded his pajamas, and took his gray suit from the stool and hung it on a peg.

"Has the mail come?"

"There's nothing for you. Only some English newspapers."

"I've asked you a thousand times to send the mail up to me here. Those papers are part of the mail too. But in this house if you ask someone something——"

"Dr. Liepach is reading the papers. I couldn't get them away from him. If he reads something, at least he tells me about it; but from you one never hears anything at all. Dr. Liepach told me the curate had told him you were designing the church windows for some American cathedral?"

Philip did not know what to do. How was he to get rid of the old woman? It was twelve minutes past seven. Before supper . . . that meant before eight! That meant that Boba might come back any moment. So he decided to tell his mother that he wanted to shave.

"Have you any hot water?"

"Yes."

"Then be so good as to tell Carolina to bring me some hot water to shave with. And give the Doctor my compliments and tell him I will come and see him as soon as I finish shaving!"

He put his large dressing case on the table, opened it, and began to arrange his shaving articles on the shelf. Then he sat down, took off his coat, and loosened his tie. The old woman stood motionless and watched him with a quiet, almost phlegmatic, interest, and then asked again, as if she did not believe he was going to shave now: "Then you want some hot water?"

"Yes, please. Only tell Carolina that it mustn't be boiling!"

The old woman shrugged her shoulders and quietly closed the door behind her, and the careful shuffling of her rheumaticky feet could be heard as she went down the forty-five stairs.

Philip again began to walk about the room and lit a cigarette. The taste of the nicotine was extremely unpleasant. Through the window he could hear the rain, and through the rain the monotonously irritating jangle of a mandolin. It was the idiot boy, Francek, who sat in the stable doorway playing his infernal mandolin continuously for evenings on end. Philip opened the window and shouted into the darkness to tell him to stop for once, because it was not as pleasant as it seemed to Francek. Through the dark curtain of water pouring down from the gutters and drainpipes under the eaves, he heard someone mumble something in answer.

"Go to the devil! You'd drive a person mad sooner or later with that infernal mandolin."

He slammed the pane of the little window; he was cold. He put on his dressing gown and sat down in front of the mirror. It was quite unnecessary for him to shave; he had shaved at midday. The clock showed eighteen minutes past seven.

Before eight! If not, then "in the café as usual!"

He stood up again to move about, and before him he saw the dead Georgian moving his jaws and talking about craniology. The dead man without doubt had possessed an extraordinary knowledge. And what had it meant when Baločanski had said over the murdered coachman that a knife in the stomach was the best way? No, Baločanski was not dangerous! He was a degenerate cowardly wretch, insane, evil-smelling, toothless! Only how he had started to shout, like a drunken coachman! He heard footsteps. That was Carolina bringing the water.

There was a knock.

"Come in!"

It was not Carolina. Regina herself had come back with the hot water.

"But I told you to tell Carolina. It wasn't necessary for you to bother yourself!"

"How does Carolina know what is necessary? She just pours water from a kettle, and it's ready! But I cooled the water. Don't be so irritable—it's not good for you. Who were you shouting at?"

"At that idiot with his mandolin!"

"That's true. He plays that wretched mandolin from early morning till late at night! But what do you expect, child? Somebody had to give him a roof! They found him in rags. Someone's illegitimate child, I expect."

"Illegitimate child! What does that mean, 'illegitimate child?' There are 'legitimate' children who are just as illegitimate! It only seems to us that something is 'legitimate,' because everything is more or less illegitimate in our life!"

"Well, I don't know, child; that's just how it shouldn't be!"

Philip lit another cigarette and moved about the room, puffing nervously. The old woman followed him with her eyes, with a slow movement of her head corresponding to his movements from the cupboard to the table. What was the matter with him? He said he was going to shave, but now the water was getting cold; it was already tepid. And then she decided to ask him why Mr. Baločanski had come to see him.

"He just came. How do I know why?"

"I was surprised, for since you've been here this is the first time he has been to see you."

Philip made no answer.

"Poor man! I don't know; I don't know why, but I'm sorry for him! He looks so nice, a fine gentleman!"

"And what do you find so nice about him? His yellow horse teeth? Or his little goatee?"

"Did you offer him anything?"

Philip did not know what to do. Should he take his coat and go out into the rain? He had no umbrella and it was pouring outside. He stopped in front of the old woman and for once spoke roughly: "Why the hell are you bothering me? Please leave me alone! Anyway, you heard every word of what that man and I said, so what do you want now? Do you want me to tell you a second time everything you've heard already?"

"Son, son. There's something the matter with you, Philip! You were always one to bang your head against a wall!"

"But Mother, I've lived these forty years, and I'll manage another ten somehow, and after that it won't matter!"

"It's not good, son, what you are doing! That man was quite right! All summer the whole of Kostanjevec has been talking about nothing else but you and her! And for me, of course, that's not very pleasant."

"And what else is there that isn't pleasant for you?"

"God forgive you, child! You meet this person here under my roof, and you must admit I can't be indifferent to that! And, besides that, I say this in your own interest: she is a wicked, fallen woman! She has already ruined so many men's lives. There was that Russian on the Turčinovo railway. He was one of those who hung around with her anywhere and everywhere! No one can hope for anything good from that woman!"

"If you want to read me a lecture, Mother, then you'd better stop it! I don't want to hear a single word about it! You know too little about it all to be able to judge!"

"What is there to know? It is enough to see things and use one's own common sense; because of that creature men have thrown themselves under trains and gone to prison, and you have lost your senses because of her—there's nothing to know about it——"

"If you want me to stay, then, please, not another word, understand?"

"I am your mother, my child, and no one in the world is nearer to you than I am. Who could be more sincere and wish you better?"

"Yes, that's true, no one in the world is nearer to me than you!"

He sat down on a chair at the other side of the table and gazed at the woman. Behind the light blue globe of the old kerosene lamp, in the glow of the milky glass, sat a gray-haired old woman with a white shawl on her shoulders; a gold chain hung around her neck, and her hands were covered with jeweled rings. This was his mother! This was the same mother who had looked at him with cold eyes through the brass-ringed circle in their entrance door when he had come back lost and desperate, and who had driven him out on to the street with her voice full of moral indignation! And since that morning, for twenty-three years, the distance between them had remained exactly the same. He went around with immoral people, he compromised her respectable roof, and she morally dissociated herself from him. How utterly ridiculous! As if for years she had not left him to suffer worse than a lost dog! All his childhood, and not only his childhood

. . . he himself, his character, everything that was important in him and in his life, everything had remained scarred, from the first rottenness in which he had been born; and this woman, because of whom he had cried for nights on end, and from whom he had inherited his unhealthy blood, this woman had dissociated herself from him, and something was unpleasant to her because it was immoral, and because this immorality went on beneath her highly moral roof! As if for the whole of his childhood he had not felt the curious eyes of that foul magpie-like backwater continually creeping over him like a caterpillar, and all because of this—this priests' harlot! As if she had not belonged to them all and had not built herself a comfortable and respectable old age out of it; and today she sat here under her respectable roof and read him a moral lecture!

He got up and put his left hand to the back of his head; he felt a sharp pain there. His eyelids were heavy, as if stuck down, and his joints felt leaden. He rummaged about for some time in his dressing case, took out a phial of sedative pills, and then drank two glasses of water. All this time Regina sat motionless and followed his every movement with the greatest interest; she showed no intention at all of leaving him alone. The hands of the clock were coming closer to a quarter to eight. Seven minutes more to a quarter to. He lit a cigarette and again began to walk restlessly.

"Why did that Russian kill himself?"

"I don't know! He killed himself! People do kill themselves sometimes! There are several suicides in the newspaper every day!"

"Dr. Liepach said he had heard from the Superintendent that this Russian was exceptionally intelligent; he had two doctor's degrees and was a university professor"

Philip pushed his left forefinger between his shirt and his tie, as if he would tear everything off in one convulsive movement.

"Mother, for God's sake, please stop bothering me! Why have you pounced on me this evening like a jackdaw? Leave me alone, please! Can't you see that I am upset?"

Regina remained indifferent, quite collected, without moving.

"To tell you the truth, my child, I am worried about you."

"And why should you worry about me?"

"To tell the truth, I am afraid that woman may not let you go."

"Who do you mean? Who is 'that woman'? What does 'that woman' mean?"

"Well, that—that common———"

"Mother, for God's sake!"

"I see you are naïve; you know nothing about women!"

"You dare to say that to me?"

"When someone is blind, it is a good thing that their eyes should be opened! And you do not see; you are blind!"

"And you think it is your duty—yours—to open my eyes? You?"

"Yes, I am your mother! You are my child! And who in the world is closer to you than I am?"

Philip stood in front of her and felt himself getting dizzy. He swayed slightly and in that moment she seemed to him a pale painted shape, a stupid clownish face in the half-light; his chest felt tight, he could not breathe.

"So you think it is your duty to read me a moral lecture? And under this roof that was built with exactly the same sort of money, if not worse, as the bills those girls tuck away in their stockings? And my childhood, my birth, the tobacconist's shop, and everything in Friars' Street, and that old woman with the jay, and the part played by the bishop in all that? Mother, Mother———"

Regina got up and her voice shook. "Only a fallen man who does not believe in God could talk like that to his own mother!"

"Yes, Mrs. Regina, you have always kept a very orderly account of your trade relations with heaven: not all those women that you are so indignant about tonight are in a position to be provided for in their old age by canons, in villas where they play cards with gentlemen and doctors! Why do you look at me now as if I had gone mad? I am over forty, yet even today I don't know who my father really was! I was tormented by that question all my childhood. My youth was ruined because of that secret, and you, who are to blame for it all, are you going to talk to me now, here, this evening, from some moral pedestal?"

Philip felt that all this was overdone, exaggerated and ridiculous, but he could control himself no longer. He had started now. The drama had already begun to unfold. There on the oval polished table against the wall, on the fringed velvet tablecloth, stood the brassbound velvet photograph album with its gold herald. In one movement he furiously flung open the old album, that record of his hellish torments as a child, and turning over the old faded pictures under his mother's nose, he grew more and more angry.

"Now, look at your pictures, take a look at your wonderful pictures, and then moralize! Who are these people? Where did they come from? Where did this chamberlain come from, this stupid bishop, this Canon Lawrence? What is all this, my lady? What are these gentlemen in fur, your brother, the Lieutenant Fieldmarshal, and you in the costume of a Colombine at the Red Cross ball in Vienna? Why is my name Sigismund? Who are these Valentis? What is this Abbot of the Holy Virgin doing here? He had a diamond cross and he used to give me a crown when I was his server. What is this black-framed picture of a nude; was it you lying there naked on a cloud? And that old woman with the jay? And who is this unknown gentleman with the top hat? Which of these faces here in this accursed book is my father? Tell me! Why are you looking at me as if I were not normal? The devil take you, and this album, and all the lot together!"

He threw the brassbound book against the wall with such vehemence that it fell apart and all the pictures were scattered on the floor and about the room.

Regina crossed herself pathetically; she was in complete control of herself and, bending down to the floor, she began to gather up the scattered pictures and put together the torn covers of the album, talking quietly and soothingly. "God forgive you, my child! To sin is human, but the most important thing is to realize that one has sinned, and repent. If this question has tortured you so much, why didn't you ask? I haven't seen you now for exactly twenty-three years, and I wrote it all down for you in case I should die! Many a time I wanted to talk to you about it myself, but lately I had no chance. Dr. Liepach, too, put me on my honor to settle all this before our wedding. Look, here is a photograph of your father!"

She got up and gave him a picture with the gold seal of a Budapest court photographer. In front of a pasteboard Renaissance balustrade was the District High Commissioner in his court dress, helmet, and heron's feathers, with his ornamental curved saber in a velvet scabbard, its chased Damascus hilt all set with artificial gems: Doctor Liepach of Kostanjevec, in 1895, plumper, shining with brilliantine and with a full, untrimmed Magyar mustache à la Attila. Flossmann: Polka Potpourri! Royal Hungarian Court photographer Löwinger. Döbrentey Tér 13. Budapest.

Someone knocked.

Three minutes to eight. "By eight. If not, then in the café as usual!" That might be Bobočka.

"Come in!"

Baločanski. It was Baločanski.

With his build, his delicate physical make-up—and particularly since he had been on the verge of paralysis and threatened by dreadful internal disorders that grew worse every day and showed themselves now in the stiffness of his joints, now in his painful stammering—Baločanski usually moved like some kind of reptile: he crawled, indeed slithered, rather than walked. But up here this evening, as he stepped through Philip's door and crossed the worn doorstep, he seemed of a much weaker physical build than ever. And as he stood with his shoulders bent and his derby in his hand, he was more like a hunchback than a man who walks upright. He bowed to Mrs. Regina as servilely as a servant, kissed her hand ceremoniously, all the time smiling pleasantly and gently, apologizing for bothering them, but he had come about something that was not only his own private business.

Regina collected the last pictures, took the cover of the album, and shut the door behind her. In a voice that was very quiet, pitched in a low, almost unnatural minor key, hushed and scarcely audible, Baločanski turned toward Philip and gave him the message from Boba, that she had not been able to come earlier because it had been physically impossible. Boba sent her kind regards to Philip and asked him not to expect her this evening, because she was prevented from coming. There was no need for her to come and the money was unnecessary. She wanted to let him know she could not go away.

Philip, still under the influence of that Hungarian court photographer, was completely confused and bewildered, and for the first few moments could not grasp what it was all about.

Boba was not going . . . Boba refused his financial help . . . she was prevented from coming . . . she was not at the café and she would not be coming there . . . but had sent Balo-čanski as the bearer of her message?

"Yes! She sent me so you would not wait in vain. She will not come this evening! She is staying at home!"

"What! At home? But this evening she had her work at the café."

"Yes, but after letting you know, I am going to the café to tell Fanika to find a substitute! She is going to stay at home this evening. We had a serious talk, she and I, that's why I couldn't come earlier. I explained to her nicely what it was all about. It's like this, I don't know how to play the accordion, and I am not a cur!"

"And she?"

"And she began to cry! Boba has always been a good sort! That's what always attracted me; she is as good as a Samaritan. On account of that little consumptive cellist whom Boba nursed for two years, everyone said she was a Lesbian, but it had nothing to do with Lesbianism, just pure Samaritanism! Boba has a heart! She always had a good heart!"

He was crying and his voice began to be lost in his tears. He wiped away his tears with his hands and the greasy brim of his derby, but they still poured down onto his mustache.

Philip went up to him.

"Well, all right, and what did she say to you?"

"I explained to her how things are: Boba, child, we are not animals."

"And she?"

"And she cried with me. She took my hand and kissed it, and

said that I was an unfortunate man! She has not been so good to me for a long while. And then she sent me to you to say that she was staying and that she is all right with me!"

Through that sniffling, half-toned, subdued voice, through that dejection, through that wet slimy mustache soaked with tears, a face looked at Philip as if from an incredible distance. The feeling of incredible distance was the only strong impression Philip got, and there penetrated into his own personal delirium the single definite thought that everything this pauper was saying was untrue.

What? Boba, who only half an hour before had wanted to go away, now told him it was all unnecessary? For two months now she had been planning this journey to Hamburg! The thing was not at all clear. He would take his coat and go with Baločanski to hear from her personally what it was all about and why.

Baločanski was not in the least put out.

"Oh, of course! If you don't believe me, then do come! But I think it is quite unnecessary for you to take the trouble in this rain! I myself told Boba you wouldn't believe me. So she wrote it all down for you!"

"Where? What did she write to me?"

"Here you are. Here it is!"

From his right-hand pocket, Baločanski pulled out a crumpled note and gave it to Philip.

Philip went up to the lamp to see better. It was some sort of a bill.

DROGUERIE PARFUMERIE APHRODITE

Account: To Madam X. von Raday Pavlinić

Items:

Perfumes, eau de cologne, soap, smelling salts, pine salts	3,724
Perfume soap, and various toilet requisites	3,141
Dispatch of perfume to H. F. Dresden	1,215
Dispatch of perfume to H. F. Dresden	4,375
On account, to Miss E.	575
Dispatch abroad to S. Paris	4,214
TOTAL Dinars:	17,244

Paid. With thanks, Aphrodite. (Signed.)

On the whole sheet of this crumpled bill there was not a single word in Boba's hand. And the second sheet was completely blank. Philip noticed something sticky on his fingers, greasy. Moist. Lower down, at the bottom of the blank sheet, was a greasy red fingerprint like a seal. Blood. He looked at Baločanski. Baločanski stood motionless and looked him in the eyes like a dog that has brought something to its master.

"What is this? This is filthy! This is no letter!"

As Philip had moved nearer to the light, he had gone around the table and the chair to see better, and so he now had the table between him and Baločanski; the lamp stood on the table. In the milky light of the glass globe he could see Baločanski only in outline. He put the chair aside and went closer to him. Only then did he notice that Baločanski was bleeding. His right trouser leg was soaked with blood, and he stood in a pool of it.

"What has happened to you? You are covered with blood!"

Baločanski discreetly touched his lips with his left forefinger, warning him not to shout.

"We do not know either the hour or the day, O Lord!"

And then he put on his derby, pulled open the door, and leaped down the stairs. That leap and the way the man ran, bleeding as he was, was like an animal. From the doorway he flung himself down the stairs, jumping perhaps ten at a time, reaching the ground floor like a fleshy ball, with a terrific thundering of the boards as if the whole wooden house were shaken to its foundations. Then he disappeared in the darkness.

Without his coat, bareheaded, Philip ran after him. He heard a noise in the room behind him, the slamming of a door, his mother and Carolina shouting, and saw the mud in front of him; from the muddy night echoed the steps of the man who had rushed off into the darkness, bleeding like a beast before the hounds.

Philip ran on through the dark autumn downpour as though he himself had gone mad, but the madman had disappeared and could no longer be heard. Philip fell into a ditch; he ran onto the barbed wire in front of the trees on the promenade. . . . At the municipal café people began to shout and run after him. In the distance behind the brick kiln, Boba's window was brilliantly lit through the green glow of her silk curtain. Covered with blood and scratches, muddy and wet as a drowned man, Philip ran into the room. On the table the candle was burning quietly. Everything was tossed about in disorder as if after a fierce struggle: dresses, cushions, books, feathers, skirts. Thrown across the bed, with both feet on the floor, lay Bobočka in her own blood: Baločanski had bitten through her throat. And everything was covered with blood: the bedclothes, the cushions, and her black silk blouse. Her eyes were open and she seemed to be looking at something.